Three Fools for Spies

By Michael Lachance

Treaty of Versailles, The Power of Love

The Camera

McKinney Sweetlock

The Long Short

21 Windows

Three Fools for Spies

By

Michael Lachance

Three Fools for Spies

Table of Contents

Prologue

Present day, it was Jan's first time out of the United States, not because she didn't like to travel, but she just never thought to go overseas. She'd been to Yellowstone, Branson - MO, Anchorage - AK, and throughout Nebraska where she was born and raised her family, but not to Europe. The thought excited her and worried her; there were so many things to see during the holiday in France and the sights themselves, but there was also the thought that nearly overwhelmed her when she watched the news, "Terrorist bomb" or "Terrorist shoot". Weren't there spies who kept an eye on things so the public was protected? And her friend, Aaron, had been to Europe many times; he worked for NATO some time ago, spoke French, and enough conversational German and Spanish to translate. She thought about her kids and what if anything happened to her.

Her daughter told her, "Mom, you're at a point in life where it's kind of now or never." Her daughter continued, "Dad's been gone for some time and you're in good health, retired, and your kids …" She smiled, "We're fine and want you to go."

First, the trip would take them to France where they would head east from Paris to Strasbourg to see the Christmas market and visit a special friend of Aarons. After France, they would go to Switzerland for the Christmas market and then a visit to Schilthorn-Piz Gloria with its beautiful panoramas. Aaron made all the arrangements and there would be three of them for this trip: Aaron, Jan, and Mary.

Mary was a kind woman, a good friend, and a bit of a religious fanatic. She collected bibles and had three that were historically valuable; she planned to bring them along and get them blessed at Notre Dame and at the Strasbourg Cathedral. "I can't wait!" She told her husband. "Europe, too bad we can't go further east to Hungary or … Russia." She sighed happily. "I'm so excited!"

The following morning, Mary, Aaron, and Jan boarded their plane to France from Omaha. Seven hours ahead of them in Moscow, Russia, a stout young man, covered in a heavy coat, hat and scarf, walked in a casual way, without worry or fear and in no real rush to get to a place. His fingers played with something small in his pocket, perhaps an extra button or some change he'd left in it. But, when he turned the corner to the airport shuttle, two Russian police officers stood there with a flyer in their hands and he was, at once, unnerved. The police officers scanned the faces and looked for someone, him perhaps?

Suddenly, the thing that he played with in his pocket was more valuable than his life and he made a fist around it. Then, he turned away, though no one was the wiser because he did it so naturally that there was not a thing suspect about it. He stopped and looked at the passersby. "By train then." That afternoon, he managed to get the train out of Moscow and had as his final destination Strasbourg, France. He got his seat on the train and then sent an urgent text; the words were encrypted the second he tapped, 'send'. "Strasbourg Christmas market, two days, near the cathedral."

The following day, Jan, Mary, and Aaron would be in Paris and then on their way to Colmar. The next day, they too would be in Strasbourg to see the cathedral and shop at the Christmas market.

Chapter One – Schilthorn – Damn Americans!

December 24th, Schilthorn-Piz Gloria, Switzerland, there was a beautiful building with glass all around that sat atop a mountain some nine thousand feet above sea level. Christmas decorations adorned the lobby and beautiful colored lights hung around the exterior. Holiday music played in the background and tourist looked and pointed at the majestic mountains that surrounded them. Tourists sat at tables on the patio at Schilthorn while other people sipped on espressos or cappuccinos and had pastries. However, three American tourists were on the verge of an international incident.

Screams erupted and two Americans, a grandma and widower, Jan, who walked thousands of steps a week, and her friend, Mary, a sixty something brunette with a petite frame and a bible in her hand, moved as fast as their legs would let them! Jan had her tablet tucked neatly under one arm and her purse under the other arm. Mary had an old school camera with a long lens slung around her neck.

Russian thugs chased them!

Jan looked at Mary. "Run!" The cable car was just ahead of them and it was nearly full for the return to Murren. "Mary, the cable car!" She turned, saw a food cart, and jerked it out to thwart the thugs!

One thug leapt over the cart, two thugs fell onto it, and the last thug dodged left … then right, but fell anyway over his fellow thugs!

"Mary!" Jan stood at the hallway to the cable car. She got her tablet out and snapped pictures of the thugs. "Ha!"

Mary huffed and then turned back to Jan. She grabbed Jan by the arm and hurried her up the hallway. "Cheese and rice, stop taking pictures already!" She looked around. "Where the hell is Aaron?"

A bearded disabled man with a cane swatted one of the thugs across his shin! "Ja! Das ist gut!"

"Ah!" the thug yelped and stumbled into a table and chairs!

Aaron looked at the snowcapped mountains and was clueless. "Ah, Switzerland, majestic mountains."

Tourists rushed to the windows and looked at the men who chased the two grandmas.

Aaron, a handsome forty something, parked himself close to the glass so he could people watch.

A robust twenty-something woman, with breast the size of the nearby mountains, stood next to Aaron. "You are American?"

"Yeah," He bowed up his stout frame and pushed back his dirty blond hair.

Mary looked around once to get some idea of where they were. "Get in that line!"

"What line?" Jan stood near a large group of teens that bundled together to stay warm. She got her tablet out and took a picture; the flash blinded several teens.

"Ah, stop that please!" A teen held his hand up over his eyes.

"I can take pictures if I want." Jan looked at Mary and then she saw a thug. "Oh shit!"

"Language!" Mary's brow went up. "Sinners?"

Jan nodded and dipped her head toward the center of the building.

The disabled man limped quickly across the floor! Then, he swung his cane and knocked another thug down! "Get on the car!" He shouted at Jan.

"Who the hell is that?" Mary asked.

A thug stood at the end of the hallway and looked for the women. "Davay, Idiot!" He fanned his hand at his men to come to the line at the cable car. "Here!"

Two thugs were upstairs and looked at the crowd. Three thugs pushed their way through the

crowd toward the glass doors that led to the cable car. One thug hobbled and rubbed his shin.

The lead thug, a tall, muscular man with a tattoo that covered half his face, looked Jan over. "Here!" He reached over and grabbed her arm! "Come with me!" He looked for his man. "Yuri!"

Yuri, a stout man with a beard, shoved his way through the crowd. "Marco, I'm coming!"

Mary drew her small, but heavy bible back, and swung it at him! "Sinner!" The leather was supple and much like the leather on a well-used whip. The bible's spine landed dead on his cheek and the impact rippled across his tattooed face!

"Du idiot!" He shook his head to recover from the smack down.

"You don't call me an idiot!" Mary kicked his shin, "get your filthy hand off of my friend, sinner!" The bible went up and then she looked for place to strike. "Praise be to the glory of God!"

"Ah!" His leg gave out! He grasped his shin and looked at the bible that hung over his head. "Suka!"

"Mary!" Jan waved her hand and pointed at the cable car. "It's leaving!"

"Rude!" A teenager yelled at the thug. "Ma'am." She motioned at Mary.

"What did he call me?" Mary asked and held her bible high.

"The 'B' word." Then, she mouthed the word 'bitch'.

Two thugs on the second level pointed at the grandmas. "They are there! Go!" The thugs nodded and rushed to the stairs.

Mary looked at the tattooed man. "How dare you!" She wiggled the bible in her hand. "Jesus wants you to repent for your sins." Then, she drew back her Jimmy Choo knee high boot and paused. "I only wear these when I'm not at church." She buried the tip of the boot in his crotch!

"Ah!" His hands clutched the family jewels and he cried out in agony. "Ah, my nuts!"

"Language!" She smiled, tucked her bible, and then pushed through the crowd toward the cable car doors. "Go Jan!" She motioned for Jan to get on. "Move or help!"

Aaron looked at the crowd and his jaw dropped. "What the hell?"

Jan stood by at the door to the cable car and blocked the door with her hand. "Move!" Teens slid past her while others did not dare to cross. "Mary!"

The operator, a nicely dressed man, waved at her to get clear of the doors. "Madam, please."

"Just let my friend get on." She put her body across the door so he couldn't move her.

The big breasted woman next to Aaron pointed at Mary. "You know that woman?"

He turned to the her and shook his head. "I wish I didn't." Then, he rushed to the stairway and down the steps toward the crowd.

The thugs fought their way through the crowd and one thug, in desperation, pulled a gun. "Klar!" His thug buddies turned and ducked. "BANG!"

Screams erupted and people frantically ducked under tables or ran for cover!

Mary got in the cable car. "They're shooting at us!"

"No, just in the air." She showed her tablet to Mary. "See, I got a picture of them."

Mary gasped. "You and that damn tablet!" Then, she shook her head. "Where's Aaron?"

Jan scoffed, "He's been here plenty. He'll find us." She had Mary by the arm and pulled her deeper into the cable car. Other people huddled on the floor of the cable car. "Why are they down there?"

"Because terrorists are shooting!" Mary yelled. "Oh God." Two thugs stood, sweaty and disheveled, at the very back of the cable car.

The operator rose from where he'd taken cover, pushed a button, and the doors slid shut; the lock released the cable car and it drifted from the pen toward the open mountainside.

Just as the cable car was about to clear the roofline, the disabled man threw his cane away and leapt from the roof of Schilthorn onto the roof of the car! "Thud!" He slid toward the edge and jammed his fingers into the metal rim to stop himself from going off the roof and to his death.

Everyone looked up!

Jan looked at Mary. "What was that?"
Back at Schilthorn, the thugs slammed their fists on the glass doors of the station and cursed the women as the car drifted down the mountain. "Yuri and Marco are in the car." One thug said.

Jan held her tablet up and filmed them. "Ha, we got away."

"No, we haven't." Mary tapped Jan's shoulder and turned her to look at the back of the car.

The car was jammed with people and descended toward the town of Murren.

 Jan squinted and then saw the thugs. "Oh shit."

A woman next to Mary pointed at the men who banged on the glass. "Do you know those men?"

Mary caught her breath, "no." She snapped and then sighed. "They're nasty, evil men."

"Oh, then you've done well to get away from them." She said and looked at Jan. "And your friend?"

Mary looked at Jan. "Her? She's evil too."

Jan smiled, tapped her hearing aid, and then got her compact from her purse. "Who's evil?"

"She wants you take her picture." Mary said and rolled her eyes.

Jan got her tablet in hand, tapped the camera icon, and then snapped a photo of the woman with Mary.

Aaron low crawled to the lobby, looked at the thugs, and then looked toward the cable car. "What the hell did they get into?" He turned away. "What do I do?" He got to the bar and crawled behind it.

The bartender was behind the bar too. "Sir, would you like something?"

"Sure, something healthy." Aaron kept his head down. "A shake."

The bartender nodded, looked over the bar top, got the blender, a few ingredients, and ducked back behind the bar. He poured the ingredients into a blender and then put the blender on high. The green, orange, and reddish mix whirled around in a blur.

People fled to other rooms or stayed on the floor while the Russian thugs searched the place.

"Stay down!" One of the thugs yelled.

Other thugs walked around and looked at people.

"Here you are, sir." The bartender poured the muck into a glass.

Aaron's eyes locked on the mulch and then he cleared his throat. "What's this?"

"A pyrolytic digestive enzyme shake." He smiled, "James Bond had this healthy drink."

"Oh, what a plus." Aaron looked at the contents, took a sip, and gagged. "Wow." His cheeks contorted and his throat buckled; he swallowed poison and his body fought to vomit it up! He took another sip to force down the horrid muck. Then, he licked his lips. "It's the second swallow that washes away the gross one."

"So, what brings you to Schilthorn?" The bartender asked.

The thugs gathered around the bar. "We can't stay, Boris … the police."

Boris nodded, "The drone has jammed everything up here, no calls out or in." He looked up and then at the people who cowered on the floor. "Don't hurt anyone and find the other American."

Aaron looked up and put his finger to his mouth. He slowly looked back at the bartender and mumbled. "I *was* with a couple of friends." He winked.

"Where are they now?" The bartender looked left and then right.

"Uh," he shrugged his shoulders. Then, he put his money on the floor and a tip. "Thank you."

"Good luck, sir." The bartender smiled. "Just to know, the Swiss police will come."

Aaron nodded and then wondered about the terrorists around the bar.

One of the thugs leaned over the bar, "You!"

Aaron choked. "What?"

"Get up!" He pointed his gun at Aaron.

Boris looked at him. "What's this?"

Aaron stood up and held the drink. "Have you had a protein enzyme drink?" His tongue convulsed.

Another thug studied Aaron's face. He edged his gun out and leveled it at Aaron's head. "You *are* one of the Americans." He walked around the bar and grinned slyly. "He was with those women."

Aaron looked at the cable car stand. "No, I wasn't."

The thug looked at the bartender and then him. "Uh-huh."

Aaron looked at the muscled thugs. "Wow, you guys are really muscular and rough looking."

The thug nodded at Boris and then looked at Aaron. "This way, please." He dipped his head toward the lobby. "Where is Marco?" He asked a thug next to him.

Another thug dipped his head toward the cable car stand. "He's made the car with Yuri."

Aaron swallowed a gulp the size of a baseball. "C'mon guys."

The thug pressed the barrel of his gun against Aaron's temple. "Where is the chip?"

Chapter Two: Small town, Nebraska

A WEEK EARLIER, on a table near the living room window, Jan talked on her phone and looked over pictures of other places that she'd been to. In one picture, the Grand Tetons rose majestically into a powder blue sky. Then, there was a picture from the Grand Canyon and another picture of a street in Anchorage. "A lot of travel in the US, but nothing outside of the US." She got her passport and looked it over. "Yes, good for another five years."

A male voice nearly shouted over the phone. "And you have your pill list!"

"Yes, I have it." She smiled. "I can't wait to go." Her jovial spirit brightened at the prospect that she was going to Europe. "Hey, this will be my first stamp in my passport."

"Mom, I just want you to be okay." Her son had the phone on speaker and his mouth right against the microphone.

"I will be, son. My knees are in top shape." She pressed the phone against her ear to hear him better.

"I know. You walk thousands of steps every day." He hedged. "But it's not your knees …

"Don't start." She puckered her lips and then pressed her fingers against her eyes. When she opened them, her hand was firmly over her mouth; a bad feeling welled up in her like gray clouds that preceded a storm. "I'm fine."

"Okay." He huffed. "So, it's you, Aaron, Mary and then you're going to meet his friend."

"Yep, then onto the Christmas markets, and then Switzerland." She looked at the time, "Hey, I got other things to pack."

"Alright, so tomorrow morning?" He knew it; she wanted off the phone because he hinted at something that she didn't want to talk about.

"Yes, I can't wait." She set her passport on the coffee table.

"Alright, mom." He knew that was it. "I love you."

"I love you too." She got a glass of wine. "I'll call you tomorrow."

"Okay, until tomorrow then." He waited for her to hang up.

"Bye." She pressed the red icon on her phone and hung up. Then, she looked over the clothes on her bed, a nice black dress with sliver sequins around the collar and a dark belt that wasn't as dark as the dress. "Okay."

Her daughter knocked heartily on the front door.

"What is this, Grand Central?" She swallowed the wine and shook her head. "Good wine."

The door rattled as someone turned the knob to get in.

"Okay!" She set the glass down, got the knob in hand and pulled the door open. "I wondered who had that hard knock."

"Mom," they hugged. "So, you're all ready?"

"Mark just called and I'll tell you what I told him." A frustrated sigh pushed through her lips. "Yes."

She went right to her mother's bedroom and looked the luggage over.

"Please, come in, Janey." She shook her head.

"You know I've been to Europe a few times and I want to make sure that you have what you need." She looked at her phone. "I'm going to text you this list."

"Great." She rolled her eyes and went to the kitchen. "Coffee?"

"Is it organic?" She went through everything in the luggage. "I think you're all set." Then, she grimaced and touched a black strap that was buried deep under a heavy sweater. Her eyes widened. "So, you have … everything." She gasped.

"Yes, I'm taking what I need for the trip." She got her wine glass and hid it.

"I bet." She pulled up on the black strap and mumbled what she read from the label. "Victoria's Secret." Then, she lifted the black lace thong up and mouthed the words, "oh my god."

"Coffee's nearly ready." She pressed the percolate button.

"Will you …" She bit at her lip. "Have some privacy when you're there?" She cleared her throat and then stuffed the thong into the dresser drawer.

Jan looked up and wondered what she was up to. "Yes, I have my own room."

Janey hands trembled as she put the clothes back in the luggage, flipped the top over, and pushed it down. "Looks good."

"Okay." She blurted out and headed to the kitchen.

"Okay?" Jan held up the coffee cup. "No cream."

"Yeah." She looked at her hands. "My hands are dirty."

Jan smiled. "You know where the bathroom is."

Janey went to the sink and scrubbed her hands. "Yeah, so it looks good."

"I'll put your cup here." Jan laughed to herself and set the cup down.

They talked about the weather over there and the threats.

Janey gulped her coffee, "Just be careful who you talk to."

"Aaron knows his way around." She smiled.

Janey set her cup of coffee down and then went to the front door. They hugged. "Alright, I love you and enjoy yourself."

"Love you too." Jan shut the door, turned her attention to the bedroom, and went in to see what Janey had done with her things. "Why is she such a prude?" Her eyes panned the clothes on top, then she rummaged through her things. "Really." She shook her head and looked at her dresser. One of the drawers wasn't completely closed. She got her fingers on the handle and pulled. There was the thong. "It's my life and my sexuality." She looked at the time; it was nearly midnight.

Her phone rang and she looked at the name. "Mary Bridgeless." She slid her finger across the phone. "Hi, Mary." She got the thong and modeled it against her waist. "Uh-huh, baby. Grandma's got candy."

"Hey, have you got an evening dress for the bateau thing?" Mary looked at her husband who busied himself with a pair of needle nose pliers and dug them into the back of a cuckoo clock.

"I'm bringing my black dress and the rest are street clothes." She got the dress from her luggage, put it against her hip, and looked in the mirror.

"Okay, then I'm going to bring my evening two-piece. I just didn't want to wear the same color." She looked at her caramel colored dress; it shimmered.

"Phil still set against going?" Jan set her dress down and then went back to the living room for her passport; she got it and took it to the bedroom.

"Yeah, he said there's no reason to leave the US." She looked at her husband who worked quietly on the clock.

"There isn't." He blurted out.

"Oh, be quiet." Mary waved her hand at him and shook her head. "Men."

"All them damn foreigners don't like us anyways." He shook his head. "You don't know the language."

"Aaron taught us some words." She said. "Bon-jur."

He put the end of the pliers to his temple and thought, "Help! Terrorist are shooting everyone."

She held up her bible. "I have my faith in God and people."

He looked at the bible. "May stop a bullet."

"Tell him to be quiet." Jan said. "And it's aide moi."

"You hear that?" She turned to her husband. "Shut up."

"What'd she say? Be quiet?" He rolled his eyes.

"I'm so excited." Mary said gleefully. "She said, help me in France."

"You mean in French." He shook his head and focused on his clock repair.

Jan looked at her things. "I'm going to be on the lookout for a rich European, a Sean Connery look alike" She went to the bathroom and looked at herself in the mirror. The faded skin spots and wrinkles were there, the crow's feet. "I'm seventy-one and still look good."

Mary forced herself to grin. "Well, you know you have to be careful over there." She thought about it. "Phil's right. Everyone wants to come to America."

"Frank's been dead ten years. So, I'm looking for a rich, good looking guy." She sighed. "I'll bring him back." Then, she laughed. "Frank wouldn't mind."

"Yeah, but love has to be a part of it." Mary said and gripped her bible firmly. "God's the center of my life and faith will help you."

"I know that's true with you." Jan looked at a Gideon bible on her dresser. "So, pray and ask God to find me a man."

"A good man."
"One that loves long walks and sex." Jan laughed.

"Jan!" Mary nearly choked.

"Okay, I better go." She set the bible to the side.

"Uh-huh." Mary pressed her bible to her forehead. "Really, don't you feel the heat on your skin?"

Jan caught her breath and thought. She's just a nut about her religion. "Okay, okay." This time, she let the phone stray from her ear. "I better finish packing."

"See you tomorrow." Mary said.

"If God allows it." Jan smirked. "Bye." She quickly pressed the "END" button.
Mary looked at her phone, "CALL ENDED." She shook her head. "Lord Jesus, I pray for Jan."

"Honey." Phil set his pliers down. "She's different than you."

"She's a sinner and just won't give her sin unto the Lord." Tears welled up in her eyes. "I …"

"Now," he got up and went to her. "Not everybody will be as strong as you are." He wrapped his arms around her.

"I know." She ignored her husband and turned to her bible. "Going to read a passage to cheer me up, Psalms."

The words were as lite as his breath. "I'm right here." He said and pulled her close.

"Stop, I can't read it with you all over me." She pulled back and went to the stairs, trotted

down to the basement, and to a nook. There was a large graphic picture of Jesus on the cross and it hung

next to her; the frame was tall, nearly three feet tall. "Dear Lord."

Phil looked at the empty stairway and bit at his lower lip. Then, he turned and went back to the cuckoo clock.

That night, Aaron stared at the clock. "Nearly midnight already." The carryon had a bulge in the middle. His fingers gripped the zipper. He pulled it back and then around the bag. The pile of shirts was neatly tucked under the two straps. He pulled at the edges of the shirts so that they were stretched out and flat. "Four-inch squares for underwear, six inches for T's and my jeans rolled up."

His large frame overshadowed the bag and his eyes perused the shirts, then the jeans, socks, underwear, T's, and all else. "Alright, either it's here or it isn't here." A heavy sigh pushed through his lips and his fingers got hold of the zipper. "That's it until the morning."

The next morning, he was up, dressed, and lay his bag in the car trunk. "Omaha, here we come."

At security, Mary had to take out each bible for a total of eight; they were of various sizes.

The TSA looked her over. "Yes, ma'am. Each bible."

"This is ridiculous. I mean, some ISIS terrorists are probably in their seats on the flight, but a God-fearing Christian …" She crossed her arms and huffed.

"Mary," Aaron said and shook his head. "We have plenty of time."

Jan was in line and had her tablet in hand.

Mary looked at the line behind her. "Great, so they'll think this is my fault."

Jan's skin cooled and she looked at a TSA agent with another traveler; their luggage was open and everything was set out! She mumbled to herself, "please no, please no."

The TSA agent at the monitor looked at Jan and smiled, then she winked and Jan's carryon moved out of the X-ray machine.

"Thanks!" Jan said. Then, she videoed the fuss that Mary made while Aaron tried to keep the peace.

"Be careful with that!" Mary nearly yelled. "It's not a Gutenberg, but it's rare."

"Why so many bibles?" Aaron lifted one.

"I want to have them blessed." She smacked Aaron's hand. "Don't touch."

"There's like eight bibles." He shook his head and then walked away. "Lot of extra weight."

"Jesus carried a heavy cross." She looked up and closed her eyes, "thank you, Lord."

Aaron stopped, didn't turn to her, and then looked at Jan. "Okay then."

Finally, Mary got through the security check and made her way toward the boarding area. "The terrorists get through, do bad things, and then we change security so that all the innocents get interrogated." She sat down in a huff and then shook her head. "I forgive them."

"The terrorist?" Aaron asked.

"Not in this life, just the TSA." She smiled. "Let's do that selfie."

They took a selfie and each of them made a stupid face. "Blah!" Jan said. "Fromage!" Aaron said. "Praise be!" Mary said.

"Talk about division of the masses." Mary passed Aaron in first, Jan in comfort plus, and then she went to her seat in "main cabin."

An hour into the flight, Aaron walked back to Mary with bananas, a candy bar, and some biscotti. "Here."

"Is that what you're eating?" Mary looked over the goodies. "Gosh, we got a pack of cookies like they used to give us at Sunday school."

"Enjoy." He smiled and returned to first.

That night, on the international leg, Jan and Mary sat together just behind first class. Jan had a fourth glass of wine and giggled. "Uh, I haven't felt this good in months."

"No kidding." Mary said. "Bottles half empty, I'll set it down."

"No!" Jan blurted out and some people stirred from their sleep. "That bottle is half *full*!"

"Shh." Mary said and looked at the flight attendant who looked at her. "She's a little …" She motioned with her hand as if she had a drink and then rolled her eyes.

The flight attendant winked and brought some coffee. "Some coffee?"

"Coffee?" Jan shook her head and could barely keep her head up. "Cof …" Her head fell back against the seat headrest.

"Okay, she's done." Mary took her glass and the bottle; then, she handed them to the attendant.

"She made a good show of it." The flight attendant smiled. "Thank you."

The tail section fish tailed!

Mary yelped!

A passenger nearby spoke up, "someone shut that drunk up already."

Mary turned to him. "Sinner!" She looked the man over one more time to be sure he didn't dare say another word. Her knuckles were white from the grip she had on her bible.

Jan inhaled, her nostrils rippled, and then she snored.

"Great." Mary sighed and looked at the video screen; an image of the plane floated over the Atlantic. "Time to Destination: 7 hours", she touched the screen and it faded to black. She mumbled the words, "Seven more hours and then ten days in France with these two. Lord, give me strength."

Jan turned onto her side from discomfort. Then, a series of farts slowly slipped from her behind and each one made a different, louder sound until the tenth fart passed with a solid "pop!"

Mary's tired expression turned sour and she fanned her nose. "Strength Lord, please." She fanned the stench back at Jan.

Chapter Three: Welcome to France!

Mary and Jan got their bags from the overhead bin.

Jan's smile was contagious, only to other passengers who had slept. "I got a good night's sleep."

"Oh, that's good." Mary yawned and rolled her eyes into crow's feet that were doubled up after a

restless night. "You missed out on the snoring and other gross sounds."

"Who snored?" Jan asked and then moved toward the exit.

The flight attendant held the phone. "Ladies and gentlemen, welcome to Paris, Charles De Gaulle. Please be sure to gather all your personal belongings …" Her voice faded. The gate agent opened the plane's door.

"What other gross sounds?" Jan looked at the back of the man in front of her.

"Snoring, farting, and God only knows what other eruptions spewed like a Cobra's venom around us." Mary covered her nose. "Dog in the cabin to comfort them; who comforted me?"

"Jesus." Jan looked up.

"Well, you're right about that." She pulled her carryon up against her. "Sneezed too."

"Who sneezed on you?" She moved forward.

"Never mind." Mary stepped up and they headed for the door. "Aaron had a bed, right?"

They turned at the door that was between comfort-plus and first class. Jan spied the alcoves. "Yep, he had a bed."

Mary looked on, stepped up, and then shook her head. "I hope he feels bad that we were in the back, jammed in, and without air."

Jan stepped onto the jet bridge. "You could have paid more and moved up."

"It's always about paying more. Why can't they just have it nice for everyone?" She followed Jan onto the jet bridge and then into the terminal.

"Good morning!" Aaron said. Then, his wide smile faded to a simple grin when he saw their faces. "Bienvenue à Paris!" He held his arms out.

"Yeah!" Jan shouted and they hugged.

"Mary?" He held his arms out for her.

"Okay." They hugged and she smiled. "Glad to be in Paris."

"Didn't sleep?"

"She said there were people who snored and farted all night." Jan walked over to a sign, "BIENVENUE A' PARIS".

"Thou shalt not judge." Mary said.

Jan stopped, turned, and looked back. Several other passengers cut to the left or right to avoid a collision with Jan. "Said the pot to the kettle." She turned back to the terminal ahead and marched off.

"Here I thought you woke up on the wrong side of coach." He laughed.

Mary gritted her teeth.

They made their way through customs and then downstairs to the TGV, France's high-speed train.

After an hour wait, the train pulled in and the doors opened. They boarded quickly and the train left a few minutes thereafter.

"Wow, this is nice." Jan said and sat next to the window.

The TGV wound its way through the countryside and Jan repeatedly tried to take pictures. "My

pictures are blurry."

Aaron laughed, "Honey, we're going over two hundred miles an hour." He pointed, "focus on the landscape further out."

After a couple of hours, the train slowed and rolled into Strasbourg, FR.

Aaron looked out. "Strasbourg, Christmas capital of the world."

Mary, "Remember there's Christ in Christmas."

Jan laughed. "What about the ornaments and wine?" She took a drink from her coffee cup. "What'd they call this? An Americano?" She tipped the end up. "Wasn't much in it."

"It's not a cup of coffee like the gas station has, five-gallon jug for a buck ninety-nine." He laughed.

"It was stout." Jan said and set the cup down.

"There's another Notre Dame here." Mary said.

"They move it from Paris?" Jan asked.

"No, it's just another one." Mary bowed her head and prayed. "Amen."

Aaron looked at the station and big signs hung on the wall, "STRASBOURG". "Okay, we get off here and change trains to the TER."

They got their things together and made their way to the door as the train slowed to a crawl. The station was busy with locals and tourist.

"This could be ugly." Mary looked at the anxious crowd.

A bustling crowd readied their belongings and made their way to either end of the TGV to get off.

"Get your things." Aaron said.

There was a silent pause and then a soft tone sounded throughout the car. "Madame et Monsieur" … the conductor announced the arrival at Strasbourg with a heavily rolled "r".

"He sounds like he's drowning when he gets to the 'r' in Strasbourg." Jan said and laughed to herself.

"Yep, okay." Aaron said and stepped into the aisle. "Let's go."

The ladies followed him off the train, down the steps, and into the hallway below the tracks. Then, they were back up the stairs and into the Gare de Strasbourg-Ville. People rushed here and there while a small group formed in front of the departure board. There were several TER or regional trains with numbers next to their destination and the time.

"Which one is ours?" Jan asked and set her things down.

"Jan, probably best to move up." Aaron motioned at the people who tried to get by and bumped her luggage.

"Your friend's going to meet us at the station?" Mary asked and had her smallest bible clutched tightly in her hand. "France has a majority Catholic population." She said proudly.

"On purpose?" Aaron chuckled.

Mary dipped her head as a librarian would do to a raucous visitor. "Ha-ha."

A woman pushed past Mary, "excusez moi."

"Sinner!" Mary snapped.

"Mary, it's no different than Grand Central or Penn in New York City." He shook his head.

"It is when they touch me." She got a wet wipe and dabbed her shoulder.

"Oh, it's fine. We have time for coffee." Jan looked at the clock. "I'm exhausted, so if you want me to keep my eyes open until supper."

"Okay." Aaron looked at the departures. "We've got a half an hour."

He got hold of his luggage and they headed to the café across from them.

"How much is one Americano?" Jan asked.

"You're using Euros, so it's apples to apples." He said and ordered an espresso.

"Americano." Jan said.

"Oui." The young lady said.

People wound their way around them and their luggage.

Mary studied the drink menu. "Guess I'll have one too."

"Americano." The girl nodded, turned, and went to work on their drinks.

A few moments later and she set the coffees on the glass counter.

"What the hell's this?" Mary looked into her coffee cup.

"Americano." Aaron said. "That's what you get."

"It's not even half full … rip off report." She held up her bible and fanned the counter staff. "Demons be gone." Then, she turned and walked off to an empty table.

Jan looked at Aaron and grinned. "Wait till she's had her moment at Notre Dame." She worked her way through the crowd and sat down.

Aaron got his expresso and walked over. "No shit."

Mary sat back, took a drink, and set her cup down. "I'm done."

"You are not." Jan said. "It's got more than a swallow in there."

"Nope, I downed it."

"Really, you could do shots at a bar." He said and sipped his espresso from a tiny cup.

"I used to." Mary laughed. "Oh, I was so wild back then."

"Topless parties at the sorority house?" He laughed and shook his chest.

"No, nothing that would humiliate me." She grinned and a sly smile came across her face. "Not like the homosexuals."

"Mary." Aaron dipped his chin and they eyed each other.

"Just saying." She looked Aaron up and down. "Gay guys do all kinds of crazy things."

"We do, but women aren't one of them." He smiled and lifted his pinky while he sipped on his coffee.

"Ouch, snarky words." Mary looked at Jan. "Don't come to my defense."

"We have ten more days together, so you two behave." Jan people watched. "We've got about ten minutes."

"Yep, we should go." He got up and got his luggage.

"What's the number?" Jan asked.

"81473." Aaron said. "To Colmar."

"I thought you said it was Little Venice?" Jan asked.

They walked to the lobby and Aaron looked at the board. "Hey, that's us!" He looked at Jan and Mary. "Well, come on!"

"Okay, okay." Jan hurried after them.

"You alright?" Mary asked as Jan hobbled behind her.

"I'm fine, just keep going." Jan said and they made their way back to the tracks.

"Track five." He got to the top of the stairs and then helped Jan. "C'mon."

"I'm alright." She smiled.

"You can always imagine you're being chased by thugs." Mary said.

"Why?" Aaron asked.

"Oh, I walk faster when I think I'm being followed." Jan looked at the train that crawled into the station.

"Uh-huh." He shook his head.

"I think you better pray about your imagination." Jan said.

"How about I pray for your knees?" She smiled and pointed at Jan's knees.

"They're fine." Jan went up the steps to the train like nobody's business and found a seat. "Doesn't matter where we sit, right?"

"No, sit wherever." Aaron caught the eye of a handsome young man. "Hello." He mumbled to himself.

"Huh?" Jan asked.

"Oh, just a handsome guy." He said and looked again.

"Not just any guy." Jan said.

"What's up?" Mary asked.

"He's a French guy." Jan looked past Aaron and her eyes met the handsome young man's eyes.

"Yes, French as we are in France." Aaron chuckled.

"Or German, we're near the border, right?" Mary looked past him and spied the young man. "He looks thuggish." She held up her bible and read.

"Thuggish?" Jan asked.

"Yeah, he's got rough looks like he hasn't shaved and his hair isn't combed." She dipped her bible and took another look.

"Right," Jan said. "He's looking at me." She smiled and winked.

"Jan!" Aaron said.

"What?" She rolled her eyes. "My husband's been dead for years. I can hope."

"Hope for what is what worries us." Mary said. "I'll find you a passage to read."

The soft bell rang, the doors closed, and the train left the station quickly.

"No, I don't need a passage to read." Jan got her book out. "Demi Moore married Ashton Kutcher."

"Honey, that was after she was married to Bruce Willis." Aaron said. "I mean how many times can you look at that mug and …" He stopped.

"What?" Mary asked.

Jan laughed. "I'd look at him all night."

"God, I think I'm going to be sick." Mary said and covered her ears. Then, she caught the young man as he looked past her at Jan. "That man is looking at you."

"What?" Jan edged up on her seat.

"What the hell." Aaron said and then turned away. "Looks like he is interested in you."

Jan got her tablet out and stood.

"Jan." Aaron shifted in his chair. "Am I going to have to catch you?"

"No, I'm just going to take a picture." She aimed the tablet down the aisle so that it was a picture of everyone.

"You are such a deceptive woman." Mary said.

Jan tapped the camera icon and snapped a bunch of pictures in the low light. "Takes one to know one."

"Christians say that to one another, not to sinners." She tapped her bible on Jan. "Good Lord, the page turned color."

"Okay, am I going to have to separate you two?" Aaron turned and looked at the young man. "Awkward."

The young man winked at him, got up, and left the car.

"I'm not chasing after him."

Jan looked on. "I will."

"Jan, he's barely thirty." Mary said.

"Oh, I think he's good looking." Jan winked at him.

The young man looked back once and locked eyes with Jan. Then, he disappeared into the next car.

"Au revoir." Jan said.

"Try A la prochaine."

"What's that mean?" The train changed tracks and Jan fell against the seat. "Sorry."

"Until next time." Aaron helped her sit down. "Keep your hopes up."

"Ah-lah-pro-chain."

"Close." He laughed. "Practice makes perfect."

"Maybe I'll practice with him." Jan's brow bounced up and down.

Mary's tongue moved in and out of her mouth as if some horrid stomach acid pushed its way into her mouth. "Are we there yet?"

The train slowed and then it stopped at Gare de Colmar. The soft bell rang and the doors opened. Jan hurried to keep up with Aaron and Mary.

"Hello!" Aaron let his luggage fall to his side and hugged his friend.

A dark-haired woman, bold cheeks and a simple smile, hugged him back. "Yes, welcome to Colmar!" She kissed his cheek. "I'm so happy to have you here."

"I'm happy to see you too; it wonderful!" He tightened his arms around her and then let them loose. "Olivia, these are my friends." He held his arm out toward Jan and Mary.

Jan stepped up. "Hi, je suis Jan."

Olivia laughed. "So, you've learned some French." She hugged Jan and then Mary stepped up.

"Je suis Mary." She looked the children over.

"It's lovely to meet you." She looked to her children who were quiet and taken by the strangers. "These are my children, Ada and my son, Alexandre. Though, he prefers Alex."

Just then, Alex, ten years old and full of energy, pulled at his mother's blouse. He spoke so fast that Aaron raised his brow in a curious way.

"I thought my French was good, but I didn't get one word." Aaron said and smiled at the boy.

"Well, he's just ready for dinner." Olivia said.

They greeted Ada and Alex. Ada, just eight years old, was so shy that she clung to her mother's side with clenched fist full of her mother's blouse.

In the distance, a stout man with a hoodie on, dressed in jeans, watched them. His phone was pressed against his hip and the phone snapped several pictures.

"Oui, un moment." She looked at Aaron. "So, we should get you to your flat."

Alex looked at the man and then the phone. He squinted to focus, but the man turned and disappeared into the crowd. "Mama."

"D'accord, Alex … un moment." She ushered her children off to the car.

"Mama," Alex said and told her about the man who had his phone aimed at them.

"Oui," she said and then told him that it's common for people to take pictures at the station.

In a few minutes, they were out of the station and in Olivia's car.

"This is so nice of you." Jan said and held her tablet up. She balanced it with one hand and tried to press the picture button with the other. The tablet moved with the bumps in the road. "Cobblestone roads."

"Yes, it has a long history in France. Especially, in the place you're staying …"

"Petite Venise." Aaron said.

Mary leaned forward, "Is it true that most of France is Catholic?"

Olivia looked at Aaron through the rearview mirror; their eyes met and his rolled. "It's quite possible." She smiled and turned her head just enough to acknowledge Mary.

Alex spoke in French and wanted to know what she asked.

"We are Catholic; my husband practices more than me." Then, she explained to Alex what she said.

Jan mumbled the words, "Mary, maybe we should ask other things." She shook her head. "So, what grade are Alex and Ada in?"

"Ah, Alex is in the middle of school. I don't know how to translate his position." She smiled. "And my daughter is at the end of starter school."

"Maybe kindergarten and middle school, like sixth grade or something?" Jan said.

"Is that private school?" Mary asked.

"It's something similar." Olivia said. "We pay to send them there, but it's open to other students. The curriculum varies and is different than a state school."

"So, they have less students per teacher." Mary said.

"I think so." Aaron chimed in. "We're here." He pointed up the alley. "We'll get changed and have a rest, then head over to your place."

"Yes, I'll come for you at seven-thirty?" She got out.

"Great, that'll give us a couple of hours to freshen up." Aaron got out and they went to the trunk.

Alex looked around and then looked at his sister. "There was a man who took photos of us."

She looked back and then at him. "Mama has said to beware of such people."

"I told her, but she didn't care." He shook his head.

"Alex, she cared, but she has her friends."

"One American friend and he's only been here once before." Alex said.

Ada rolled her eyes and then shook her head at him. "You worry too much."

"Okay, that's it then." Aaron said and hugged Olivia. They walked to a gate where their host waited.

"Allo!" The host waved at them. "Please, I'm Tolley."

Olivia spoke to her in French and then Tolley welcomed Jan and Mary.

"It's good you're here. Please." Tolley motioned with her hand toward a door.

"Bye." Olivia walked back to her car was gone in that next second.

Jan, Mary, and Aaron got in the apartment.

"Wow, this is nice." Jan said.

Aaron laughed, "We're off to a good start. I hope it ends as nice."

Mary set her bible on the counter. "Okay."

Chapter Four: My Tablet!

Aaron rubbed the sleep from his eyes and looked at the window. "Is it morning?"

"Aaron?" Jan asked from the living room.

"Yeah, I'm up."

She laughed, "Mary's ready and I'm ready. When is Olivia coming?"

He pressed his fingers into his eyes and pushed the blurriness out. Then, he studied the hands on his watch. "Ten minutes."

Too late, Olivia pressed the buzzer on the door and looked up at the window to the apartment.

Mary opened the window and looked at Olivia. "We're coming."

"Yes, okay." Olivia nodded.

Aaron was dressed, splashed his face with water, and then put a towel to his face. "Should have planned for dinner tomorrow."

"You have jet lag?" Mary asked.

"It's rare." He set the towel on the rack. "Keys?"

"I've got them." Mary went to the door with Jan.

"Good, need someone responsible in this group." He smiled and Jan winked at him.

They got to Olivia's house in Colmar; the house was a charming home on some land with a turned under garden.

"Yes, the garden is very good for us." Olivia looked at Jan and Mary. "We have beets, radishes, lettuce, carrots, and more." She pointed. "We use everything from it through the season."

Alex waved from the window. "Allo Aaron!"

"Bon soir, Alex." He waved back and then they went in.

The foyer was long with a stairway to the basement right by the front door. The hallway ran the length of the house from the living room past the kitchen and den to the other end of the house with two bedrooms and a bathroom.

François, her husband, shook their hands and nodded more than he spoke to them. "Welcome." A slender man with salt and pepper hair, he was curious about Aaron. "So, you've come after all these years."

"Yes," Aaron replied. "All of them."

"How lovely." Jan said and held her tablet up. She snapped pictures of the foyer, the hall, and the bathroom.

Aaron couldn't resist the temptation to say something about her photography. "Yep, that's what the toilets look like in France. It's crazy that it's just like our toilets in the states."

Jan held up the tablet and snapped another picture. "Huh?"

"That they sit just like we do for hours on end." He smirked and bumped her with his shoulder. "Literally."

"Ha-ha." She put the tablet up and blinded him with the flash.

"Ah!"
Alex and Ada laughed.

François helped his wife get the food to the table: sliced tomatoes, zucchini, squash, and dried meats.

Mary took some photos and then held the bible up. "Do you read the bible?" She asked Alex.

Alex looked at her, looked at the bible, and then looked at her again. "Mama!" He smiled, turned and walked away.

"Is he afraid of the bible?" She shook her head.

"It's in English, so he can't understand any of it." Aaron said. "Don't you have one in French?"
"Why ask." Jan said and smiled at Ada. "Take a picture with me?"

Mary looked the food over and then went to Aaron. "What's for dinner?"

"Vegetables, dried meats, and fromage." He touched her shoulder. "It'll be fine."

"The meat looks … flat, lifeless." She gritted her teeth and pursed her lips. "She's our host so …"

"It's fine. Dried meat is thin." He chuckled. "And all prepared meats are lifeless, hello."

After dinner, Ada played the piano for them.

Aaron leaned forward to clap and the chair slid out from under him! "Hey!"

They laughed. Mary and Jan took a picture.

"So, you get up to … not help me, but to take a picture?" He shook his head. "You people suck."

"Aaron, d'accord?" Alex asked and held out his hand.

"Now, here is a true gentleman." He took Alex's hand and got up. "You know you're overweight when you turn on your side to get up."

"You're not overweight." Jan said.

"Thanks, Jan."

She laughed heartily. "You're fat!"

Olivia laughed and then translated to her family; the family erupted in laughter.

"Glad to be the joke this evening." He shook it off and got the chair upright. "The fire is nice."

"Well, it's just for you." Olivia said and they locked eyes.

François looked at his wife and then Aaron. He crossed his arms and sat back against the chair. He mumbled something to his wife about her behavior toward Aaron. The words were a little harsh and dismissive of his wife's friend from so many years ago. "Twice in one year, why?"

"François." She rolled her eyes at him.

"Twenty years before April of this year, right Olivia?" Aaron's words unsettled François.

François looked at Aaron and sneered. "And back so soon."

"Well, yes, but you were here in April though." She smiled and looked toward the kitchen. "Perhaps, some dessert."

"Yum!" Mary said and got up. "I'll help."

"François, what do you do?" Jan asked.

Ada went to Jan and had her phone in hand. "Selfie?"

"I'd love too." Jan said and hugged Ada.

François looked around the room and then at Aaron. "I'm …" He was lost and searched for the words in English. Each word he spoke was with a heavy accent and did not translate directly to English. "It's a post to look over …" He thought about it. "The dealings of people with anger that is displaced." His eyes slowly panned our expressions and then he tilted his chin up and looked toward the kitchen. "Olivia …" Then, he asked her in French to translate what he did for work.

She came in the room with Mary in tow. They had their hands full with cake and croissants.

"Gosh, it smells wonderful." Jan said.

The kids hurried to the table, but were met with Olivia's soft smile. "Our guest come first, thank you very much." Then, she looked at her husband. "So, he's the human resources person that has to manage the affairs of employees who have had trouble."

Ada and Alex stepped back. "Aaron," Alex said.

"Non," Olivia said, "Jan, Mary." She motioned with her hands to come sit. "Some wine, Mirabel perhaps?"

Jan sat down and Mary helped set the desert plates around the table.

"So, his job is anger management." Mary said frankly. "Yes, I'd love the wine."

"Olivia?" François asked.

"Yes," then she translated. "It's the short version." And she laughed.

After dessert, Jan, Mary, and Aaron's expression were worth a thousand words. "WE NEED SLEEP!" Aaron said it politely and in French, "Bien que nous soyons fatigues, nous sommes vraiment reconnaissants pour ce merveilleux repas."

"Of course," Olivia said. "We've got quite a day planned tomorrow, the Christmas market."

Just then, Alex spoke up and was worked up about something. "Mama."

They listened and François dismissed his concern.

"What's wrong?"

Olivia looked at François who shrugged his shoulders. "Well, you know it's known that we have to be careful."

"Because of terrorist." Jan said.

"Jan." Mary said.

"Yes, and Alex felt that there was some man that watched us; he thought it was unusual." She smiled, but her smile was less relaxed and less natural.

"We were loud and American. People always look." Aaron said and nodded at Alex. "Merci, Alex."

"No problem." The boy said.

They laughed and then sat down for desert. Afterwards, they looked at each other and their red eyes and sunken cheeks were the sure signs of utter exhaustion. "Thank you so much." Aaron said.

Back in their apartment in Petite Venise, they got their things ready for bed. Mary and Jan wrote in their diaries and Aaron laid on his bed with his tablet.

"I'm done." He said and went to the living room. "I just can't keep my eyes open."

"I can't wait to do the market tomorrow." Jan said.

"I'm curious about Sunday." Mary sat at the counter that abutted the kitchen.

"If they go to church?" He asked. "François will, but Oliva won't."

"I'd like to go to the service in Strasbourg." She grinned.

"Well, it is a Catholic church." He said.

That night, a man dressed in a heavy-long coat and chapeau stood by their building. From the main street, a cobblestone street, he looked at the dim glow that emanated from their apartment.

Aaron and Jan were fast asleep. Mary read a verse from the gospel of Mark and then prayed.

The man got on his cell phone, said something that was barely audible, and then walked away.

The next morning, Olivia pressed the buzzer. She held a sack with croissants: some with chocolate and some with powdered sugar.

Aaron studied the expresso machine. "How hard can it be?" Then, he turned his attention to the door. "Better let her in." He pushed the button for the door below.

Olivia knocked on their apartment door and the door eased open. "Hello?"

"Come in!" Jan said and was so jovial. "Oh, I'm so happy to be here." She hugged Olivia and then kissed her on the cheek.

"Yes, well I'm happy to have you. Good morning." She set the bag of croissants down. "So, I've brought croissants. I know Aaron likes chocolate and there are plain too."

"Hey Olivia." Mary said and they hugged. "We're nearly ready."

"It's still quite early, just half past eight." She looked at the espresso machine. "Have you figured it out?"

Jan laughed. "He pressed the button and the cup filled up, then over."

"His cup runneth over." Mary said.

"Yeah, she wasn't going to let that one slide without a religious reference." He tapped the expresso machine. "Damn thing."

"Yes, well it's the operator." Olivia set the coffee in the container. "The upper button is for one cup; the lower button is for two cups."

"But there's only one spout." He rolled his eyes.

"No, in fact there are two within." She pressed the top button and the cup filled with a single pour. "See."

"See my butt." He shook his head, got the cup, and went to his room. "I'll be back."

"We've got a good ride to Strasbourg." She took the croissants out. "The Christmas Market is really beautiful."

"Where are your kids?" Jan asked.

"In school." Olivia said and made another expresso.

"So, they have school too." Jan smiled politely. "I didn't know if it was the same as the US."

Olivia laughed and offered her the espresso. "Yes, we work too." She put a croissant on a plate. "We have school and stores just like the US." She fanned her hand down as an extension of her statement.

"I feel funny for asking." Jan said and sipped her espresso. "Sorry."

"It's her first time outside the US." Aaron said. He wore jeans, a nice polo, and had a scarf wrapped around his neck.

"Things are quite the same. The language though, no." Olivia sipped an espresso.

Steam rose from the coffee and Jan and Mary savored the croissants.

"My goodness, this is so delicious." Mary said. "Wow, we definitely don't have this in town."

"Perhaps, you can take a recipe back." Olivia offered.

"Or a boyfriend." Aaron said. "I'd rather have the latter than the former."

Olivia laughed. "So, everyone knows?"

"Except your hubby." He said and got his coat.

"Yes, well François does not believe it's possible for such a thing." She put the croissants on a plate and set them to the side.

Jan rolled her eyes. "with Aaron, it's possible."

Mary mumbled, "sinner."

"Yes, I know, Mary." He tapped her shoulder.

"What's this?" Olivia got her keys out and stood by the door.

"I'm a sinner before God." He walked out.

"In the eyes of God." Mary finished her coffee, set the cup down, and then went to the door.

"Oh, who cares. It's your life, do what you want." Jan got her tablet and took a picture of the food. "This was lovely, Olivia, thank you."

"Yes, you're quite welcome."

From Colmar to Strasbourg, they talked about the small cars, diesel gas only, roundabouts, and good eating.

"Can you get stuck in a roundabout?" Jan asked.

"I hope not." Olivia laughed. "It would be quite maddening to be trapped and go around and around."

Aaron laughed. "Let's try it."

"No," Mary said. "I want to get pictures of the church."

"Oh, the nativity scene will wait for you." Cars passed by in blurs.

"I want time to Christmas shop too." Mary said. "Things made in Germany, France, and …"

Jan held her tablet and looked at the landscape. "You said it's not acres, it's hectares?"

"Yes, it's quite small compared with an acre which is nearly three acres to one hectare." Olivia said and looked at the road. "Ah, we're nearly there."

"Remember, please don't take pictures of the police or security." Aaron said.

Olivia nodded, "yes, just to be careful of who is near you."

"Anybody touches you, shove their hand away." He finished.

"Yes, sarge." Jan saluted. "Unless they're handsome and are looking for …"

"God, please don't finish that sentence." Mary said.

"God won't, but I might." Jan smiled slyly and her brow bounced around.

"So, we have just a turn here and then to find a parking space." Olivia looked around.

"We'll take the tram." He said. "There!"

"Yes, I'm turning." She parallel parked handily.

They walked to the tram where a mix of tourist and business people jockeyed for a good place to board.

"So, I've got the tickets." Olivia said.

"Be sure to tell us how much we owe you." Jan said.

"If she wanted us to pay, she'd say so." Mary took a selfie and waved. "This is great."

They caught the tram and made their way to Strasbourg Cathedral. Olivia pointed up the cobblestone street to the main entrance. "Its actual name is Cathedral of Our Lady of Strasbourg."

Around the cathedral, there were wooden stalls set up in rows and decorated with wreaths, garland, and colorful lights. Many of them had any number of Christmas décor, candies, and mulled wine.

"It's wonderful." Mary said. She stopped, got her Canon EOS, and focused the 28-200 zoom. "I love my camera."

Aaron pulled at his collar. "It's a little chilly."

"Oh, don't whine. I thought you loved the cold." Jan had her tablet in hand and took several pictures.

"From the inside of my house or a warm train." He shook off the chill. "Windy."

"C'mon." Mary said and marched off to the entrance.

Once inside, Mary went to the Holy Water Font.

Jan snapped a picture of Mary and the blast of the white flash blinded everyone within ten meters.

"For the love, Jan!" The words blew out of Mary's mouth and nearly knocked Jan to the ground. She rubbed the white glow from her eyes. "My gosh." She stumbled into a column and hit her head.

Several Asian tourists were blinded and pressed the buttons on their cameras which set of a series of flashes! "Click!" "Click!" "Click!"

Other tourists were mad about the flash, but Jan didn't understand anything they said in French or German or Italian or Greek.

Olivia laughed quietly. "Perhaps, they will chastise you."

"Oh, they'll get over it." She aimed the tablet at the ceiling, "click!" The flash ricocheted off of the ceiling much like lightening does off clouds. Then, she turned and her bag caught the lip of the Holy Font; this particular basin was larger, made of stone, and on a pedestal. She walked off and jerked the basin over!

The stone basin smacked the marble floor! "CRACK!" The holy water splashed across the marble floor and around the shoes of the tourists!

"Oh, gosh damn-it!" Jan said and turned. She jerked the basin to her and it knocked several people over!

An elderly German couple slipped in the tsunami of holy water and they fell onto the marble floor! "Schweinhund!" The man threw his hands up, turned to get up, slipped, and fell back on his wife!

"Frederick!" The wife belched and then she knocked him off of her.

"Jesus, Jan." Aaron said. Tourists offered to help the couple as well as Aaron, but the man knocked Aaron's hand away.

Jan had her hand over her mouth. "I'm so sorry." She walked over and took their picture. The flash blinded them and then she tucked her tablet and offered to help them up.

"Jan!" Aaron shouted.

A crowd gathered and tourists from Asia snapped bunches of pictures.

A voice erupted over the speakers, "SILENCE!" Then, there was silence. Everyone looked up!

Mary looked up, "Yes, God?"

Then, the voice growled over the speakers again and the words reverberated off of the stone walls and stained glass, "This is a church!" A moment passed and then, "SILENCE!"

"Perhaps, no more flash photos." Olivia whispered.

"How else am I supposed to get pictures?" Jan offered her hand to the woman. "I'm so sorry."

The man was up, but his wife lost her footing and slid around in a circle on the marble floor.

People in the crowd leapt to avoid being knocked down themselves by that poor German woman.

Finally, Jan and Aaron got her up and he swiped at the water stain on the woman's backside.

The woman looked at Aaron, her pale cheeks turned an ashy red and she slapped him! "Ah, du biest!"

"So sorry." Aaron said. "You're … all wet."

The German man was in a rage and waved his hand at Jan and Aaron. He got his wife by the arm, pulled her close, and then they turned and marched off.

Jan couldn't resist and took a picture of their soaked behinds. "Holy ass."

Aaron scoffed and shook his head. "Going to send you to your room if you can't behave in public." He went to Olivia and they walked away.

The crowd thinned and Jan went the other way. A man, with a hoodie pulled over his head, had his gaze fixed on Jan and her tablet.

Olivia stopped at a saint and looked at Aaron. "She's quite a lot to manage."

He looked for Jan. "Uh-huh, that's what the Pope said."

Olivia laughed. "I don't imagine she'd get near him." She tucked her arm into Aarons. "She's far too dangerous."

He tightened his arm around hers and they walked toward the front.

Mary talked quietly with a priest and held her bible out for him. "Just a blessing for my bible and, maybe, your signature?"

"My name?" His thick accent made it difficult for Mary to understand.

Mary held a pen out and opened the bible. "Yes, so I know who blessed it."

"Father Latour."

Mary spelled his name out and then drew a line next to it. "Just there."

"Madam, this is highly unorthodox." Father Latour said and tucked his hands. "Please." He smiled politely and wished she'd go away; despite how it felt as a thought, he prayed for her salvation.

"Alright, a selfie then." She turned and got her camera up. "C'mon." The bible looked like it floated in front of them.

Father Latour turned away. "Madam!"

"SILENCE!" The voice roared over the speakers.

Mary snapped several pictures as Father Latour made his way behind a barrier. "Definitely not a *devout* Catholic." He said.

Jan and Mary looked over the postcards, rosaries, and other collectibles.

Aaron and Olivia were outside and waited on the girls. He sent a text to Mary, "when you're ready. We're out front."

"Aaron is out front." Mary said.

"Oh, I'm ready." Jan looked at her and then turned to the massive wood doors.   "What'd you think?"

"It's magnificent." Mary said. "A beautiful place to worship." They went outside and stopped on the steps.

"I love it." She aimed her tablet up. "Get a picture of the top."

Mary looked at several French military men who were armed and on patrol. "Look out Jan."

"What?"

"Don't take their picture." Aaron said.

"What if we take a picture of the building that's behind them?" Mary asked.

"Yeah, or bump into the hotties." Jan smiled wide and then made her way toward them.

"Jan!" Aaron reached for her and missed.

"Hi," Jan stopped right in front of them. "How about a picture."

The sergeant, a stocky sandy blond with a beard, smiled politely. "No, it's not possible." He motioned for his men to move on.

"That's too bad." Jan waited. After the men passed, she aimed her tablet at the church. Then, she waited, lowered her tablet, and got a picture, several in fact, of the Army men's butts. "Wow, even in khakis, their butts stick out."

"Really." Aaron said. "Okay, they did."

Olivia laughed. "Yes, it's nearly time for some lunch and there's been such excitement already."

Aaron looked at the men. "I know I'm hungry."

"Olivia, do young French men dig older American women?" Jan caught up to her.

Olivia smiled at Jan, "I don't know. Anything's quite possible."

"Good." Jan raised her balled fist to celebrate.

"Wow, look at all the Christmas stalls." Mary said. "We have time to stop."

"Of course," Olivia said. "Please."

"We'll never eat now." Aaron shook his head. "We'll look at some after lunch too."

Jan got her tablet and took pictures of the handmade ornaments.

"Are the decorations made in France." Mary asked.

"Anything made in China?" Aaron asked.

"Probably not China." She pointed at the ornaments. "There are wood carved trains, hand blown glass, and handmade soaps with balsam. Things are made in Germany, Belgium, France, Italy and other EU countries."

The man with the hoodie from the church pretended to look at croissants, but kept a closer eye on the foursome, particularly Jan.

"Oh, look at these." Jan held up a large hand-blown glass ornament with "NOEL" and holly leaves on it. "This is beautiful."

Mary got one in hand. "Try not to slip in the water." She looked behind Jan.

Jan looked behind her. "Oh, ha-ha."

A handsome young man with dark hair and a thin beard came from behind a curtain. "Bonjour, can I help?" His soft cheeks were a rosy red and his full lips barely had the strength to part when he smiled.

Jan was smitten and looked him up and down. "Bonjour you." Her smile beamed like a light from a lighthouse looking for distant ships. "How much are you?"

"Jan!" Mary shouted.

Jan looked at Mary and then at the young man. "How much is this?"

"Really Jan." Aaron chuckled and looked at Olivia. "Did you take your pills?"

"She's not at all bashful." Olivia said.

"Ah, it's marked on the side." He pointed at a tag that hung from the top of the ornament.

Jan mumbled, "I wish he was."

Mary got her bible in hand and smacked Jan's shoulder. "Be healed."

"Stop it." Jan held the ornament up. "I love your balls."

"Good Lord!" Mary said and stepped away.

Aaron and Olivia cleared their throats.

"Yes, well, I have worked them with my hands for many hours." He waved his hand over the ornaments. "Do you prefer just that one?"

Aaron spoke out. "One's never enough."

"I'll take that one too." Jan pointed to a red glass ball with gold and silver drizzled around it.

"Ah, it's very nice." He got the one from Jan and the other ball. "I'll wrap them nicely for you and, if you like, you can come by when you finish your walk to get them."

"Oh, I'd love that." She got a card from her bag. "Here's my number in case I forget."

He took the card, winked at her, and tucked it into his pocket.

"If you had your phone, that would help." Mary said and looked at Aaron.

"Jan, we have lunch reservations." Aaron said.

"I'll put the name Jan on your package." He set them aside.

"And what's your name?" She got her credit card out.

"Philip." His smile held her gaze.

"Uh, I think as soon as you pay, we should go." Aaron said and tapped her shoulder. "We don't want to be late."

Jan smiled, signed the bill, and got her credit card back. "See you later, Philip, merci."

"Je vous en prie." He winked at Jan.

"Okay, how about lunch." Aaron said.

Jan tucked her tablet under her arm and turned. "Don't be jealous."

Just then, the man in the hoodie made a mad dash at them, snatched the tablet, and ran off!

Jan yelped! "Hey!"

Aaron turned and ran after him! "Stop him! Thief!"

Mary screamed, "Sinner!"

The hooded man darted around people like a rabbit running through the brush!

The hooded man looked back several times! Each time he looked back, Aaron was closing in on him.

Aaron huffed! "STOP!" In the split of a second, he looked for any military or police; there were none. "Police!"

Jan and Mary talked with Olivia about what just happened.

"It's not as common, but people steal." Olivia was on her phone and alerted the police.

"I can't believe it. I just tucked it and he got it." Jan wiped the tears away. "All my pictures."

Marry hugged her. "Aaron will get him."

"Oh my God, Aaron … he, I hope he doesn't get hurt." Jan trembled.

Aaron turned another corner and chased the man past the square and down a quiet street. People were shocked and got out of the way! Then, another turn and the pursuit went on! With every slam of his foot on the cobblestone street, Aaron's legs ached.

The hooded man cut down an alley and ducked into a nook. The darkness in the alley, even on this sunny cold day, seemed to overwhelm the light. Aaron turned into the alley and skidded to a stop. His cheeks blew in and out, his lungs burned, and his throat itched! "Where the hell is he?"

Clearly, there were fewer people than before. He'd been lured into a trap before and knew that he had to back off. "Damn dirtbag," it was quiet, eerily quiet. A cat walked across the alley, stopped midway, and looked at him. "Meow." Then, it walked on. "The police are coming!" His eyes squinted and tried to focus on the shadows. "In French maybe." He inhaled. "La police arrive!"

Suddenly, the hooded man stepped out from the shadows. "Not soon enough." He held the tablet up and, with a heavy French accent, "Come get it."

The police ran up to Jan. "My friend chased him toward the square."

"He shouldn't have run after him." The officer said. "Allon-y!" Several of the police ran toward the square.

"Just give it back." Behind him, people wandered by without a clue that he faced off with a thief.

The hooded man studied Aaron and then looked at the tablet. He spoke with a soft French accent. "Not worth the trouble." He tossed the tablet onto a pile of garbage, flipped Aaron off, and then ran away.

"Jerk." Aaron waited a moment and then walked into the alley.

"Qu'est-ce que vous faites?" A policeman shouted at Aaron. He blew his whistle!

Aaron picked up the tablet and turned. "J'ai la tablette des mes ami."

"Ah, you are the American who chased the criminal?" Several other policemen rushed in.

"Yes." The police escorted Aaron got back to the cathedral. When he made the corner to the cathedral his mouth dropped.

Jan was arm in arm with two good looking cops. Olivia took a picture. "Olivia, here!" She hugged a young, bearded Army man who eased away mid hug.

"Non, madam, pas possible." He brought his rifle to his chest to add an extra barrier to keep the loving American at a distance. "S'il te plait."

Jan frowned.

Mary pulled at Jan's jacket. "Jan."

The policeman questioned Aaron. "Your passport please."

Aaron handed his passport to the policeman.

"And what can you tell me about this person?" The officer took a picture of Aaron's passport with his mini-tablet. He studied the screen and then got a reply. "Okay."

"Uh, he was about five-ten maybe." He pondered. "I guess he was stocky, it could've been his heavy coat. Oh, he had a hoodie over his head and it covered part of his face, unshaven, strong jaw."

"So, the color of his skin?" The policeman used a stylus and tapped away at a tablet. "Did you speak with him?"

"Yeah, I did and he was white." Aaron looked at the crowd that passed slowly by them. "I caught up to him in an alley and said that the police were coming."

"It's good that you didn't follow him into the alley." The policeman said something over his radio. "How did you get the tablet back?"

"He came out from a spot in the alley and said it wasn't worth it. Then he tossed the tablet down." Aaron bit at his lip and wondered if the crook broke her tablet.

The policeman extended his hand. "Thank you, here's your passport."

Jan came to Aaron. "Thank you. I'm so glad you weren't hurt." They hugged. "My hero."

"Your tablet madam." The policeman handed it to her.

The bearded military man waved goodbye, "Adieu, mon cher!"

His buddies taunted him. "Quel Belle fille!"

"Get me a date with him as a reward." Aaron whispered and dipped his head at the bearded Army man.

Jan turned and winked at the bearded hottie. "I'll try."

Aaron got her by the her arm. "No, uh let's just hold on a minute."

Afterwards, Jan, Aaron, Mary, and Olivia sat at lunch in a second-floor restaurant with a large window that faced the square. Beautiful green and red garland adorned the window and there were many poinsettias at the base of the window. The tables were round with four leather recliner style chairs to each and velvety red table clothes.

"This is nice." Aaron got his serviette and placed it over his lap.

"Bonjour," the server looked at each of them with a heart-felt smile.

Olivia ordered the drinks, "deux espressos et deux Americanos, s'il te plait."

The server nodded and left.

"I just can't believe he did it in broad daylight." Jan said and looked her tablet over. "At least it's not broke."

"Aaron, I can't believe you chased after him. You could have been hurt." Mary bowed her head. "Thank you, Lord." She looked up. "My heart's still pounding like a runaway train."

"Mine too, thank you." Jan gripped Aaron's forearm and her eyes welled up.

"You're welcome." He let his hand rest on hers. "It's done and things are alright."

Olivia sipped her water and had a worrisome look. "Yes, thank goodness."

Jan turned her tablet on and studied the screen. The screen scrambled and then went to the desktop. "That's funny."
"What is?" He asked.

Olivia asked, "Mary, did you look at your ornaments?"

"Oh." She got her bag. "They are terrific."

Jan turned to Aaron. "The screen was scrambled." She handed him the tablet.

"Looks okay now." He pressed the home button, then the power button, and then the home button again. "It went to the homepage, seems fine."

Jan got the tablet in hand then fingered a corner. "Oh no."

"What?" Aaron asked.

"He broke it." A portion of the plastic was split apart.

"Oh?" Aaron leaned over and looked at the corner.

"See, it's cracked." She got her fingers into a small opening along the edge.

"No, it's the case cover, just snap it back." He reached over to help her.

"Oh?" She pressed on the edge and it clicked back into place. "Thank God."

"Thank God that Aaron didn't get hurt." Mary said and handed her small wooden Christmas train to Olivia. "Made in Germany."

"I'm fine." He drank half his water. "And thirsty."

After lunch, they roamed the Christmas market and bought more Christmas things. Jan picked up her ornaments, shook the young man's hand for a while, and then let go only when he pulled away.

Olivia glanced at the time. "Perhaps, we should get back."

Aaron looked at his phone. "Wow, no kidding. It's nearly three."

"Lunch was wonderful, Olivia, thank you." Jan said.

"It was wonderful." Mary looked around. "Where do we need to go to get back to the car?"

Olivia happily pointed the way. "The way we came, through the market and toward the entrance of the cathedral."

By four-thirty, they were back in their apartment.

"I'm going to take a nap." Aaron nodded at Jan and Mary. "See you later."

"What time is Olivia coming back?" Mary asked.

"About six I think." He said and plopped down on his bed.

Mary and Jan went to their room and wrote in their diaries. By five, the sun was just a glimmer of orange over the rooftops and the street lights were on.

The hooded man stood a few blocks away and held a phablet. The bright screen showed a map of the area and a little yellow blip from the apartment with Mary, Jan, and Aaron just up the street. A single tap with his finger and the coordinates lit up right next to a blip that pulsed, "TARGET ACQUIRED."

Jan looked at her tablet. "It's nearly charged." Then, the screen flickered. "Dumb thing."

"How about you?" Mary asked. "You doing okay?"

"Yeah," she said and pushed the sleep from her eyes. "It was different; that's for sure. I can't say I've never been robbed now."

"But you're safe and you got your tablet back." Mary went to the bathroom. "You want to wash up?"

"You go ahead. I'll do my hair after." Jan ran her fingers through her hair. "Ick."

"Okay," Mary closed the door.

Jan looked at the screen and it flickered. "Great." She set it down and went to the kitchen.

Aaron emerged from the bedroom with a half-crooked smile across his worn face. "Hey."

"You better splash some water on your face." Jan made a coffee.

"Or have a glass of wine." He rubbed his eyes. "You doing okay?"

"Yeah, but the screen flickered again." She stepped to the side so he could get to the fridge.

"How about I check it when we get back?" The wine, a Moscato, poured easily into the glass. "Oh, that smells so good."

"I thought you were a fan of gin?"

"I am, but I don't have any gin." He chuckled.

That evening at Olivia's house, they sat at a round table. The children were full of energy with the guests in the house, strangers only a day ago; now, they were their friends.

"So," François handed Mary some vegetables. "Tomorrow we go to Auberge."

Olivia looked at Aaron. "You've been,"

"Yes, I remember it and the food was awesome, very authentic." Aaron said.

"Yes, it's authentic, but for German food." François said. "Not French."

Aaron shook his head at François and huffed. "Yes, those damn Germans."

"Il neige, Aaron." Alex said.

"What's that?" Jan asked. "These greens look wonderful."

"He said, it's snowing." Aaron got the bowl with the greens.

"Is that bad?" Mary asked and held the plate with the dried beef. "This beef is great."

François nodded at Mary, "Not for here, but on the mountain, maybe."

"I'm glad you like it." Olivia got the dried beef and passed the vegetables to Ada.

François raised his glass. "To new friends."

Everyone raised their glass and spoke. "New friends."

"And no more thieves." Jan swallowed her whole glass of wine. "No more."

"Maman?" Ada asked.

Olivia translated for her daughter.

"Oh." Ada smiled and was delighted to know what they said.

"One great meal after another and wonderful company." Mary set her bible to the side, "amen."

Olivia looked at Alex, "and tomorrow we go to Auberge and have a different kind of prepared meal."

"Different?" Jan asked. "How?"

Chapter Six: Mountain Top and Duck, Duck ... Rabbit

The next morning, they were up and Jan looked out the window and then at her tablet. "Weather app has zero Celsius and there's snow all over."

"It's winter." Mary said and got her bible from the counter. "Who got jelly on my bible?" Her cheeks reddened.

"Oh, gosh I'm sorry." Jan got a paper towel and wiped the cover off.

"Jan." Mary got the towel from her and shook her head. "You know what this bible means to me."

Jan smiled politely. "Yes, I do." She got her coffee and sat in the living room.

Aaron opened the door to his room which opened to the living room. "Don't drink too much. We're going to that café up the street I thought."

"I just want to have a warm up." Jan said.

"And a jam up." Mary mumbled.

"What?" His brow rose slowly and mouthed the words. "What is it now?"

Jan mouthed the words, "her bible."

"Oh." He went to the bathroom. "Leave in ten minutes or more?"

"I'm fine." Mary said.

"Yep, ten minutes to relax." Jan sipped her coffee. "And tonight, we're going to that mountain restaurant?"

"No, this afternoon, we'll go around one." He splashed his face and cleaned up. "I love my cologne."

"It does smell good." Mary said. "Where's it from?"

"Norway, Geir cologne for men." He dried his face and then spritzed himself.

"You're a man?" Jan laughed. "Kidding."

"Another comment like that and I'll trash you in French to every hot guy I see." His shirt was a light blue and he pulled at the collar. "I look good."

Mary laughed, "you mean you're going to sin in French."

"Oui, sin." He shook his head.

Along the cobblestone streets of Petite Venise, Mary, Jan, and Aaron made their way past the beautiful seventeenth century homes.

Jan stopped, held her tablet up, and aimed it down the street. "My gosh, the houses are beautiful."

Many tourists made their way past; some of them stopped at store fronts and admired the souvenirs.

Mary had her camera and snapped several shots. "They are beautiful." She walked across the street to the canal and took a selfie. "A blue house, yellow house, and a light green house. I love the colors and the Christmas decorations."

A musician played an accordion and the soft sounds floated around them.

Aaron inhaled deep. "Yeah, it is a neat place tucked into the east of France. Most people come to France and they go to the Eiffel Tower, the Louvre, Montmartre or walk the Champs Elysees." He drew in a deep breath and paused. "It's off the beaten path." He sighed gently. "Let's find a nice café."

"Do they have the gondolas?" Jan asked.

Mary pointed at a boat. "Something less romantic." Her camera flashed. "Looks like a Jon boat."

"What?" Jan asked and looked over the rail at the boat.

"Jon boats are flat bottom boats for freshwater; they're usually not very big." He pointed up the canal. "There's a couple of gondolas."

"Oh, yeah." Mary took several pictures. "Hey, let's do a selfie."

They lined up and looked at the camera. "Click!"

"Alright, onto the café." Aaron said.

A block away, the man who stole Jan's tablet was dressed nicely in dark slacks, an open collar French blue Oxford, and a dark blue blazer. He pushed his wavy dark hair from his face. When he raised his arm, his bicep nearly burst the blazer's seam. Aaron was right when he told the police that the crook was stocky; it wasn't his heavy overcoat. The sun brightened the soft dark whiskers that covered his face. He reached into his jacket and got a phablet out. His fingerprint unlocked it and his eyes danced around the screen. Then, he mumbled a few words in French. "Mon petit ane."

Jan and Mary sipped on Americano coffees and Aaron had an espresso. Two half-eaten croissants with butter sat next to their coffee.

"Let's not eat too much." Aaron said and sipped his espresso. "We've got lunch on the mountain."

Mary spoke up. "Yeah, so what's the deal with that place?"

"Auberge is a charming restaurant with breathtaking vistas." He said. "It won't be on a scale like Schilthorn, but it's still nice."

"I can't wait to see it." Jan said and played on her tablet. The screen flickered. "You told the cop that he tossed my tablet."

"Yeah." He leaned over and looked at it.

"The screen flickers every once in a while." Jan pursed her lips.

"I'll check on line to see if there's a way to adjust it." He rested his hand on her shoulder.

"German food, is it like sauerkraut and schnitzel?" Mary asked

"Can be, but they have other meats and very authentic." He looked at his watch.

"What time is it?" Mary asked.

"Nearly noon." Aaron held up his watch.

"Already?" Jan asked.

"Yep." He took another sip and then raised his hand at the server. "I'll get the bill and we'll have to get going; Olivia's going to pick us up at twelve-thirty."

"Oui." Jan said.

"Oui-oui." Mary said and finished the croissant.

A man, in a coat and hat, followed them.

By one, they were with Olivia and the kids. Jan and Mary were in the back with Alex and Ada. The kids talked in a frenzy about all kinds of things. Olivia tried to translate most of it and Aaron got a few words. His translation amounted to clues of what the kids did at school, after school, and on the journey to get them.

"So, Ada had math and played the harp." He said.

Olivia chimed in. "Well, she had math yes, but she did not play the harp in math class." She laughed.

"Yes, I know that." He shook his head. "And Alex had horse lessons in downtown."

"Yes, just next to the highway." Olivia laughed. "You should stay longer to better your understanding."

"Didn't Alex say, petit-ville?" Aaron asked.

"No, it was petite ferme." She said.

"Maman!" Alex shouted.

"Alex, un moment sil te plait." She said firmly.

"That meant a little closed?" Aaron asked.

"No, it means a little farm." She turned and they began the journey up the mountain. "It's a lot of snow."

"No kidding." He looked ahead and there was snow piled as high as three or four feet to the sides of the road. "Wow, the trees are covered with snow."

"Yes," she laughed. "It's winter."

"Tell them Olivia." Mary said. "They keep checking the temperature." She held her bible. "This keeps me warm."

Olivia looked at Aaron. "Yes, I see that."

"She tears out the pages and sets fire to them." He chuckled. "She's on her fifth bible now."

"Oh, shut up." Mary smacked him with the bible.

"Maman!" Alex shouted.

"Oui, Alex?"

Alex went on about the thief and asked if it looked like the man at the train station.

Olivia was firm when she answered. "Non, Alex."

"He asked about the crook?"

Olivia looked back at him and then at Aaron. "Yes, but to confirm what he asked will make his mind run on and on. So, I said no so that he doesn't worry at the train station or have nightmares."

"Oh."

Jan leaned forward. "What's going on?"

Aaron turned to her, "nothing, tell you later." He grinned.

"Oh," she leaned back. "How about a selfie?"

Alex made a goofy face. "Oui, selfie!"

They continued their journey up the mountain and made turn after turn. The road wasn't as clear higher up and, now, was snowed over.

"It seems we'll stop up here." Olivia looked for a place to park.

"Are we here?" Jan asked.

"It's here if we stop, but the restaurant … no, it's not here." Olivia pulled into a place and the car tires crushed the snow beneath them.

"Why stop then?" Aaron asked.

"We have to walk." She said, shut the car off, and gathered her purse, scarf, and keys.

"Walk?" Aaron looked around. "Walk where?" He huffed. "We're surrounded by snow; it's like a winter wonderland."

Jan and Mary got out.

"Mary, look how nice it is." Jan said, got her tablet up and snapped pictures.

"Yes, well Christmas is for wonderland." Olivia got the keys to the car.

"Olivia." François walked up and wore a heavy coat, gloves, and hiking boots. "Ah, you're not quite dressed for the walk."

Aaron smiled, "I didn't know we were going to walk. I'll be hungry when we get there."

"Yes," he said and got Ada. "Perhaps, we have an extra coat."

"No, I'm fine. This windbreaker is pretty tough." He pulled the collar up.

"Here, but further up … I don't know." François looked at Alex, "Allez Alex."

Mary took pictures. "This is perfect." Jan followed her up the snow-covered road.

Olivia got her gloves on and checked that the car was locked. "Okay, we should go."

"How far?" Aaron asked.

François and Ada were some distance behind Jan and Mary.

Olivia rolled her eyes and laughed, "Aaron, it's a good walk." She took his arm in hers. They trudged through the snow; it was nearly four inches thick and slushy.

Alex looked at Aaron and waved for him to come over. "Aaron, selfie!"

"Oui, Je viens, Alex." He got his foot stuck and his shoe came off. "Damn snow."

"Aaron, the children." Olivia's brow went up.

"Yes, sorry." He stood next to Alex and got his phone out.

Olivia laughed. Jan and Mary stopped to take a picture too.

Mary focused, "ready?"

Alex reached behind Aaron and got hold of a snow laden branch just above Aaron's head. Then, he pulled hard and ran!

A dump truck load of snow fell from the branch and showered Aaron.

"Ah!" Aaron shook and turned. "Alex!"

Laughter broke out amongst them and other passersby.

François waved his hand at Alex. "Alex, non."

"Oh, Aaron, you are white for Christmas too!" Olivia laughed heartily.

"Hang on!" Mary said. She aimed her camera and snapped several pictures.

Aaron shook and wiped the snow from him. "It's gone down my back." He looked at Alex who had fled to safety up the road. "I will get you!"

"Ah, non, Aaron, sil te plait!" Alex shouted.

Ada mumbled something about waking a sleeping bear. "Tant pis pour toi, Alex."

Jan looked at Ada. "What'd she say?" She took more pictures of Aaron.

"It's too bad for Alex as he has woken a sleeping bear." Olivia translated.

Mary and Jan walked on and laughed.

Jan, "That was perfect."

"I hope you're not mad." Olivia got him by the arm. "I'll warm you."

"No, more surprised and frozen than mad." He smiled to reassure her. "Truly."

She swiped the snow away that clung to his scarf and collar. "There, you're rid of it." Then, she took his arm in hers.

François looked at them arm in arm and bit at his lip. Then, he turned and shouted, "We will be late!"

"Your husband doesn't like me." He said and looked ahead at Jan and Mary who were at the turn to go up the next leg.

An SUV beeped at them to get by.

"What's he doing?" Aaron asked.

"Well, he has all-wheel drive, so he can make it. I don't." She said and they got over. "Alex! Ada!"

The SUV pulled ahead and, at the corner, honked again at Jan and Mary.

Mary got her bible out and yelled, "Stop honking that damn horn sinner!"

Frustrated, the man pressed and held his horn for a few seconds. Finally, he got past them.

Jan gave him the finger! "Jerk!"

"Jan!" Mary said. "Not the finger."

"He's lucky I have my tablet in my other hand or he'd of got both fingers." She stopped and took a picture of the back of the SUV.

Suddenly there was a rumble and the ground trembled.

"Where's Jan and Mary?" Aaron asked.

Olivia looked ahead. "Well, either they have made the turn and are safe going up the final hill."

"Or?" His happy expression faded to worry.

"They have fallen from the mountain." She grinned.

The ground rumbled and then … the snow bank gave out at the corner near Jan and Mary!

Jan screamed! Mary turned and snatched Jan, screams erupted! "Ah!"

"Avalanche!" François yelled and grabbed his children. They ran to the side and away from the snow.

"Jan!" Aaron yelled and ran up the road. "Mary!"

Olivia yelled, "Stop Aaron! Wait!"

Aaron stopped, grabbed Olivia and dove for cover!

A bunch of snow whooshed by and covered the road! Then, it was done. Everyone stood to the sides and huddled with their loved ones.

"Jan!" "Mary!" Aaron yelled.

The snow that covered the pine trees was gone and all the pine needles glistened.

François pointed at the spot where Alex and Ada sat. "Reste ici!" He ran toward the corner.

Aaron got to the corner and the onslaught of snow knocked down some pine trees and buried other trees. He yelled, "Jan!" his eyes scanned the trees, the snow, and the valley below. "Mary!"

"What?" Mary yelped.

"Mary?" He looked around. "Jan?"

"We're right here." Jan said. She and Mary clung to the other side of a huge pine tree's trunk.

Mary had her bible in hand. "Thank God."

"Jesus Christ." Aaron said and grasped his heart. "I thought you two ..." He stopped, got his senses, and rushed to them. "Here, let me help you."

"Really," Jan said and held out her hand.

"We came for lunch, not an avalanche." Mary said.

"No shit." Aaron got her up and then grabbed Mary.

François got hold of Jan and helped her back on the road.

Mary was up and on firm ground. She looked around and then saw the SUV parked at the restaurant. "When I get up there, I'm going to kick his ass."

"Who?" Aaron looked at the restaurant.

"The honker." Mary said and marched off.

"Mary," he got Jan and looked at Olivia. "Mary, don't do anything rash."

In no time, they were in the parking lot and Mary looked the SUV over.

François looked at the SUV. "It's from Germany."

"How can you tell?" Jan asked.

"The tags are German." Olivia said.

Mary went inside first and then François, the kids, Olivia, and Aaron followed. They stood by the door. A woman, the owner, somewhat of a dirty blond with tits the size of Mount Rushmore, walked up and hugged Olivia. They made small talk and then the owner waved for them to follow her.

After they sat, Mary asked the owner a question. "Pardon me, who owns that SUV?"

The owner pondered.

"Mary, let it go." Aaron said.

"It's a man, just there." She pointed and rolled her eyes. "He's here always … with an attitude."

"That so." She looked at Aaron.

"Okay, I'll go say something." He stood.

"No, I'm fine." The bible rested softly in her hands and she prayed.

"Aaron?" Olivia asked.

François looked around, "perhaps, better to just …" He shrugged his shoulders.

"Amen." Mary set her bible down, smiled at the kids and walked over to the man.

The man, a brusque-heavy set German, was loud and waved his hands wildly as he talked. "Ja!"

Mary walked up and stood at the head of the table. In front of her, four German men, all heavy set but smaller than the driver, sat on the sides of the picnic like table.

"You." He rolled his eyes, "das kind hast kommen." He stood, "You are not welcome here. Go back to your table."

"You honked your horn and caused an avalanche that nearly killed us." Her cheeks turned an ashen red.

Olivia looked on. The children eyes were locked on the pending confrontation.

"Apologize." Her fists were balled as tight as a rope around someone's neck.

"What?" He moved from his chair and stepped halfway around the table. "You come here and you want to tell me something!" His pale complexion turned red. "You stupid tourist … you walk the middle of das road and then you tell me apologize …" He shook his fist at her. "You get the hells out of here!"

"I'm an American and …" She brought her hands up to her chest and was calm.

"Oh," He threw his hands up. "An American. Well, we should bow down to your power." Then, he got a glass of water, put his fingers in the water, and flicked the drops at her.

"Oh shit." Aaron said and his jaw hung open.

"Should you get her?" Olivia asked.

The owner watched and smiled.

Other people nearby edged back from them.

Mary took a napkin from the table, wiped her face off, and waved for the man to come to her. "Why not come closer and do that?"

Jan shook her head and turned to Aaron. "You better get involved."

The brusque German roared, "You gets the hell out of here or you get worse!"

"Gosh damn-it." Aaron looked at François who was pale with fear. "Don't worry François, nothing like a good old fashion fist fight before lunch."

François 's heart skipped a beat. "Non, please."

The brusque German looked at the faces of his buddies who looked at him to do something. He made his way around to Mary. "Ja, okay, no problem Amerikanisch, oh zorry, dummer American."

His buddies roared with laughter.

"I don't' need to know what that translates to." Mary drew back one leg and set it firmly in place. Then, she lowered her hands to her midsection and smiled.

He held the glass in hand, towered over her, bent at the waist, and put his fingers in the water.

"Got one last chance … apologize." She loosened her fist and wiggled her fingers around.

He raised his fingers, bent them in and was ready to flick the water on her. "To hell wit you dummer Amerikanisch."

In the few seconds that followed, Mary used both hands to grab his shirt and locked her fingers into it. She used their weight to fall backwards and pulled him onto her feet! Then, she shoved her legs up and threw him over her! The brusque German flew through the air and smashed into the people and tables behind them!

Tables, plates, napkins, glasses, people, a small dog, and lots of salt and pepper shakers went airborne!

The other diners were awestruck at Mary's courage and the fact that she threw the man!

Olivia's eyes widened, "Oh my."

Alex smiled, "yeah!"

Ada raised her hands up and cheered, "MARY!"

The German lay flat on his back and couldn't move. A moan eased through his tightly pursed lips. Debris from the massive body slam lay all around him.

Jan looked at Olivia and leaned over to her. "She has a black belt in judo."

"Ah." Olivia looked at Mary. "Well done!"

The owner nodded at Mary and went to the kitchen.

Mary walked over to the man while the customers around him moved in a daze. She hovered over him and looked at a table nearby. She stepped away, got a glass of water, and came back to him. Her legs straddled his waist. "We kicked your ass in World War One, World War Two and … today." She poured the water over his face. "You owe me an apology, sinner."

"Zinner?" He whimpered and his eyes welled up. "Zorry."

She balled her fist and drew back. "What?"

"I …" He choked on the word and his bottom lip trembled.

Alex rushed over and held his phone up. "Youtube!"

"I *so* zorry." Tears streamed down his cheeks.

Mary winked at him, handed him the glass, and went back to her table. "So, have you guys picked what you want?"

His buddies rushed to him and helped him up. The brusque German cried out in agony.

"Welcome back kick ass." Aaron smirked and nodded at her.

"That's quite something." Olivia said.

"Oh, he's just a sinner." She got her menu and then glanced back at the German. "Sinner!"

The customers, with the help of two servers, got the tables and chairs back in place.

Mary looked back again and the German bowed his head to her. She turned back to her menu. "I think I'll have the duck."

Alex came up to Mary and they hugged. "You are super!"

Ada nodded, "Cool."

"Cool," Mary said.

Jan chimed in. "Cool."

The owner came back with three bottles of Crémant d'Alsace. "Merci beaucoup." She patted Mary's shoulder. "I prayed for that." Then, she set the bottles on the table and extended her hand to Mary. "I'm Efi."

"I'm Mary, that's Jan."

"Aaron." He nodded at her.

"So good to have you here. Now, how about some lunch." She took out her tablet and pencil.

Olivia, "I'm going to do rabbit."

"Oh, rabbit." Jan's expression soured. "It's dark meat?"

"Well, it's the taste … yes." Olivia said. "But they prepare it quite well." She pointed to a door. "You can see for yourself."

"Oh, they let you watch them prepare it?" Jan asked. "I want duck."

Alex smiled. "Oui, you can." Something sinister came to mind and he winked at the owner.

"I think I'll have the lemon chicken." Aaron handed her the menu.

Alex spoke to Efi and she laughed. "Yes, okay." She looked at Mary, Jan, and then Aaron, "He wishes that you watch us prepare your meal."

Mary got her camera and Jan held her tablet.

Jan got up. "Oh, I'd love that."

François, "Poulet."

"Oui, François." Efi made the note.

Alex clapped his hands together in excitement, "hamburger."

"Moi aussi." Ada smiled.

"Why not take a picture?" Mary got her camera ready.

François looked at his wife, "Oliva?"

She nodded, "c'est d'accord."

Efi spoke to Alex and told him that it was a good experience for them.

François replied in French that he didn't want Mary to kick the owners butt if it was too much of an emotional experience.

Olivia rolled her eyes and told François. "Everything will be fine."

"I'm going." Aaron got up and got his phone out.

"Maman!" Alex stood.

Ada pulled at her mother's sleeve.

"Yes, okay … why not. Everyone will go." She threw her hands up.

Efi laughed and then announced to the restaurant, "We'll be back shortly!"

Mary walked by the Germans and they stopped talking.

Mary, Jan, and Aaron got their coats. Alex teased Aaron with a push.

"Keep it up." Aaron pushed him against the wall.

Outside, the sun shined brightly and the snow-covered mountains glistened.

"Wow, I didn't notice it when we came up, but there's so many pine trees." Aaron said. "Must've been the cloud cover."

Mary laughed, "or the avalanche." She took a picture of Aaron, Alex, and Ada. "Together." She waved her hands to show them that they needed to be closer.

"Oh, I want one." Jan said.

"S'il te plait, prende un photo avec Jan." He looked at Alex's eager smile.

"Okay!" Alex shouted.

Efi laughed. "I've known them for three years and they have more energy each year."

"Some good," Aaron said.

"All kids are good, Aaron." Jan said and hugged Ada. "I'm just in love with Ada."

"Ouoi?" Ada asked.

"Elle aime tu." Efi said.

After the pictures, they trudged through the snow and got to the back of the restaurant. There was a door to the kitchen and an older bearded man, fifty perhaps, with a cigarette between his fingers, stood by it. He wore a lazy chef's hat atop his head. The white apron clung to his waist, because his gut hung over it and held it in place. "Efi."

She nodded, "Marc, deux canard et un lapin."

The chef grinned and flicked his cigarette to the ground.

Efi turned to the cages with rabbits, ducks, and some chickens. "So, you want duck."

Jan's face paled. "What?"

Mary stopped, "Yeah." Then, she looked at the ducks who quacked wildly!

"Two ducks." Efi pointed at the mallards that wandered around in the snow and quacked for help.

Alex pointed and exclaimed, "Fresh!"

Ada laughed. "Canard."

Marc walked to a large wooden stump, pulled hard on a bloodied meat cleaver, and held it up. The sun shined on the edge of the blade and nearly blinded Mary and Jan!

Jan swallowed a gulp of worry. "Well, hang on."

Mary got her pocket bible in hand and licked her dry lips. "Is he …"

Chapter Seven: Quack!

The ducks quacked wildly! The chickens clucked loudly! The poor rabbits hopped to the corner of their cage in fear!

Marc sung Alouette, "Je te plumerai la tete."

"What's he singing?" Jan asked.

Alex held his phone up for a picture. "Okay! Alouette!"

"He's singing Alouette, a song about picking a bird apart. He just said, I'll take your head." Aaron's tongue suddenly felt a surge of acid shoot up his throat; he swallowed hard to get the sick feeling back down. "Okay."

Marc had the duck by its neck! "Quack!" "Quack!" He made his way back to the stump, got the duck's head under a metal hook, and brought the cleaver up over his head!

Mary gulped. "Oh Lord."

Jan covered her eyes. "Ah."

"Quack-quack!" The other fowl looked on as their brother faced the guillotine.

"THUMP!" The cleaver landed dead in the stump.

The quack was over.

Jan looked at Mary who waivered, turned, and passed out, face first into the snow. "Mary!"

"Really." Aaron said.

"Et la tete!" Ada shouted and sang on.

Alex stopped filming and went to Mary. "Oh non."

Efi went to her. "Mary!"

Marc laughed, tossed the duck to the side, got up, and got another one. "Deux canard and un lapin."

Efi looked at him and shook her head. "Marc."

Back inside, Mary drank her glass of wine in its entirety. "Yes, I'm from Nebraska, but I … I never really butchered anything, not screaming for mercy anyway." She poured another glass of wine.

"You flung Kong across the room, but you pass out over a duck." Aaron laughed.

"Well, the duck didn't try bury me in an avalanche." She fanned her face.

"So, tis your first time to see that?" François asked.

"Yes," she swallowed a gulp of wine. "More wine."

Jan shook her head. "I've butchered chickens, but I don't know. That poor duck just screamed."

"Here we are!" Efi announced and sat the plates of food out. "Lapin pour Olivia." Then, a server handed her the hamburger meals for Ada and Alex. "Et pour toi." She set the duck dinners in front of Mary and Jan. The body of the duck was there, grilled. "Et canard."

"Uh," Mary said and looked the duck over. The head hadn't been cleaned; the feathers and eyes were there and the duck stared at her. "I don't think ..."

Jan got crackers, pushed them in her mouth, then got her napkin and set it over the duck's head.

Mary's stomach convulsed and then she vomited on the plate. "Oh God, I'm so sorry." She got up and turned.

Everyone shoved themselves away from the table. "AH!"

Ada and Alex convulsed at the sight of the yuck.

The Germans chuckled.

Mary looked at the Germans and, in that instant, they were silent again. Then, she rushed to the bathroom.

"Damn!" Aaron let out. "Come on!"

Efi's eyes widened. "Okay, so no canard for Mary." She quickly got the mess cleared away and sprayed a heavy dose of lemon scent around them.

Olivia looked at the kids. "C'est d'accord."

"Oui, mais," Alex said which translated to, "yes, but." And then he said, "it's very bad to have that in my eyes and, now, to eat."

Olivia ate her rabbit. "I'm eating."

Ada looked at her hamburger and ate. "Alex." She rolled her eyes at him.

François turned away and quietly ate his chicken.

Mary came back, water had freshened her face and she was more composed. "I'm sorry."

"Oh, it's alright." Olivia said. "Perhaps, just some soup or salad."

"Let me have a minute." Mary's tongue darted in and out of her sour mouth. "Gross."

"You kicked that guys butt across the restaurant and passed out over duck." Aaron laughed.

"You don't want to be next, Aaron." Mary snapped at him.

"Tension." Jan said.

It was after four when they finished lunch. Efi hugged Jan and then Mary.

"Sorry about the mess." Mary said.

Efi smiled, "You're not the first."

Mary asked. "Would you take our picture?" She held her camera up to a server.

"Oh, and with my tablet too." Jan handed the tablet to the server.

The server snapped several pictures from each device and then handed them back.

"Terrific!" Mary said.

Jan looked at her tablet. "Wow, that's great."

"Au revoir," Efi said.

"Au revoir." Jan said.

Ada and Alex hugged Efi.

Moments later, they were on their way back to the car.

"The guys left already." Aaron said.

"Yeah, they didn't want to honk at you." Olivia said and chuckled.

"Aaron!" Alex had a snowball in hand.

"What?" Aaron turned and ducked!

"Ha!" Alex ran off!

A snowball fight ensued and the result was a lot of red faces. By the time they got back to the apartment, it was after six.

"Yeah, we're on our own for supper." Aaron said and set his things on the counter. "If we eat anything."

"What a day." Jan said and took off her coat. "I'm exhausted."

"Uh, hello." Mary said.

"Well, you kicked someone's ass." Jan said. "You must be exhausted too." She went to the window and opened it.

"Kind of cold out for that." Aaron said.

Mary went to her room and wrote in her diary.

"How many times will I be able to take in the fresh air in Colmar?" She inhaled deeply. "It's wonderful."

"Jan, you are a neat lady." He went to his room. "I'm going to change; my clothes stink of ... never mind."

Something caught Jan's eye and she looked down at the path to the main street. There were a lot of shadows. A cat rushed from one dark spot to another. She rubbed her eyes and then focused. "Who is that?"

There, at the corner and on the opposite side of the path, was a figure that stood on the periphery of light and dark.

"Can I help you?" Jan said aloud.

"Who are you talking to?" Aaron asked from the bedroom.

"I don't know, a person in the shadows down there." She got her tablet and aimed it. "Take their picture."

The person slid further into the darkness and was gone just as the tablet's flash lit up the entire square!

She lowered her tablet and looked around. "They're gone now."

"You wanted some mystery and men. Maybe, it's an admirer." Aaron was in his pj's and sat on the couch with his tablet.

"Maybe a stalker."

"Don't act scared now missy." He crooked his head over the back of the couch and looked at her. "You talked and talked about finding a hot guy."

"Yeah, but not one hiding in the shadows." She closed the window and pulled down hard on the lock.

"What's this?" Mary had her diary in hand. "You going to write?"

"Some man hid in the darkness so as to admire his beauty from afar." He chuckled. "Wish it was me."

"Jan?" Mary studied the window.

"Oh, I thought I saw someone hiding in the shadows across the street." She looked at the grainy picture. "Nothing to look at."

"Okay," Mary said, went to the window, and opened it. "Sinner!" She shut the window, turned to Jan and smiled. "See, all good."

"Really, Mary can go down there and snap his ass back over himself." He laughed. "That was crazy."

"Oh, anyone could do it." She said. "He was a jerk."

"A lot of men are." He replied.

"My husband wasn't." Jan went to the bedroom. "Time for my diary."

"Yeah, I want to ask you something so I can fill mine out." Mary followed her in.

"And for dinner?" He asked.

"Let's see after we write." Mary said. "And we leave for Zurich tomorrow?"

"Yep, tomorrow at three." He replied. "I'm going to miss Olivia."

"Yeah, she's a wonderful lady." Jan said.

"Well, time to move on." He lay back against the couch and read emails.

The girls worked on their diaries.

The person in the shadows looked at the window once more, looked at their dimly lit cell phone, and then made a call. His French accent made his English coarse and broken while he spoke. "She's there, I hear them."

A Russian female voice erupted over the phone. "Do not let them see you."

He moved away from the corner. "Oui."

She barked at him. "Keep a recording of everything they say!"

He looked up. "Okay, okay." Then, he got a cigarette and lit up.

"I know they have it." She huffed.

"I will not lose them." He exhaled and big white plume floated around him.

"You better not!" She barked again. "If you fail us, you'll wake up dead."

"Eh?" A puzzled look came over him.

"Just go!" She hung up.

"Stupide." He growled at her. Then, he peered around the corner again and studied the light from the bedroom where Jan and Mary wrote in their diaries. An ear piece cord hung down and connected to his phone. His finger tweaked the volume.

"Did you write about the beheading?" Jan asked.

His eyes widened. "Beheading?"

"I can't believe I passed out." Mary said.

The man lowered the volume, pressed his fingers against his weary eyes, and checked around him. He was the only person on the street.

"We leave for Zurich at three." Jan said.

Then man sent a text, "Leave 4 Zurich @ 3." He tapped, "SEND".

Chapter Eight: Two Spies, Two Lunches, One Way Out

Mary sat up, held her bible to her chest and prayed.

Jan was in the bathroom and looked at the clock. "ten in the morning!" Her face was covered in an anti-aging cream. "I love this stuff." The cream darkened as the time passed. "Rose and lavender."

Aaron pushed his hair back and looked at the tiny creases across his forehead. "Aging sucks."

Mary went to the bathroom and got ready next to Jan. "Are we doing lunch with you?"

Aaron, dressed in jeans and a polo, sat down in the living room. "No, I'm going with Olivia and then we'll catch up afterwards."

"How's that going to work?" Jan washed the crusty mud pack off. "How do I look?"

"That's wonderful." Mary looked her face over. "The crows' feet are gone."

"Good, for what this stuff cost." She smiled. "Should have taken a layer of skin with it."

"What are you two scheming about?" He sat up to hear them.

"Nothing." Jan said.

"Nothing." Mary said and pulled her hair back. She applied the same cream. "How long does it take to dry?"

"About twenty minutes." She worked her way out of the bathroom. "I'm going to get dressed."

"We'll go to Petite Venise and meet with Olivia. Then, you and Mary can wander, have lunch." He laid across the couch with his tablet. "We're going to do lunch at Café Noot."

Jan eased the door open to the bedroom. "If we end up at the same café for lunch, will that be a problem?"

"Well, Lucille Ball, as long as you don't come to our table." He shook his head.

"I think I watched one episode of that show." Mary said and looked her mask over.

"I Love Lucy." He sat up again. "It was on in the fifties. She was a basket case and always got into trouble."

"Are you saying Jan and me are a couple of basket cases?" Mary peered out of the door.

"I don't want you to flip me over the couch. So, no I don't think you are a basket case. Jan, on the other hand, is a basket case." He laughed.

"Jan, do you want me to get him?" Mary looked at the bedroom door.

"No, he's been good on this trip." She opened the door and wore a black blouse with bits of gold on the collar and shoulders and black heavy slacks. "Too much?"

"You look great." Mary said.

"When we get to Zurich, what are we doing?" Jan went to the kitchen. "It's nearly eleven."

"Get into our apartment first." He stretched. "And then have dinner, no tours."

"But Wednesday, we have a tour." She got an espresso and went to the chair in the living room.

"Jan, you look beautiful." He held his tablet up and took her picture.

"Yeah, it cost a lot of money to look good." She sipped her espresso.

Mary washed the mud off and then got a towel. "What's our tour about?"

Aaron tapped his screen and looked at the reservation. "It's a four-hour tour of Zurich: the Goldcoast, the Silvercoast, a trip up a mountain in a cable car and then back to the train station."

"I'm hungry." Jan looked at the kitchen.

"Didn't you have the croissant?"
"Yeah, but that's not enough. There was barely half left." She chuckled. "What did you eat?"
"I had …"
The doorbell rang.

"Must be Olivia." Aaron got up.

"I'll get it." Jan went to the door. "What train are we on?"

Just a block away, a Frenchman watched their apartment and eavesdropped on them. He sat in a Renault Zoe, a compact car and was too big for it; his knees pulled up against the steering wheel. His finger tweaked the volume on his ear piece and he heard Aaron, "TER 85542 to Mulhouse and then SBB 457 to Zurich." He tapped away at the screen on his phone and then tapped the arrow to send a text with that information.

Jan pressed the buzzer and waited a moment. Then, she opened the door. "Olivia?"

"Yes, it's me!" She came up the stairs.

"Is that a highspeed train." Mary went to the bedroom.

"Yeah, but I don't think it'll be that way for the whole ride. It's mountainous." He stood and went to the door. "Bonjour!"

"Yes, bonjour." They hugged, then she hugged Jan and Mary. "So good to see everyone."

"Yes, we're nearly ready." Jan looked at the bedroom and her luggage was packed.

"I'll be ready in just a minute." Mary pushed the bedroom door shut. "Hey Olivia!"

Jan, Olivia, and Aaron went back to the living room.

"So, have you your tickets?" Olivia and Aaron hugged.

"Yep," he held his phone up. "eTickets."

"After lunch, it's quite quick. We can load your bags when we return, then to get the children and on to the station." Olivia got comfortable on the couch.

"We're so thankful for everything." Jan said.

"Oh, it's not a problem. I'm glad you came." Olivia forced herself to smile, but sad feelings about her friend's departure made it hard to be happy. She held her hands out. "Okay, so I'm going to miss everyone."

"I know I'll miss you, but I'll be back next April." He held his phone up. "C'mon Mary, selfie time."

"Wait!" She rushed from the bedroom.

"Wow, hot red blouse and black slacks, nice." He said and videoed Mary.

"Turn that damn thing off." She swatted at the camera.

They got comfortable on the couch and then, several clicks from the tablet, camera, and phone! Afterwards, they went to the street and then walked right past the thug in the Renault Zoe.

The Frenchman held his phone just above the dash and videoed them.

Further down the street and right at the bend on the Rue De Ecoles' and Rue Wickram, the handsome man who stole Jan's tablet took video of the Frenchman in the Renault. His blazer shifted with the breeze and exposed the butt of his pistol.   The handsome man's phone rang and his eyes scanned the screen. "Elliot." His eyes were locked on the thug. "I'm working on it." One swipe and the call ended. He walked up to the Renault, stood just at the driver's door, and tapped the glass. "Bitte."

The Frenchman waved his hand at Elliot. "Touriste stupide."

"Bitte, hast du …" Elliot tapped the glass like a woodpecker tapped a tree.

The Frenchman, red faced and grossly frustrated by the man at his window, furiously rolled his window down. "Je ne parle pas Allemande, imbecile!"

Elliot tightened his balled fist and punched the thug in the jaw! The Frenchman's face shot to the opposite side and then he slumped over onto the passenger seat; he was out cold. Elliot reached in, took the Frenchman's ear piece and receiver; then, he dropped them to the ground. The case shattered under the weight of the heel of his shoe!

A young French couple, with a map of Petite Venise in hand, stopped and stared, their jaws hung open.

Elliot looked at the couple and then spoke in a soft southern drawl. "He called me an idiot; I just asked for directions to Petite Venise." He shrugged his broad shoulders and smiled.

The couple looked at each other. Then, the man's hand slowly rose and he pointed up the street. "It's just there, a few minutes' walk."

Elliot walked over and the man stepped to the front of his wife. "It's nice to know there's still good people in the world who choose to be a blessing to others rather behave like sinners." He smiled, waved at them, and then slowly strolled up the street toward Petite Venise. At the corner, he turned briefly and waved again. They reluctantly waved back and waited for him to go on.

Soldiers walked the street, their machine guns hung across their chest and their hands were around their pistol grips; they were ready to defend people.

Jan saw the men, smiled, and got her tablet from its pouch. She held her tablet high, then waited. "Just get a picture of those beautiful buildings." She aimed and had the soldiers in the picture.

"Told you it's against the rules to take pictures of the soldiers." Aaron chastised her.

Mary held her camera up and took a picture of the street and homes. "Seventeenth Century homes, decorated in beautiful Christmas decor."

Olivia laughed, "Why fight their urge?"

"She's been single too long." Aaron said.

Elliot waited at the corner and watched the three Americans.

The soldiers smiled and walked past with no thought of the cameras.

"Bonjour!" Jan waved and her smile was contagious.

Two of the soldiers smiled back and nodded.

"Wish I was thirty years younger." She turned and locked eyes with Aaron.

"You must've been a handful at school." He said.

Mary laughed. "I wouldn't know. She went to pub."

"Why do you say that?" Jan asked and snapped a picture of the homes behind her that included a picture of the men's butts.
"Because you don't follow any rules." He huffed.

"I wasn't in the military like you." She tapped his shoulder. "Love the Christmas lights."

There was a palm size camera in Elliot's hand; he snapped pictures of the Americans. Then, he put the camera away, pulled at his collar, and walked toward them.

"Hey." A twenty-something woman with Sophia Lauren cheeks said. Her dark bangs swung to and fro just above her eyes. "Are you Americans?" She was a shapely woman with her breast tucked in a push up bra. The soft orange colored dress she wore was practically seamless and followed her curves with precision. Her tangerine and light brown shawl rested on her shoulders and dangled down to her waistline. Along with her sunshine colored gloves, her boots were dark orange and she looked like she walked off a page from Vogue.

Aaron's brow went up.

"Yeah!" Jan said and went to the woman. "I'm Jan."

"Did you get a good picture of those hot guys?" The woman asked, shifted her purse to her other shoulder, and extended her hand.

"I sure did." Jan's brow bounced up and down and she shook her hand.

Mary mumbled. "Sinner."

"I'm Natalya." Her smile was crisp and easy to look at. She had the slightest accent, Eastern Europe.

"You're from America?" Aaron was puzzled by her accent.

"Yes, New York, but my father is from Romania. He works in Great Britain." She nodded and shook hands with Mary. "I heard you and had to say hello."

"Hi." Mary said. "It sounds like a hard accent."

"Perhaps," she smiled and her teeth were in sharp contrast to her body with their nicotine and caffeine stains.

"Aaron." Olivia said and pointed at her watch.

"So, are you here on your own?" Aaron asked.

Elliot stopped and then stepped over to an alley where he wouldn't be seen. The word passed just under his breath. "Natalya." He got his camera out and snapped pictures.

A Frenchman played the accordion nearby.

Elliot walked over and tossed a few Euros into the man's accordion case. The camera was at his waistline and clicked pictures. His head turned ever so slightly toward them and he listened intently.

"Yeah, so I'm on my own here. My father was going to join me, but he had a change in plans at the last minute." She looked around with a concerted effort as though she was looking for something particular.

Aaron looked around too and mumbled to himself, "What's she looking for?"

Mary looked at Aaron to get a feel about Natalya.

He shrugged his shoulders.

"You're welcome to join us." Jan said.

"Yeah, I was just going to dump them and run off with my friend here." He motioned with his hand at Olivia.

"Hello." Olivia smiled politely.

"No way, I don't want to be a burden." She held her hands up. "But I'd love the company."

Mary smiled at her, "Yeah, we're going to go eat right now, but we have to leave for our train by …"

Olivia stepped up. "By two-thirty."

"Well, we'd better go. It's twelve-thirty now." He said and held his phone up. "Can I get your number? We can text you when we're ready to meet up again."

"Yes, of course." She got her phone and looked at the screen. A couple of swipes and then she studied the screen. "33-456-454-1122."

"That's a prefix for France." Aaron's brow rose.

Olivia was puzzled at the thought that she had to look up her own number.

"I got it here so I wouldn't use my phone, too expensive." Her smile was too broad and her cheeks looked like they ached from the force it took to keep that smile.

"Okay," Aaron said. "We'll see you in a little while."

"Yes, until we meet again." Natalya said.

Jan, Mary, and Natalya walked away and chatted amongst themselves in a fury.

Olivia and Aaron walked down Rue Des Ecole.

Olivia looked back once. "That's so funny to have her show up just when we sought to go our own ways."

"Just coincidence." He said and took her arm into his.

"Perhaps."

Natalya pointed up a street. "There's a great pizza place just there."

"Oh, you know this town?" Jan asked.

"No, not really. I saw the pizzeria and thought … why not?" She looked around them again.

Elliot was at the next corner and walked into a Christmas shop; he stood by a large bay window and admired Jan for her forthright personality. "Jan, you're a neat lady."

"Can I help you find something?" The shop owner, an elderly woman with far too much blush, asked.

"You speak English, how nice." His smile was lackluster, but enough for this exchange.

"Yes, well I heard you say, neat lady." She clapped her hands over each other and her brow went up as her patience waned. "There are a lot of nice Christmas ornaments and souvenirs to buy here."

"Just browsing." He looked for the girls and saw them disappear at the next corner.

"There are other shops." The woman pointed at the door. "Perhaps, you should browse them."

"Pushing consumers out of your store doesn't make you a living." A smirk crossed his handsome face, he eased past her and went out the door. Then, he jogged to the corner.

"American browsers." She scowled at him.

He stood at the corner and looked for the girls. "Where'd they go?"

At the pizzeria, they stood in line and looked at the pictures of pizzas, calzones, sandwiches, and snacks.

Elliot walked slowly past the shops and stopped. "Lunch time." He ducked to the side and then went into the pizzeria.

The girls got their food and sat down.

"So, you're from Nebraska. The Cornhusker State." Natalya cut her pizza up.

"Yep, we're just farm girls." Mary said. Then, her curiosity peaked. "Wow, do a lot of New Yorkers know that?"

"You're not a farmer." Jan turned to Mary.

"I know something about farming." Mary said.

"Just not ducks." Jan laughed.

"I'm sorry." Natalya said and used a fork to eat her pizza.

"Oh, just a thing between us." Mary said. "Do a lot of New Yorkers use a fork to eat pizza?"

Natalya caught herself and then lowered the fork, "nouveau New Yorkers, yes." She turned to Jan. "Have you met any interesting people here?"

Jan set her pizza down. "Besides you? No."

"Yes." Mary said.

"Oh, who?" Natalya asked and took a very small bite of her pizza.

"She got robbed in Strasbourg." Mary said.

"Yeah, but I didn't meet that guy." Jan got her tablet out and took a picture of the food.

"What did he rob you of?" Natalya looked at Jan's arms and neck; she made a mental note of all of the jewelry: three rings, two necklaces in gold, a watch, and the tablet.

A few tables away from the girls, Elliot took a seat with his drink and a slice of pizza.

"Oh, he took my tablet, but Aaron got it back for me." She held her tablet up and showed Natalya. "Not worth much, but it has all my pictures."

"Yes, pictures are worth a great deal." Natalya sat up straight, "must've been a fight to get it back."

"No, Aaron said the guy told him it wasn't what?" She looked at Mary.

Mary finished the story. "Think he said it wasn't worth it. The police were coming and Aaron had him cornered." She bit into her pizza, pulled back, and all the toppings slid off onto her chin! "Uh."

"That's quite funny." Natalya chuckled. "I don't like that when it happens, better to use a fork."

"You should see her eat duck." Jan laughed.

"Ha-ha." Mary said and pulled the pizza cheese with the toppings from her mouth. "They need to find a way to keep the cheese and dough from coming apart."

"Oh, I'm sorry. I meant that it was funny the thief gave the tablet back." Her full lips gripped the straw to her drink. "Most of the people who steal are gypsies or drug addicts. They would have fought to keep it."

"I guess, but he didn't." Jan said.

"Did your friend ID the man?" Natalya set her drink down and eyed Jan's tablet.

"ID the man?" Jan asked and chuckled. "Do you work for the police?"

"Oh, sorry." She laughed it off. "I … too many crime shows." She said. "Mmm!" She took another small bite.

Elliot looked at Natalya and mumbled to himself. "SVR, so neat and tidy. Foreign Intelligence Service of the Russian Federation." His camera was just above the table's edge and took pictures.

Jan swallowed and nearly choked on the glob of cheese. She washed it down with water and then looked at Natalya. "No, we … well, Aaron didn't get a good look at him. He wore a hoodie or something."

"It's good you got your tablet back; I hope the crook didn't break it." She eyed the tablet.

"Oh," Jan lifted it up and looked at the screen. "The screen flickers now. But the guy threw it down."

"He's sounds like a pig of a man." Natalya said.

"He was." Jan replied.

"Yeah, a real sinner." Mary said. "Gosh, I didn't give thanks."

"What?" Natalya asked.

"Mary's very religious. She prays and gives thanks about everything." Jan rolled her eyes.

"Stop it." Mary said to Jan. Then, she bowed her head and spoke quietly. "Dear Lord, thank you for this food and good … almost good company." She paused, "amen."

Jan and Natalya were quiet.

Elliot looked on. "Amen."

"It's too bad about the screen." Natalya held her hand up. "May I see it?"

Jan was surprised. "Oh, sure." She handed her the tablet.

"Hmm, I work in IT. Perhaps, I could look at it for you." She tapped the home button and a sly smile crossed her face. Her other hand reached down into her purse and unzipped it.

"Oh, that's alright. Aaron's a computer guy and he'll take care of it." Jan smiled and held her hand out to get it back.

"I'd be happy to." The screen had four dashes across it for the passcode. "It's no trouble."

"Natalya!" Elliot stood right next to her and roughly patted her shoulder. "Good old Natalya."

Natalya jumped and moved her hands to knock his away! She looked Elliot up and down. "Do I know you?"

Jan was taken by the handsome man. "Hello."

"Oh, come on." He looked at the tablet and Natalya. "What, no hug?" He pulled the tablet from her and handed it back to Jan, "can't get a hug with that in your hands." He forced himself on her.

Natalya pushed back. "Get your hands off of me, Elliot!"

Elliot's wide smile made heavy creases in his cheeks. "C'mon, don't be like that. After six months together." Natalya reached to her backside for her gun.

"So, you do know each other?" Mary asked.

"He's a piece of …" Her mouth froze. "An unpleasant business associate who I never wanted to see again." She eyed him.

"One more hug." He leaned over, grabbed her, and pulled her close! So close that her tits pushed up his chest and against his chin. A whisper pushed through his lips. "Don't do it."

Her eyes were full of rage and disgust, his eyes were subtler, but warned her.

He pressed the blade of a small knife against her hip. "You'll be down before you pull that piece."

"You hope so." Her lips were an inch from his and her soft red cheeks were an ashen red now.

Jan and Mary were dumbstruck.

He turned to the girls. "You know what, we're going to go outside and talk, try to patch things up."

Mary looked him over. "Natalya?"

"Yes." She said. "Old friends. I'll just get my bag."

He got the knife to her back and pushed it gently against her. "Honey."

She forced a smile, got her purse, and stood. "I'll be back."

"Maybe." He laughed. "Enjoy your trip, ladies." They stood in front of the pizzeria and talked.

Mary and Jan looked at each other and wondered.

"What the heck was that about?" Jan asked.

"Weird." Mary took a bite of her pizza and the cheese pulled off again. "Damn it." She opened her mouth and the chunk of cheese fell out. "Maybe I should use a fork."

Elliot tucked the knife. "I know you're fast, dangerous."

"Then, you know I owe you." Natalya opened her mouth and then slammed her teeth together.

"For what?" He looked at the girls and waved. "Hey!"

"Get your filthy hands off of me, Americanskiy." Her cheeks were darker now, angry.

"Yeah, I'm sorry about that, but you're messing with two innocents." He dipped his head at the girls.

She stepped closer to him, wrapped her arms around him, and gently rested her lips on his. "I'm going to kill you, get the tablet, and walk away like I own this village."

Just then, there was a click. He pressed his semi-automatic pistol against the side of her chest. "Not if I kill you first."

The girls came out and stood a few feet away.

Mary spoke up. "We have to go, because It's nearly two-thirty."

"I can call." Natalya said. "Seems my *ex* has me under the gun."

Elliot lowered the pistol and slowly tucked it back under his blazer. "Don't."

She got her phone and called Aaron. "Hello, yes they are ready."

He smiled at Jan.

Jan looked at Mary. "Selfie!"

"What?" Mary rolled her eyes. "No." Then, she shook her head vigorously.

"It's the pizza place, Chez Claude." Natalya said to Aaron. Her eyes burnt holes in Elliot's face. "We'll wait here." The phone faded to black and the call ended. "He's coming."

Jan got her tablet out. "Oh, C'mon."

Elliot pondered. "Why not." He pulled Natalya close to him and motioned for Jan and Mary to stand on the opposite side of him. "Yeah, just stand there and that'll put me in the middle."

Jan held up the tablet.

Just then, the couple that saw Elliot punch the Frenchman earlier walked out of the pizzeria. "Oh, let me help you."

"Thanks!" Jan said and handed the man her tablet. "Just tap the icon."

"Yes, no problem." He looked at the tablet and then his eyes widened. "You found Petite Venise then."

"I sure did … with your help." Elliot's pistol was under his coat and he tapped Natalya's back, "Smile."

Natalya jumped. "One more tap and I will …"

"Say …" The man thought for a moment.

"Cheese." Mary said.

"Well, in French, it's fromage." Elliot winked and blew a kiss at the man's wife.

"Fromage, okay." He aimed the tablet. "Fromage!"

Everyone said, "fromage!"

He tapped the camera icon several times. "I took a few."

"Terrific." Elliot said.

Jan looked the shots over. "Oh, perfect. Thank you!"

"Yes, no problem." He got his wife's hand and hurried off.

"So, Natalya and I have to run too." He pressed the gun into her. "Don't we?"

"Yes, it's important that we go." She gritted her teeth. "There's so much I want to do to him." She gritted her teeth.

Mary mumbled, "sinner, big sinner."

"Hey," Aaron walked up with Olivia.

"You've got a new friend." Olivia tucked her arms.

"Yeah, this is …" Jan paused.

"Oh, I'm Elliot." He dipped his head and did not shake hands. "So, like you, we have to go."

"Oh, okay. Yeah, we need to get to the train station." Aaron said and nodded at Elliot.

"Where are you going next?" Natalya asked.

Elliot spoke up, "Oh, honey. That's their business, not ours." He shook his head.

"It's alright." Aaron said. "We're going to …'

"Nope, wouldn't stick our nose in your personal stuff." He moved another step back. Thanks for visiting, have a good trip." Elliot looked at each of them. "Better keep that tablet close, don't want anyone to take it again."

"Right." Jan said and then she wondered how he knew.

Aaron looked Elliot over. "No, we don't."

Elliot ushered Natalya off. "Goodbye!"

"Yes, until we meet again." Natalya said and fought with Elliot while they walked toward another street. They disappeared down the street, turned a corner, and were gone.

"Okay, that was awkward." Aaron said. "Did he really know her?"

"I guess." Mary said.

"She said his name I think." Jan said.

"Well, we should get to the children and then the station. It's two-thirty." Olivia pointed toward the car.

They walked off and passed the alley. It looked like Elliot and Natalya were in warm embrace with their lips pressed against each other. "Just turn and wave." Elliot said. They turned and waved at the foursome.

Mary, Jan, Olivia, and Aaron smiled uncomfortably and waved back. In minutes, they were at the car and on the road to get the kids.

At the train station, they stood on the platform at five to three and the regional train was there. Ada and Alex hugged Mary, then Jan and then Aaron. "Goodbye."

Olivia's eyes teared up. "I'm going to miss you."

"I'm going to miss you too." He hugged her and kissed her cheeks.

"Oh Olivia, you've been so kind." Jan said and they hugged.

The conductor blew his whistle!

"Ah," Olivia looked at the train. "Go, they are leaving in just a minute." She wiped her tears away.

They got on board and took a seat midway in the car. A wave from each of them, the doors closed, and the train rolled out of the station.

Elliot and Natalya were in a warehouse that abutted the alley. She sat on the floor with her hands tied in front of her with plastic straps. He had her gun and purse. "So, how'd you find out?"

"Go to hell." She kicked him. "I'm not the only one, Elliot."

He shrugged his shoulders. "Do you know where they're headed next?" He aimed the pistol at her face. "They'll have to use dental records if you don't tell me."

"Ah!" She kicked her legs at him. "Professional courtesy. I didn't hurt them."

"You Russians don't know what that is." He looked away and thought. "Alright, so the chase is on." He leaned in and put his lips an inch or so from hers. Heat built up between them. "Know this." He kissed her. "The closer you get, the more dangerous this game gets for you and your people."

She spat in his face. "You stole from us!" Her hand slowly moved around her backside and then her fingers pinched a tab on her blouse. A sly grin bubbled up on her face.

He wiped the spit away from his lips. "So, how much time do I have?" The exits were marked and the alley door was cracked open.

"They will beat the hell of you." She kicked at him.

"It's beat the hell *out* of you." He pushed her legs apart. Then, he looked at his Omega Seamaster; it glowed with the time. "Just after three." The train left and they were on the way to Zurich. Time was on his side to get back what he hid with Jan, to save them, and to get the item to his people.

Her eyes drifted over to the cracked exit door. "They are coming."

"How'd you find out?" He pulled a pair of plastic gloves out and put them on. Then, he got a sealed gray plastic bag from his coat pocket. The seal on the bag was serrated and his fingers gripped the edge and pulled. The bag opened and he pulled out a cannister; the cannister was a faint orange with a small red cap. "CS42" was embossed on the side in bold white letters; beneath the ID was one word, "TOXIC" in black and red.

She looked the can over and smiled. "What is CS42?"

"It's similar to the Russian Po-210." The can hung just near her face. "A similar radio isotope that your people used to kill Litvinenko."

"Ah!" She thrashed her legs and tried to head butt him. "You!"

"How'd you find out?" His fingers massaged the red cap and then danced with it until it was off. "Was it the dirtbag in the Renault?" He grinned at her. "If it was, he's out."

Her eyes were hooked on the aerosol can and she squirmed. "You do this to me and I promise that my people will get you."

"They might, but you will die badly." He smiled. "Did you see Litvinenko near the end? Skin wrinkled and then it dripped in pieces to the floor; his lungs filled with moisture, poison."

"Hell with you!" She kicked at him.

He shoved her legs back and then yelled, "How did you find out!"

A heavy huff punched through her lips, "You think we are Russian, so we are stupid." She shook her head to get her hair out of her face. "My people know you made the handoff in Strasbourg."

The wind gently pulled the exit door back and then pushed it shut, "Bang!"

Elliot jerked to his side and his pistol was aimed at the door. Sweat on his forehead slowly drifted past his brow and down his cheeks. The sweat flung off when he shook his head.

"Frightened?" She laughed.

He tucked his gun and aimed the aerosol at her face. "Why haven't you hacked the cams for surveillance or used a drone or satellite?"

She sneered. "Because there are some who felt that to push the EU any harder would result in another type of NATO buildup, a separate military sponsored by the EU."

"Don't antagonize a resting bear." He nodded. "So, it's old school cloak and dagger."

Car tires screeched to a stop up the alley, near the street! Several Russian thugs got out, checked their guns and then one of them looked at a phablet. "Syuda!" He pointed up the alley.

"It's really just sleeping gas." He smiled, pressed the button, and a faint orange mist came over her.

Her mouth opened to scream and then she fell silent, her head flopped to one side.

"Sleep well, Natalya." Then, he aimed his pistol at the door, got up, and ran to the exit across the building. Once he was outside, he disappeared.

Chapter Nine: Are We There Yet?

On the train, Aaron tucked his laptop bag above them. "That whole thing with that guy and her was strange."

"I know." Mary said. "She was all about what happened with Jan's tablet."

"What?" He turned his attention to Jan.

"Yeah, she wanted the details, but that's just curiosity." Jan smiled. "It's the same in David City. You say, oh someone took my tablet and everyone wants to know what happened."

He shrugged his shoulders and sighed. "Yeah, I guess so." The passing landscape caught his attention. "I just hope that we didn't make a mistake by leaving her with him."

Mary looked up from her bible. "She acted like she didn't know him, but then she said his name and was like oh we'll go talk."

"Maybe he was an ex-boyfriend, a hot ex-boyfriend." Jan said. "Like to have him force me down an alley."

"God, I think I'm feeling nauseous." Mary said.

"Don't be jealous." He laughed.

Mary got her camera out, took pictures of them, and the landscape.

Jan's tablet rested against the window and videoed everything. "How far is Mul-house?"

"Mulhouse, it's one word … about forty minutes." He sat back and closed his eyes. "Going to keep an eye on who comes up to us next."

"Me too, sinners." Mary looked at her camera and adjusted the focus. "Jan."

"What?" Her tablet beeped.

"Sinner."

"Oh, be quiet." Jan shook her head. "Not everyone is a sinner."

The time passed quietly and a cat nap overtook them. Thirty minutes later, the train slowed and wound its way along the tracks that brought them it into Mulhouse, France. The conductor walked past and other passengers got their things together. The train eased into the station and the platform was full of people. The train stopped, a gentle bell rung, and the doors opened.

Aaron looked up and stretched. Then, he jerked upright. "We're here!"

Jan yawned and Mary sat up.

"Go!" He shouted. "We've got to hurry!"

Jan got up and looked at her things. "My tablet fell down."

People boarded and eased past Jan and Mary.

"Get your luggage, I'll get your tablet, and let's get off." He reached under the seat and grabbed the tablet.

"Do you have it?" Jan stood by the door with her luggage.

Mary talked to the conductor, "Can you hold the train for just a minute?"

"Non, they must come." He looked up and down the platform. People wandered around and most of the doors were clear. "Ma'am, I'm sorry, but that's it." He blew his whistle.

Jan and Aaron hopped off with their luggage and Jan held her tablet. She looked her things over. "Purse, tablet …"

The doors closed to the regional train and, immediately, it pulled out of the station. Each car passed by faster and faster until the last car shot past. The red lights on the last car faded into the distance as the train wound its way out of the station bound for Basel, Switzerland.

"Luggage, wallet, passport." Aaron looked at Mary. "You got everything?"

Mary nodded, "Yes, I think so." Her camera hung around her neck. She looked at her bag and her purse. "Yep, three things: purse, camera, rollaboard."

"Whew." Most of the passengers were gone from the platform. Aaron looked at the timetable. "SBB to Zurich is twenty minutes out." A heavy sigh pushed through his lips. "I need to catch my breath."

"Do *you* have everything?" Jan asked and looked his stuff over.

"Yeah," there was his rollaboard and he had his passport and phone in a belt pouch.

"Where's your black case?" Mary asked.

"What?" A surprised look came over him.

"The black bag with your tablet." Jan said.

"My bag!" He frantically looked around them and then down the tracks. "It's stowed in the rack above our seat." His face paled. "Great, our tickets for the tours, my cash, my tablet, the keys to my car …"

"Alright, don't panic." Jan said. "Let's go to the office and ask for help."

Aaron shook his head. "Damn-it."

"You have your passport and wallet though?" Mary asked and touched his arm.

"Yeah, I …" His fingers dug into the pouch and pulled out his wallet. "My passport." Then, he got his passport out.

"So that's good." Jan said.

"Right, stay here and I'll go to the office." His things lay against Jan's luggage and he hurried up the steps to the main walkway. "Just wait there!" Then, he was gone down the walkway.

"It's cold out here." Jan pulled at her collar.

Mary looked around for a place to get warm. "It is cold."

"Hey!" Aaron shouted at them from the raised walkway.

"What?" Mary asked.

"Do not get on the SBB! Just stay there so I know where you are!" He waited for them to acknowledge him.

"Yes, we understand." Jan said.

Aaron ran off to the main office.

"I hope he can get it back." Jan said. "I feel terrible."

"Why?"

"Well because he had to get my tablet and forgot about his bag." She bit at her lip.

Mary hugged her. "It'll be alright." She had her bible and prayed. "Amen."

Aaron got to the door and went into the Chief of Operations office, Gare de Mulhouse, FR. "Bonjour."

The young man behind the window, nearly two-hundred centimeters tall or six foot-six and husky, bent at the waist and looked at Aaron. "Je suis Adam Bruette, Chef des Operations." He answered a call over his radio. "Oui, un moment …" Then, he nodded at Aaron.

The words flowed a in frantic but understandable rhythm in French. His bag was on the train to Basel, Switzerland. Aaron forced himself to smile at the conclusion of his plea for help.

"Je vais telephoner Basel et les faire verifier, mais le train n'arrivera pas avant vingt minutes."

"Vingt minutes?" Aaron's anxiety climbed. "We'll miss our connection to Zurich."

"Oui." Adam understood some English. "You will."

"D'accord, merci-beaucoup." Worry took over his normally happy expression and his cheeks sunk. "Great."

Adam stepped away and got on the radio.

Aaron tapped the window, "J'ai besoin de parler a' mes amis."

Adam nodded.

Aaron pushed through the heavy glass door and headed back to the platform. He looked across three sets of tracks and there was a light snow fall. Mary stood by with their luggage and Jan was not to be seen. "Hey!"

Mary turned sharply. "What?"

He shouted. "Do not get on the train to Zurich!"

"Okay!"

"We're going to miss our train! The guy is working to get my bag!" He looked up and down the platform. "Where's Jan?"

"Potty break." She smiled. "It's going to be okay."

Aaron caught his breath, because he wasn't sure. All those people on the train with his lone bag overhead. Someone could grab it by mistake and he'd never see it again. How would he get in his car? And what about the several hundred dollars tucked away in a side pocket? His tablet had passwords to all his bank accounts and email. "Jesus."

Mary cleared her throat and spoke in a firm, strong tone. "Aaron, it's going to be okay."

He nodded and went back to the office.

Adam talked with another associate.

Aaron took a seat and looked at his phone. "This sucks."

Jan opened the door and walked out from a maintenance closet. "It's got heat."

Mary walked over and went in. "Good, I'm frozen."

The SBB luxury train to Zurich pulled in and then its doors opened.

Jan looked over. "Oh, that's our train."

"Yep, but we're not going on it." Mary pulled the door shut.

"Too bad, it was first class too." She frowned. "What matters is that he gets his bag."

Adam tapped the glass. "They checked the train and there's no sign of your bag."

Aaron's heart sunk right along with his expression. "Well, thank you."

Adam nodded. "You should catch the next train to Basel and then look yourself."

"Yes, what do we do about our trip?"

"What was your final stop?" Adam went to the security door, opened it, and stepped out.

"Zurich." Aaron shook his hand.

Adam pondered. "Then, take the TER to Basel, from there you can catch a train to Zurich; it's not a problem."

"Alright." The air felt dry, too dry to say another word. "Thanks, truly." He walked out, went back to the main passageway, and then to the platform. The SBB train to Zurich pulled out of the station and its horn blared. "Damn."

In the parking lot, the Frenchman from Petite Venise stopped at the Mulhouse station. He got out and pulled at the collar to his camel colored coat. The side of his face had a reddish, brown bruise. His fingers rubbed the lump on his cheek where Elliot hit him and he gritted his teeth. "Allemande imbecile." The translation amounted to, "German Idiot." His phone lit up and rang. "Oui."

"Your last chance. Natalya is on the way." There was sigh, "You do whatever is necessary to get the woman." Then, the phone went blank, "CALL ENDED."

A growl slipped through his pursed, chapped lips. The cold air came out as a heavy white mist from his mouth. He looked at the station placard, "GARE DE MULHOUSE". His heavy coat covered his gun and he inhaled, closed his eyes, and then walked to the station.

For Aaron, the steps to the platform looked like a descent into a terrible place; the gray and wet steps didn't smile at him and looked as though they wanted him to tuck his tail and go back to America; the trip was over; it was a hard walk into travel hell. "Lost luggage, there's never a happy ending." He looked at his Amex card and shook his head. "Have to buy the damn tickets for all the tours again."

Jan looked at him and smiled. "So?"

"The chief called ahead." He came down the steps. Each foot hit the next step like dead weight and then drug off the step. "They didn't have it."

"Okay, sorry to hear that." Jan said.

"Where's Mary?" He looked around. "Thought I said to stay here."

"Yes, daddy." Jan smirked. "Mary!"

"Coming." She kicked the solid metal door and then came out of the maintenance closet. "Hey."

"Oh my god." His head shook before he told it to. "What happened to stay right here?"

"Aaron," Jan said and touched his shoulder. "I'm seventy-one years old with double knee replacement, a bypass surgery survivor, and thin skin." She smiled. "We were cold."

"Sorry."

"It's alright. Let's focus on what to do next." Jan said.

He looked at the solid steel door and the lock. "Was it locked?"

Mary smiled. "Not anymore."

"Lost my bag and, now, you two face arrest for breaking and entering." He huffed.

"Oh, the door was like that." Mary said.

"Besides, who will know?" Jan looked down the track. "Do we catch the next train?"

"Yeah, we'll go to Basel and talk with the conductor or operations people to see if they have my bag." He retraced his footsteps and then did it again.

The Frenchman looked at the timetable board and read each number. His eye caught Zurich's next train, but that was two hours away. "Hmm, they've gone?" Then, he saw Basel in fifteen minutes. "No matter, I know them." The bell sounded and a lovely female voice announced the next train to Basel.

Adam, with a cap on and his dress jacket, walked at a brisk pace to the platform where Aaron slowly paced, and Jan and Mary trembled from the cold. Adam's legs flicked in and out as he descended the steps with ease.

The Frenchman looked over the main walkway at the platforms. "Les American, ou est ils?"

Aaron, Jan, and Mary looked at Adam who was at the base of the steps now and waved at them.

"Monsieur Moreau!"

"Adam."

"Yes, good news." His radio blared and he got the mic in hand. Then, he spoke French into the mic with a sense that his word was final. After that, he turned to Aaron, "The train with your bag will return from Basel in just a few minutes on its way to Paris." His smile was contagious, "Bonjour les filles." He dipped his hat at Jan and Mary.

Jan's smile was more than contagious; it was an invite to get her number, a car, and a home in the country. "Hi."

"Jan, really." Mary said. "Hello sir."

"Okay." Aaron was dumbfounded, "What does that mean for us?"

"I will hold the train and you can look for your bag." The radio voice called for him. He turned, got his mic in hand, and told them that the train would hold for a few minutes.

"Wow, that's nice of him." Jan said. "I like nice guys." She got her compact and looked her face over.

On the other side of the platform, the train to Basel slowed to a stop.

"But what about the train to Basel?" Aaron looked pale, frantic with worry. "I mean isn't there like three hundred people on board?"

"Oui, and they will wait." He said firmly.

In the distance, the train from Basel blew its horn, changed tracks, and lined up with their platform.

"Are you sure about this? I mean isn't it a big deal to hold not one, but two trains in France?" Aaron's worried look made Adam smile; Adam felt like he could save the day.

"It's a very big deal, but I am the Chief of Operations." His hand rested on Aaron's shoulder. "It will be fine." Then, he looked at the train from Basel. "That's your train. Where were you seated?"

"Uh, maybe mid-way?" The train slowed as the engine passed them.

Jan spoke up. "Like the fifth or sixth car in."

"Okay, so everyone get on and look for the bag, get it, and get off quickly." He looked at their things just as a station agent walked up. "Watch their things."

The agent nodded at him and stood by their luggage.

Two other trains arrived and their doors opened. Hundreds of people headed to other trains or out of the station!

The Frenchman looked at the platform and saw them! "Ah!" He rushed through the wave of people that pushed past him. "Bouge toi!" In the melee, he had to shove past people who flowed against him!

The train from Basel to Paris stopped and its doors opened. People poured out while others waited to board.

Adam pointed with his mic at the door. "Okay, go and look. I'll go this way."

They got on and scoured the cars for Aaron's black bag.

The Frenchman got on the Paris bound train at the first car. "I will not lose them this time."

The passengers tried to exit and ran into either Jan, Aaron, or Mary; they said words in French that weren't nice.

An older Frenchman flipped Mary off! She let him have it. "Sinner!"

Aaron's eyes scanned every single inch of every space in the overhead bins.

The Frenchman rushed up the first car, but was met with other people who fought to get seated. "Eh!" A woman shoved him back and he pushed her into the seat. "Tais toi!"

"Non, you shut up!" She shouted back and swung her fist at him. "Cochon!"

The Frenchman got to the end of the first car, pressed the button for the door, passed to the next car, and waded through people who stored their luggage and sat down.

Aaron's face lit up like a Christmas tree!
Two girls sat right under his bag and looked at him. One girl looked up. "Ton sac?"

A smile blew up on his face, "oui, merci!"

The college age woman got up, got his bag, and handed it to him. "Je vous en pris."

"I got it!" He shouted to Jan who just came to the sixth car. "Tell Mary, let's get off, get our things … all our things and get on the other train!" They exited and waved at Mary who was in car five.

Adam saw them and got off. "You have it?"

"Yes, thank you … thank you very much." Aaron shook Adam's hand heartily.

Adam held Aaron's hand a little longer and then winked. He pressed the button on his mic and waved at the conductor for the Basel to Paris train. "Oui, clair."

The Frenchman was in car three now of the Basel to Paris train. "Where the hells?" Everyone had a seat and then the soft bell rang, the doors closed, and the train to Paris eased out of the station. He rushed to the next car and then stopped suddenly! "Merde!" There, across the platform and boarding the train to Basel, were the three Americans. "Les American! Arret! Arret!" He yelled!

Mary and Jan were on board.

Adam handed Aaron a card. "If you should be here again." He smiled. "Call me."

"Yes," he blushed. "I'd like to see you again."

The radio blared that the train must go. Adam got his mic in hand and cleared the train to Basel. "Oui, you must board."

Aaron rushed up the steps with his black bag and luggage and then he turned to Adam. "Until we meet again."

The soft bell sounded and the doors closed. The engine revved and the train slowly pulled from the station and headed to Basel.

The agent walked up to Adam. "It's your first time to do something like that."

"Meet a nice guy?" Adam asked.

"Non, to hold two trains with nearly six hundred travelers for one man." The agent patted Adam's shoulder. "Hope it was worth the complaint from HQ."

"Sometimes, it's good to be a blessing to people in need." They nodded at each other and then headed up the platform, back to the walkway bridge, and his office.

Aaron settled in and looked at Mary, then Jan.

"Well?" Jan asked.

"What?" A puzzled look wasn't going to dissuade them.

"You got a date or his number?" Mary asked. "I may be Catholic, but I'm not blind to love at first sight."

His cheeks were flush. "It's cliché, not reality."

"Why is that?" Mary asked.

The train sped up and traveled at eighty, then ninety kilometers per hour.

"He may want me to be his boy. You know, do the laundry, cook and clean." He looked at his reflection in the window. The seat next to him was empty. "Better than being alone though."

"It is." Jan said, reached across the table and rested her hand on his. "You got your bag, we're on our way to Switzerland, and it ended with a phone number of a nice guy who held up a thousand people for you."

"I think it was more like six hundred." Mary got her phone out. "Let's do a selfie. Everything worked out."

"Leave it to a Catholic to put a damper on things." Jan shook her head.

"How'd I do that?" She held her phone up.

"Really, six hundred vs. a thousand."

"It's alright and it did end well. I got his number and my bag." He crossed over to the girls and they bunched up together.

A man stopped and offered to take the picture.

"Oh, yes." Mary handed him the phone.

"Fromage?" Then, he paused for a moment. "You're the Americans from Petite Venise."

"Yes, it's us!" They shouted and passengers looked their way. "Fromage right?"

"How funny to you again." He looked around. "And your other friends?"

"Oh, they weren't with us." Jan said.

"Okay." He focused the camera. "Fromage then?"

"Cheese!" He snapped several pictures, handed the phone back to Mary, and nodded at them.

"Thank you." Aaron went back to his seat. "Now, we have to figure out how to get to Zurich."

"Yes, no problem." Mary had her bible out and prayed. "Dear Lord, we need to get to Zurich, amen."

"We've been lucky so far." Jan said. "Amen."

"Amen." Aaron bowed his head slightly. "Either way, we'll see when we get to Basel." He got comfortable and pulled his black bag close to him. Then, he thought and looked through his bag. "I didn't even look to see that everything was in it." His fingers quickly unzipped the bag and he went through all of it.

The Frenchman raised hell with the conductor to stop the train.

In French, the argument got ugly. The conductor's face was red with anger and he waved his hands about. "Non, we do not stop this train! We are already late and you have no emergency!"

"Stop this damn train or it's you who will have an emergency!" The Frenchman shouted.

Just then, two Gendarmes stepped into the car armed with machine guns.

"Ah!" The conductor flagged them to him. "Talk to this madman!"

The Frenchman shoved the conductor to the side! He rushed past, but the conductor grabbed his coat, and pulled him back.

"Arret!" The Gendarmes yelled! "Arret!"

Passengers ducked behind their seats!

The Frenchman punched the conductor, but it was too late.

The Gendarme aimed his machinegun. "Arret! Police!"

The Frenchman slowly raised his hands.

The other Gendarme radioed that they planned to arrest a man.

The conductor still had a firm grip on the Frenchman's coat and saw the butt of a pistol tucked into the Frenchman's waistline. His hand trembled and he turned to the Gendarme. "Pistolet!"

The Frenchman looked at the Gendarme and then at his pistol.

Chapter Ten: Zurich, Finally.

The Gendarme was a superior shot and his eye lined up with the sight at the end of the barrel to the machinegun; that sight was aimed at the chest of the Frenchman. "Non, non." The other Gendarme made the call that the man was armed.

The train slowed.

Two French Army men came from the other direction and paused. They had their rifles ready, but not aimed. "Claude."

"Oui, un moment, Michel." The Gendarme leaned in to make sure of his shot. "Monsieur," he locked eyes with the Frenchman just as the train stopped at a small station. Sirens wailed from police cars that rushed up to the station. "You have a choice."

"Oui." The Frenchman said.

"To put your hands behind your head and lock your fingers or …"

"Or?" The Frenchman took a look at what he was up against.

"Get shot."

The door to the car opened and other police entered.

"Attend!" The partner Gendarme shouted.

"I don't get shot." He raised his hands slowly and put them behind his head. Then, he locked his fingers together.

The conductor stood, raised his head, sneered at the Frenchman, and then moved away. The Gendarmes moved in and took him into custody.

At Mulhouse, Adam and the agent stopped for a cigarette on the walkaway.

"Excuse moi," a lovely lady said.

They continued in French.

The agent's eyes were hooked on her tits in a push up bra. "Oui?"

She reached over and put her fingers under his chin. Then, she slowly lifted his chin so that his eyes and hers met. "Has the train to Zurich gone?" Natalya's smile warmed the man's heart.

Adam spoke up. "Yes, some time ago."

"So, I've missed it?" She asked.

"What's your ticket for your train?" Adam asked and noticed no ticket in her hand.

"Ah, I haven't a ticket yet, but I want to catch the next train to Zurich." Her sly grin didn't work on him.

"I'd be happy to help. I'm Raphael." His hand shot out and nearly punched her. "Oh, sorry."

"Natalya." She looked at Adam and then Raphael. "I'm looking for my friends. Three Americans, one man and two women. Perhaps, you saw them?"

"Yes, of course." Raphael admired her face. "You've had some sun in winter?"

Her face had a tinge of orange from Elliot's spray. "Perhaps."

"It's against the rules to say anymore, Raphael." Adam got between her and his agent. "What's your concern? Are you Gendarme or police?"

"Non, as I said, a friend and I've called, but they didn't answer." She held up her phone with Aaron's name on the screen. "We're supposed to go to Zurich together."

Adam thought for a moment and then let his guard down. "They missed the train and are headed to Basel."

"You're so sweet." Her hand went up to Adam's cheek and he pulled away.

"Good day," he tipped his hat and looked at Raphael. "We have work." Then, he turned to her. "You can get the next train to Basel in twenty minutes … good day."

"I will." She nodded and looked Raphael up and down. "Perhaps, you can show me … please."

"It's alright." Raphael looked to Adam.

"Watch what you say to people." He eyed Raphael. "You think too much with your …"

"Says the man who held two trains." His brow bounced up and down.

"Yeah, yeah, okay." Adam scoffed and walked away.

"So, come with me." He motioned for her to follow him.

"I'd love to." She got his arm in hers. "What can you tell me about why my friends missed their train?"

"Well, it seems he forgot his bag on one train." They crossed the platform and went down to the lobby.

"I see."

Aboard the train to Basel, Aaron sighed. "Everything is here. The tickets, my cash, my tablet and my car keys."

"How far is it to Basel?" Jan asked.

Aaron looked at the monitor. "Maybe twenty minutes."

"What do we do about Zurich?" Mary had her bible in hand and turned a page.

"Have to ask when we get there." The black bag fit nicely at his feet.

At the small train station, two Russian thugs drove up. They looked at the police cars and Gendarme trucks. "Not good." The arrested Frenchman was escorted to a police van and thrown in the back.

The two Russians looked at each other and one said, "call her."

The train to Basel slowed and wound its way to the connecting track for the Basel station.

The conductor announced, "Ladies and Gentleman, this train is arriving Basel, please gather your personal belongings before you depart."

"Let's make sure we get *all* of our stuff." The shoulder strap was in his hand and his luggage was in the aisle.

Jan and Mary stood in the aisle and then walked to the end of the car. Everyone else was up and waited for the train to stop.

Finally, the train stopped, the soft bell rung, and passengers quickly rushed out the door.

Jan got off, turned, and stopped!

Mary nearly knocked her over. The people behind Mary stopped suddenly.

"Jan!"

"What, I'm waiting for you." A puzzled look came over her.

"Move!" Aaron shouted and got hold of the hand bar at the door. "Go!"

Jan moved away.

The people behind Aaron were upset and shouted over the crowd to get out of the way!

"Trying to get us beat up?" Aaron pointed at a spot behind an iron beam that was anchored in concrete. "Here's a safe place to stand."

"I was just waiting for you." Jan said and her smiled faded to a frown.

"Sorry dear, but you've got to get clear of the doors." He smiled. "You're my good luck charm and I appreciate that you waited."

"I don't know. I kind of wanted to see what they would do to her."
Mary chuckled. "Just kidding."

"Uh-huh." Jan said.

"Let's let them pass and then we'll head out." Aaron patted Jan's
shoulder to reassure her.

Mary read from her bible and shook her head.

"Alright, let's go see what it's going to take to get a train to Zurich."

Jan and Mary got their luggage and trailed after Aaron to the escalator.
Upstairs on the main concourse, Aaron went to the SBB service window
where a young man sat and waved for him to come ahead.

"Hello."

"Yes, can I help you?"

"We missed our train to Zurich and ended up here." The tickets were
in his hand.

"Your tickets please." The young man smiled and held his hand at the
pocket under the security glass. His fingers typed away at the keyboard in
seconds. "So, just up that concourse, track five."

"What's that?"

"Your train to Zurich; it leaves in approximately twenty minutes." He
dipped his head toward the track.

"Great, thank you." Aaron paused. "And we just show them these
tickets?"

"Yes, that's all."

Aaron hesitated, but nodded anyway, and went back to the girls. "He said that it's track five and we leave in twenty minutes."

Mary looked at a large clock and then at the concourse. "Track five is right there. Departure at six-ten." Her stomach growled. "I'm starving and we've got twenty minutes."

"Let's get some food." Across from them was a nice sandwich shop with a case full of fruits, sandwiches, pastries, and sides.

"I'm hungry too." Jan held her tablet up and snapped a bunch of pictures of the concourse. "We should stay in Basel for a couple of days."

"I'm not sure there's a lot to see. I think it's a major financial hub." Aaron looked the sandwiches over.

"Yes, may I help?" A lovely blond girl with a petite frame looked at each of them. Moments later, they had their hands full with food.

"Okay," Aaron waved his hand toward track five. "C'mon, we've got like five minutes!"

They made their way to the escalator and down to the platform; there was the train and two conductors.

"Wow, where is everyone?" Mary asked. "Must be an off day."

"Or they're on board." Jan stopped to balance her baguette and pie in her hand.

"Hello," He showed the conductor the tickets. "We missed our connection."

"It's no problem." His hand went up by the door to show them aboard.

"And are we able to have the same class?" Aaron asked.

"Be thankful we got on the train." Jan said.

"Yes, it's fine." He nodded and his hand was stuck in the air.

"Okay." Aaron helped Jan and Mary aboard and then they looked for seats. "Wow, that worked out."

"Sure did." Jan sat down. "My gosh this is nice, big leather seats and tables."

Mary and Aaron stowed their things. Jan gave her bag to Aaron.

The soft bell sounded, the doors closed, and the train eased out of the Basel HB.

The sandwiches, drinks, and deserts were upon the table and, shortly thereafter - minutes in fact, they were nearly gone.

"That was so good." Jan wiped her mouth. "Can't believe it all worked out fine."

"Yes, it did. I messaged the host that we're late." He got his Coke and finished it. "Time for water."

"So, what are we doing in Zurich?" Mary looked at the schedule.

"Nothing today, get settled in at the apartment." He got his schedule out. "Tomorrow, we have that day tour; the tour will take us up the coast to a ferry, we cross Lake Zurich and then ..." He rubbed the soreness from his eyes. "We've got a cable car ride on our last day and a visit to a famous restaurant on a mountain."

"Another restaurant on a mountain, maybe another avalanche." Mary said.

"Knock on wood." Jan rubbed her belly. "I'm stuffed and need a walk."

"Sinner fat." Mary chuckled.

"I'll ask forgiveness." Jan shook her head.

"We have one cable car ride or two?" Mary held up a paper with a tour. "Schitt something?"

"Really, Mary!" Jan looked away.

"Hey, I'm just saying what's spelled here." She held the paper up.

"Uh-huh. It's Schilthorn Piz-Gloria." Aaron got his paperwork. "They filmed James Bond there." Then, he moved the leftovers and set the paper down. "Should be the highpoint of our trip here. It's a beautiful place on the mountain. We go to Murren, then take a train to the cable car, and up to the top."

"Sounds exciting." The train wound its way around mountains and Jan had her tablet out. She snapped picture after picture.

"Hopefully, you're not bothered by heights. The cable car has glass all around and, it says, it's about two miles up." He turned the paper for Jan and Mary to see.

"I'm ready." Mary held her camera up.

"I'm excited about it." He put the paper away and looked out. "Slowing down. Must be close."

Two soft bells sounded. "Ladies and Gentlemen, we are arriving at Zurich Hauptbahnhof. Please get your personal belongings and be sure to check around that you have everything, thank you for traveling with SBB."

Another train passed them and Jan jumped.

"You alright?" Aaron touched her forearm.

"Gosh, just scared me." She shook it off. "We must've passed ten trains that zoomed by."

"Just wasn't expecting it." He got his things, "got my black bag, luggage."

"Purse, camera case, luggage." Mary looked at Jan to get up.

"I'll wait until it stops." She edged to the side of her seat.

"Not a lot of people on board." Aaron got up and waited in the aisle.

The train stopped, the soft bell rung, and the doors opened.

"Zurich, finally." Jan said.

"Finally." Aaron said and helped her with her things. "We got all our stuff?"

"Yep." Mary said and scooted out.

They were out the door and up the platform. Then, into the concourse at Zurich's main train station. There were Christmas ornaments and a wonderful Christmas Tree near the main entrance covered with Swarovski crystals. The main concourse was filled with stalls and merchants who peddled their wares.

"Oh, we have to shop." Mary said and set her luggage to the side. "Jan?"

"I'm in!" She looked around. "Gingerbread houses, candy canes, hot chocolate, candy … oh look! Swarovski crystal!"

"Try not to do anything illegal, like take pictures of the cops or army." He winked.

Hundreds of passengers passed by along with security and police.

"Haven't spent a lot yet." Mary looked in her wallet. "Visa, Mastercard."

"Guess I'll wait here." He laughed.

"No, we can all go." Jan said.

"Right, with your bags in tow?" He got her carryon. "I'll wait while you two kill twenty minutes. Besides, I've got to figure out how to get to the apartment."

"Alright." They piled their things against his legs. "See you later."

Several announcement bells rang like bells at the gates for race horses and the girls were off!

"Yeesh." His cell phone vibrated. A swipe and a tap, then he read the text: "keys are in mailbox, key to mail box is under box." He shook his head. "That's helpful."

"Ah!" Jan looked at the case with all the handmade crystal ornaments in it. She got her tablet and took a picture.

Mary looked around like a scout for a group of bank robbers. "Can't get anywhere near the tree." There was a three-foot section of protective glass around the base of the tree to prevent people from taking the crystal ornaments. "Not everyone is a thief." There, a few feet away, was foot stool. Mary slid over, got it under her foot, and dragged it back to the base of the tree. She got up on it, but didn't stand upright. "In position …" she got her camera ready, brought it up to her eye and then stood up. "Okay, go!"

She took a bunch of pictures within inches of the crystal ornaments and the tree. "Oh yeah, he won't know a thing."

"Excuse me." A woman's voice floated up to Mary.

"What?" She didn't look down yet.

"You must not be so close." The woman insisted.

"I'm not stealing, just took a few pictures." She lowered her camera and then looked down at three Swiss police officers, two woman and one man. "Oh."

"Yes," the woman helped her down. "Merry Christmas."

"Merry Christmas." Her soft complexion paled. "Am I under arrest?"

"Did you take anything?" Her radio blared an announcement.

"Mary!" Jan shouted. "What the hell are you doing?"

"Just took pictures." She kicked at the footstool.

"And, is this your footstool?" The policeman got it in hand and held it up.

"No." She lowered her head. "I'm sorry."

"Yes, well, please don't do that again." The policewoman said.

The policewoman returned the stool to a man who held his hand out.

"Are you crazy? Aaron will go nuts." Jan smiled at the man who owned the footstool.

"Sinner." Mary said and got Jan by the arm. "Just borrowed it."

"You took his stool, sinner."

She stopped, bowed her head, "please forgive me father for I have sinned … good thanks, amen."

"Huh?"

"Got a pass on that sin." Mary's brow bounced up and down. "Ha-ha.'

They picked up knickknacks and got back to Aaron whose eyes were half closed.

"Hey!" Mary said. "You ready for bed?"

"Yeah, actually." He perked up a little. "Good, you didn't get into any trouble."

"No, nothing." Mary exclaimed quickly.

"Yep, all good." Jan looked at the tree and then at Mary. "No trouble at all."

"Let's get to the apartment. It's rush hour here, so just keep your things close and beware of pickpockets." He handed them their bags and then they headed to the main entrance. "We'll grab a street car and head out."

A Russian thug, with a tattoo over half his face, six foot-five inches tall and muscular, stood near the main entrance. He looked at a picture of three Americans on his phone and then looked at the crowd. His eyes panned each face; he made a mental note and then mumbled, "het." The word was Russian for "no."

Many people went in and out of the main entrance and then streamed off in between the stalls; there were ten rows of stalls and so the Russian saw only so many people at a time.

Another Russian stood a few rows away and looked at the picture of the three Americans on his phone and then his eyes perused the faces of people who passed by.

Aaron led them to the left exit and stopped to look at the tree. "Oh, that's awesome." Far above his head, his phone nearly floated in air and then "click-click-click."

Mary took some more pictures.

Jan looked at her tablet screen and it flickered. "C'mon."

The Russian at the far end looked at Jan and saw her tablet over her face, but not her. He looked elsewhere. Mary had her big Canon camera with its huge zoom aimed at the tree. The Russian looked past her. A handsome Swiss cop bumped Aaron and he turned to look at him. The Russian missed Aaron.

"Hi." Aaron looked him up and down. "Is the tram out here?"

"Yes, it's just there, five meters." His pearly whites were just visible past his full lips.

"Just five meters." He replied.

"Yes," the cop chuckled.

"I'd ask for a selfie, but I know it's not allowed." His phone was at the ready.

"I'm afraid not." The policeman nodded and walked away.

"My heart just broke."

"What?" Jan asked. "He was a cutie."

"He was." Aaron looked at the doors. "Let's get going. I'm exhausted."

"Mary!" Jan shouted at her and waved at her. "Let's go."

Out on the street, it was rush hour! A melee of trams, busses, cars, bicyclist, motorcycles, and pedestrians were in a rush to get home.

"Wow." Aaron walked across the closed street. "We need to get over there."

"Alright, just don't go fast." Jan made her way over the snow-covered street and back up onto the sidewalk.

They made their way through the hundreds of people that crowded the streets and stopped at a light. Jan and Mary stood to the side of Aaron.

"Just go." Jan said.

"Jan?" Mary looked at the traffic that filled the five lanes across their path. "There's trams, cars, and busses in front of us."

"Yeah, but they have to stop for pedestrians. I read it." She put her earmuffs on.

In the distance, an ambulance siren roared and its blue lights bounced off of every metallic thing from the tram to the bus to the cars! And the siren wailed up and down over and over!

"Go Aaron! They'll stop." She edged ahead and pushed Aaron.

"Stop it!" He pointed. "There's an ambulance!"

The ambulance was a block away and its blue lights got brighter and brighter; the siren wailed so loud that the sound pierced every ear! Cars fought to get out of the way, but they were bumper to bumper.

"They have to stop though." Jan took another step and was up against Aaron.

Someone bumped Jan and she turned sharply! She jerked her rollaboard around and knocked Aaron into the street!

Tires screeched! People screamed!

Chapter Eleven: The Chase is On!

Aaron lay on the street and just inches from the bumper of the ambulance! "Ah!"

"Aaron!" Mary shouted and leapt to grab him.

Aaron covered his face, "Ah!"

Jan got turned around and back to where she started. Then, she took in all the excitement. "See, I told you they would stop."

A couple of tourists and Mary helped Aaron back up and then the ambulance took off! The light turned green for the pedestrian traffic and everyone went on as if nothing had happened, just like Jan.

"C'mon, let's go." Jan walked across.

Anger surged through Aaron's chest and up to his face where it melted the snowflakes.

"Keep your cool. She's older and doesn't hear well." Mary patted his back.

"She won't hear a thing if I shove her in front of something." He huffed.

"There's the tram, right?" Jan pointed at a number seven tram.

Aaron was tight lipped and nodded.

"Mary, that's it?" Her tablet was out and she snapped a bunch of pictures. "Look at the beautiful Christmas lights over the streets!"

"They are wonderful." Mary said and raised her brow at Aaron.

Jan leaned over to Mary. "Is he mad?"

"Uh, yeah, you shoved him into the street and an ambulance nearly ran him over." Mary got her bible out and tapped Jan on her back with it. "Be healed sinner."

"Yeah, but it stopped." She smiled. "They're supposed to stop."

"Right, that's what matters." She shook her head at Jan. "Shame sinner, shame."

At the apartment, Aaron got the key from under the mail box and when he put the key in the mailbox lock, the door fell off. "Great." He got the key to the apartment, set the door back in place, and then went up to their BNB.

"Puke green toilet, shower, and tile … nice." Mary's eyes panned the walls of the bathroom. "It's nearly seven-thirty and my stomach knows it."

"Just a few minutes to shut my eyes." He said and let his things fall in a room with a futon. "You two take the bedroom."

"Okay," Jan didn't hesitate to go to the bedroom. "Let's rest for an hour and then go get something to eat, maybe walk around, and look at the decorations."

"Yeah," Mary said and saw Aaron's worn expression. She whispered to Jan. "Let's let him rest."

They winked at each other and then there was silence.

A half-hour later, another train from Basel slowed to a stop at Zurich HB. Natalya got off, sighed, and uttered under her breath. "I'm coming to get her Elliot and get what you took."

Three Russian thugs walked up to her and nodded. "Natalya."

A block away from the BNB, Elliot reclined in a red Audi S8 sedan. His phablet was dim and he studied the signal that moved around an apartment. Then, his phone rang, "Blue Moon." His fingers swiped between screens and then he answered. "Hello, mom."

Jan had her diary in hand and sipped her coffee. "I love these Americanos."

"Me too." Mary sipped on hers and then took out a mini bottle of whisky. She wagged it in front of Jan.

"Ah," Jan's eye brightened. "From the plane?"

"Yep, two of them." Mary sat up from the bed and got the cap off. "Helps when you write in your diary. I know I can remember more."

They laughed.

Elliot laughed, "Yeah, I'm alright." His happy expression faded. "No, I … probably not for Christmas, but …" A pause hit and his mother told him it was fine. She had plenty to do: bake for her friends, wrap gifts for a charity, and work Christmas eve. "Did you get what I sent?" He asked and chuckled. Then, he hung onto his smile; it was much better than his current mission. She didn't hear his question. "Did you get my gifts?" He repeated.

A word bellowed from the speaker, "Oh!" She was so happy. "Yes."

A sigh of relief came from him. "Good, I know Santa has you on the nice list." A text popped up, "SVR - Zurich."

Natalya talked with one of the thugs who had a tattoo over half his face. Then, they walked toward the main entrance. "Savarine is upset at the lack of progress." Her phone vibrated and she read the text. "That idiot Frenchman was arrested."

"Should never have used him." The thug with a tattoo on his face said. "Savarine is too ambitious."

Natalya drew back and slapped the hell out of him! "No Marco, we should not have used him." She kissed him and ran her hand down his tattooed face. "We must get it back … and do not ever say of Savarine that she is too anything."
"And what of the Americans?" They embraced.

Her gaze drifted to a man who held a cleaver. The cleaver came down on a chunk of beef and sliced right through it like a hot blade through butter. He tossed it on the grill and it sizzled!

Marco nodded.

She turned and headed to the door with her threesome in tow.

Christmas music played and people were in merry moods; except for the four Russians who were on a mission to recover what an American spy stole.

"I know. I love you too." Elliot said.

Elliot's mother caught her breath and swallowed her sadness. "So, you be strong and we'll see you soon."

His teeth sank into his bottom lip and his fingers pressed into his eyes to push away the lies. "I will."

"You're a good man, son." She cleared her throat of the emotion that surged up it. "Merry Christmas and I love you."

Elliot sat up. "Merry Christmas mom. I love you too."

"Bye son." She waited.

"Bye, mom." He pressed the "end call" icon and sniffled. Then, his phone buzzed with a text. "SVR – Zurich ???" He tightened his grip around the phone until his knuckles were white and then he threw the phone against the passenger door. "Instead of being with my family, I'm here!" The driver's side door flung open and he got out and paced. "Damn!"

"What did you think about that guy?" Jan was gleeful.

"Huh?" Mary pondered. "Oh, the hottie?"

"He was. I wonder what that was about at the pizza place." She got the pen and tapped her forehead with it. "Intrigue, they are lovers and split up over another …"

"Sinner?" Mary shook her head. "I'd rather not know anything else about a guy like that." The pen dangled around her forefinger and middle finger. "He was too forceful."

A sly grin came over Jan. "Yeah, I know." Then, she turned and went to the chair. "Men are soft nowadays." Her eyes glowed, "when the mood hit Steve, he took me and whoa!"

"Okay, I haven't eaten and have no strength to repel your sinful comments." She pulled the pillow over her head.

"C'mon, you have to imagine a man who knows what he wants and just holds you. His lips hover over yours and then he plants one on you." A happy sigh slid through her lips, "ah."

"Okay, stop the smut." Aaron said.

"Oh!" Mary threw the pillow off and sat up. "Knock please."

He knocked and shook his head. "Talk about sin." Then, he went to the living room and got his shoes on. "Dinner." His watch glowed, "Wow, it's nearly nine."

Mary and Jan got cleaned up.

"My hair." Jan said. "It's too puffy."

"Water and then spray." Mary said.

Moments later, they were on the street. "Catch the next tram." He said. "Maybe Jan will shove me in front of it."

"I didn't mean to do that." She got hold of his arm. "I would never want anything bad to happen to you."

They validated their tickets just as the tram pulled up and got on.

"Where to for dinner?" Mary asked and set her small bible in her coat.

"Christmas Market is on a street along the river. Let's go there and then find a place to eat." The tram map was just above the seats and he studied it.

Elliot huffed and sat back down in the Audi. His phone vibrated and was caught between the door and the passenger seat. His hand swiftly dove between the door and the seat, got the phone, and brought it out. "Okay." A swipe and a tap on text messages. His thumbs tapped away at the screen in quick and precise strokes. "SVR – Zurich. IK."

"& mule?"

His thumbs tapped. "On track." He deleted the text and swiped back to the track. "Where are you, Jan?" The blip lit up. "At the Christmas market on Niederdorfstrasse." The car start button was dimly lit; a quick tap and the engine roared to life! The needles maxed and then recoiled to their norms. "Let's do some Christmas shopping."

Natalya was on her phone. "Yes, but to track them." Her eyes locked with Marco's.

Two thugs walked up and nodded at Marco. Now, there were six of them.

"What do you know?" Natalya asked.

"They have checked into an AirBnb apartment." He pointed, "42 Gasometerstrasse."

"Two of you wait by the apartment for them and do not touch them, not yet." Natalya said. "I'm going for something to eat. You just to keep me informed about what they do and when the leave." She turned to Marco. "When they are out, I want video and audio in the apartment."

"Yes," Marco said.

"They left the apartment and went to the Christmas Market." One of the thugs said. "About twenty minutes ago."

She got close to him. "I've been here for at least forty minutes and no word."

The thug looked at Marco and shrugged his shoulders.

She turned to Marco. "Well?"

"I did not get that message, so we stayed and watched for them at the station." His face paled.

"Excuses will be the death of us, literally." She turned back to the thug. "Go to the apartment and plant the bugs." She huffed and pushed her hair back. "I do not want any more excuses."

At the apartment, an internet company van pulled up and parked. One of the thugs got out and wore a toolbelt; he nodded at his buddy and went to the door. His buddy stayed with the van and kept a lookout.

Elliot drove down an alley just off Niederdorfstrasse, found a place to park, and eased into the spot near an apartment building. He eased back the slide on his Sig Sauer 9mm and looked at the shell in the chamber, "never be too careful." He got out and tucked the gun to his back.

Jan, Aaron, and Mary stopped at a Mediterranean restaurant.

Aaron inhaled deeply, "smells good."

Mary studied the men inside. One of them wore a turban and all of them spoke Arabic. "Is it safe?"

"Huh?" Aaron looked at the menu posted on a placard outside the restaurant. "Safe for what? Food?"

"That one guy has a bandana around his head." Mary looked at Jan.

"The food looks good." Jan said and pointed at the many plates of food behind glass at the counter.

"Mary, really." Aaron shook his head. "You could go to Minneapolis and find guys there who speak Arabic."

"We're not in Minneapolis." She got her bible in hand. "Is there a McDonalds or Burger King near here?"

"Yes, and we're not going. You don't fly eight thousand miles to eat fast food." Aaron went up to the door. "It's fine."

"You eat first and we'll see." She hesitated.

Jan walked in. "I'm hungry."

"Ditto."

Aaron and Jan ordered and Mary watched from outside.

"Is she with you?" The man with the turban asked.

"Yes, she's got down syndrome so it takes her a minute." Aaron said.

"Oh, so sorry to hear." The man waved at Mary. "Hello!"

"So are we." He replied and turned to Mary. Then, he went to the door and opened it. "Get in here!"

Mary trembled from the cold. "Yeah, I'm freezing."

"Hello," the man said. "What can I get you?"

Elliot walked past the restaurant and looked in. Then, he went to a bar across the street and had a drink.

Afterwards, they sat at a table and Mary ate up.

Natalya happened to be on the same street, walked past the Mediterranean restaurant, and then looked up the street. "They must've stopped to eat."

Marco looked around. "There are at least twenty restaurants here."

"Let's eat and then we can wait for them to go back to their apartment." She said and pointed at a restaurant up the street. "You got their itinerary for tomorrow?"

"Yes, they have a tour at eight in the morning and will be on it until five." He handed her his phone.

She took it and looked at the bright screen. "Fine." She handed it back to him. "And we must keep a look for Elliot."

Marco nodded. "So, to kill him?"

Natalya grinned. "Do you worry about him?"

Marco lifted his chin up and his chest puffed up. "No."

Elliot stood to the side of the window frame and saw Natalya. Marco, and the other Russians in the street. "The Brady Bunch has arrived … the chase is on."

Chapter Twelve: Who's the Mole!

It was early the next morning when Jan threw water on her face and applied her anti-aging cream. "It has to sit for twenty minutes." Her eyes were closed tight and the tan cream covered her face.

"Alright," Mary said and had her hair in curlers. "I think it's after six."

"My eyes are covered."

The clock on the nightstand had "6:12 AM." "We have to be there by eight." Mary looked down the hall toward the den. "I think Aaron's still sleeping."

"Let him sleep." Jan grinned and then her grin faded. "No facial expressions during cream application."

Outside, the internet van was parked across the street. One of the thugs listened intently and made a couple of notes. Then, he sent a text, "Marco, they leave for their tour at 8."

Marco replied, "abbreviate U idiot!"

The thug thought for a moment. "Leave 4 tour @ 8."

The reply from Marco was, "U said so already idiot!"

The thug thought for a moment more and then tapped out. "I have, LOL."

Aaron rubbed the sleep from his eyes, got his things, and stood at the door. "Is the bathroom free?"

Jan's face cream was crusty, hard. "In about five minutes."

Mary poked her head out of the bedroom. "She's got her cream on."

An hour passed and they were on the tram headed to the bus station for their tour.

Aaron looked over the paperwork. "Lake Zurich, the city center, then to the Goldcoast, a Ferry to the Silvercoast, and then a cable car to the mountain top."

"Lunch?" Jan asked.

"We stop for an hour and a half." He turned the paper over. "It'll be a great tour."

"Did you hear back about the heat?" Mary asked. "The apartment was cold."

"Yeah, Michael's going to check it." He looked at the map again.

Elliot drove alongside the tram and then cut across the front of it!

The tram driver pressed a button and honked at the crazy driver! The tram slowed and then stopped at Zurich's main train station. The threesome went to the tour busses across the street and looked for their tour. After a talk and ticket exchange, they boarded a bus with twenty other people.

Elliot lowered his window, watched them board, and waited.

"Are they on the bus?" Natalya asked and adjusted the ear piece to hear clearly. The small café inside the main station was cozy and she sipped on an espresso. "Good."

The bus pulled from the lot and onto the street. Marco and his two thugs stood at the corner. "Why don't we just hi-jack the bus?"

Natalya's eyes rolled. "Fool! We do not want an international incident."

"What?" Marco was good at his job, but not so good with complicated thoughts.

"Three Russians hi-jack a bus in Switzerland. The allies would love to hate us more." Frustrated, she growled. "We are SVR-RF; we work in the shadows."

"Yes," Marco looked at his men. "In the shadows."

"Follow them." Steam drifted into the air from her espresso. Another sip and then a bite of her croissant, she was ready. Her thumb tapped out a number and then a call. "Savarine, 3395."

Marco and his men got in a black BMW and followed the bus out of the city and toward the Goldcoast along Lake Zurich.

The two Russian thugs in the internet van went into the apartment. "C'mon." Ivan jimmied the lock and they were in. He took out a scanner and scanned everything. "Andrei, make no mess, put back like it was." They carefully went through the clothes, luggage, closets, all the kitchen drawers, and they even looked in the washer and dryer. When they finished with something.

The scanner had a numerical reader and it remained at zero. "Ivan, Nichego na skaner." Andrei whistled at his buddy.

"Yes, you have nothing. I heard." Ivan shook his head.

Michael, the lessor of the apartment, got his key in the lock, but had trouble turning it. "What the hell." The key wiggled, but couldn't quite get the pins lined up. Then, he forced it and the lock turned.

Ivan and Andrei turned toward the front door! "Go!" They scurried to another room, pulled ski masks over their heads, drew their guns, and waited.

Michael rounded the corner from the hallway. "What the hell?"

Ivan rushed over, swung the butt of his pistol, and struck Michael on the head. The force knocked him to the floor!

"Ah!" Michael held his hand to the side of his head and trembled. "Please."

"Money!" Andrei yelled and aimed his gun at Michael's head. Then, he looked at Ivan, "Go!"

Ivan rushed out the door.

Michael's hand trembled and he handed his wallet to Andrei. "Here."

Andrei pulled cash out and shook his head. "Twenty francs?" He pressed the barrel against Michael's head, "ten minutes … you stay down or you die." Then, he tossed the wallet back to him, fled from the flat, and out to the waiting truck. The trucks tires screeched and the truck sped down the strasse!

Michael reeled from the pain and looked at his blood covered hand. He sat up and called the police.

The tour guide pointed at the houses. "So, this is the Goldcoast of Lake Zurich. Most of the homes on the lake are quite high priced, some are more than four million dollars."

"Not in my price range." Aaron took pictures.

"And coming up, you have a famous American who has lived here for some time." The guide talked with the driver.

"What American lives here?" He looked at Jan and then Mary.

"I don't know." Jan had her tablet up and snapped one picture after another. "Movie star probably."

"Don't know either." Mary said and took pictures and then a selfie.

"So, has anyone come to a conclusion about this small mystery?" Most of the faces on the bus were puzzled. "No?" He smiled. "I'm surprised, so I give you a clue." A slight pause and then he cleared his throat, "Algonquin."

"That doesn't do a damn thing to help me." Aaron shook his head. "No idea!" He shouted at the guide.

"You are American?" The guide asked.

"Yes."

"So, it's actually for Switzerland, not American. The clue is for the home that this famous American resides at, Chateau Algonquin on Lake Zurich." He waited a moment more.

"Tina Turner!" A person in the back shouted.

"Yes! You've had time to look it up on your phone!" He laughed heartily.

"Tina Tuner lives in Zurich?" Aaron's puzzled look surprised Jan.

"I thought the gays love Tina Turner." Jan asked.

"Do they?" Mary took a picture of Aaron. "Why?"

"I'm not speaking for all the gays out there." A smirk wasn't enough, so he smiled. "I like Tina Turner's songs, but not enough to be a groupie."

The bus slowed and then swung into a space.

"Ah! There is her house and, sometimes, you can see her at the market." He pointed.

Mary sat up and took a picture. "You can't see the house with all the trees. What kind of tour is this?"

"A good tour!" The guide said. "We go now to our ride up the mountain."

"But we haven't taken the ferry yet." Jan said.

"No, it's a chateau something that wasn't accessible by a road for years." Aaron said. His fingers danced on his phone and he had the information. "The Dolder Grand, opened in 1899 and was only accessible by a mountain train until a few years ago."

"What happened?" Mary took several selfies.

Jan turned to her, "What's with you and the selfies?"

"They have a road now and you can drive up." Aaron said.

"Ladies and gentlemen, we will arrive at Dolderbahn and take a wonderful train up to the Dolder Grand." The guide pointed to a spot and the driver swung in.

"So, please to gather your personal belongings." The driver pulled around and parked. "The bus will meet us at the top and from there we go on to the ferry."

"This is nice." Mary stood.

They lined up at the Dolderbahn and the train slowed to a stop.

The guide held up his hand. "Please, board the train."

Aaron looked at two men. One had a tattoo down the side of his face and the other looked beefy and rough. "Interesting couple."

Jan took picture after picture with her tablet.

Marco looked over the crowd and then at Jan. "She's here." His finger pressed against the tiny button on a cord to his phone.

Another BMW sedan pulled up, Natalya got in the passenger seat with two thugs. "Do not do a thing. You just follow her." She tapped, "End Call."

Marco leaned over to his buddy, "just to follow."

The tour group boarded the train and then Marco and his thug stood at the door. The guide held up his hand and blocked them. "Are you with this tour group."

Marco bent at the waist and got in the guides face. "We are now."

The guide gulped and then lowered his arm. "Of course."

Once at the top, they exited and the guide walked with them to the far side of the Dolder Grand. "Ladies and Gentlemen, so that is the Dolder Grand, completed in 1899, the rail used to be the only way to access the resort." He pointed at the hotel. "You see there is a modern addition that was completed in 2008 that is meant to accent the original resort."

Aaron spoke up. "You look like that didn't happen."

The guide walked up to him and leaned over so that they were the only ones to hear what he said next. "It didn't." He smiled politely.

"Indeed, and unfortunate."

Jan held her tablet up and took photos. The screen flickered and this time it went on for a couple of minutes. "That screen flicker's getting worse." Frustrated, she turned the tablet off and waited.

"What's up?" Aaron asked.

Marco and his buddy got close to them. In fact, they were just a foot or so behind Jan.

Aaron turned and nodded at Marco who grinned. Then, Aaron turned his attention to Jan. "Jan?"

"That flicker's gotten worse." She fought to keep her happy expression. "Uh."

"I promise I'll look at it when we get back." His phone took super pictures and he snapped away. "Mary and I will have plenty of pictures to pass on too."

Mary snapped a selfie of her with the hotel. "Yeah."

"Mary, you keep taking selfies. There are three of us on this trip." Aaron had his camera turned for a selfie. "C'mon Jan."

"Sorry." She hurried over and they posed with the hotel in the background.

"Perhaps." Marco said and forced himself to smile. The muscles in his cheeks pushed back and fought the idea of his smile as something they'd never done. "I can take photo."

"Oh," Aaron hesitated and then slowly handed his phone over.

Jan looked at her tablet. "Tablets back on. I want one too."

"Yes, of course." Marco said and looked at his buddy. The phone clicked away. "Just one more." He tapped the screen and handed the phone back to Aaron.

"Thanks." Without saying so, Aaron lowered his camera and snapped several pictures of the two men.

"Ah, your tablet." His smile widened and took on a look that resembled the Grinch's wide and devious smile.

"Alright, we ready?" Jan asked.

Marco's buddy stood a foot or so behind him and spoke in Russian. "Hand it back to me and I will run."

Behind them was a crowd of tourist and a busy road.

Marco looked around and then brought the tablet up to take a picture. "No." The focus on the tablet went in and out.

"You have it in hand. Just give it to me." The thug said. "Marco."

"Everything alright between you two?" Aaron asked and then spoke under his breath to Mary. "Like a married couple dickering over who gets to do what."

"Yes." Marco said. His big finger tapped the icon and the tablet snapped several pictures.

In the distance and behind Mary, Jan, and Aaron, a black BMW swung onto the road and stopped by the curb. Natalya got out and looked at Marco. She shook her head gently and her hair swung softly across her face.

"There you go." He said and resisted the temptation to walk off with the tablet.

Jan walked up to him. "Thank you." She touched his chest with her hand. "Wow, you're strong."

He forced a smile again and then looked at Natalya. "Yes, I am."

Natalya shook her head again to be sure he did not make a scene. Then, she got back in the car.

"Thanks." Aaron said and leaned over to Mary. "Like a Russian accent."

Mary nodded.

The tour bus pulled up and beeped the horn. Everyone boarded and they were on their way to the ferry.

A red Audi pulled into the parking garage above them and Elliot got out. From the higher point, he saw the bus drive down the road, the black BMW, and Marco and his buddy. The phone in his coat buzzed. "We're secure." He turned away.

Marco and his buddy got in the BMW with Natalya. She kissed Marco. "Back to your car, then you follow the bus. I will go to the Silvercoast and we meet together there."

Elliot pressed his fingers to his nose and looked at the ground as his supervisor talked.

"So, you should have found a mule that was headed home sooner." The female voice said.

"She's fine." The wind blew against his face and chilled his cheeks.

"Your arrogance is showing. It's far more dangerous now and if they get it from her, the whole thing is a wash." The wind whooshed by. "She's not an asset and she could get hurt … or worse."

"It won't happen." He said. "I've got it in hand."

In a very firm tone, she made clear what she wanted. "Uh-huh, I want you to re-think how this will play out and get it today. Echo four is in Zurich and will pass it along." Then, there was silence.

"Echo four isn't up for the challenge. I'll get it and deliver it." The wind was stronger now and it was harder for him to hold his place. His soft pale cheeks were worn red by the gusts. "It's under control."

"Is it?" She cleared her throat. "Right now, I see you on the upper parking deck and the SVR agents just drove off."

"It's fine." The clouds cleared, the blue sky was beautiful, and the satellite was over him.

"Two of them were a foot from your mule." She took a drink.

Elliot knew that she planned to lay into him now that she soothed her vocal chords. "I know." Then, he looked at the street level. Two men got out of a black Chevy SUV and pulled up their collars. "Don't do this."

"Your order is to get the device, deliver it to us, and debrief." She huffed.

"I understand." A few steps and he was at the concrete barrier. To his right, the two men went to the parking garage door and entered. "The satellite isn't the only thing that has eyes."

"You go rogue on me and I promise that the price will be far higher than you can imagine, Elliot." She coughed.

He sighed, "No names, at least that's what I was taught." Then, he looked at the ground. "Who's the mole?"

"Turn yourself over to Echo four and we'll find a remedy that works."
She muted the call and told the two men to move in. Then, she unmuted
the call. "Sorry, you were saying?"

"No, Beth." The parking garage door to his level was to the right and
he looked at it. He dragged his foot along the ground and made a line in
the salt and sand. "Sorry, but nope." Then, he tapped end call, looked up,
and shook his head.

Beth looked at the satellite live feed of him and then nodded at a tech
who sat at a desk with three monitors around him. "Echo four approved."

A couple of hotdog American agents, twenty-somethings, raced up the
stairs! "Go!" One agent said. They drew their guns and hurried to the third
level where Elliot waited.

The driver's side door to the Audi was open and the engine idled
quietly. Elliot looked around and then eyed the exit. "Six minutes for them,
two minutes for me."

The door flung open, the agents saw Elliot and they drew down on
him. "Don't move!"

Elliot smiled, swung himself into the car, jerked the door shut, and revved the engine!

"Elliot!" One agent shouted and then pressed the button for his lapel mic. "Echo four, he's running!"

From fifty or so feet away, they stopped, aimed at the tires, and paused. "Elliot, don't do it!"

Elliot shook his head, put the car in drive, jammed his left foot down on the brake and floored the gas pedal! The back tires spun wildly and smoke billowed from them!

"Shoot the tires!" The agent said to his partner.

His partner aimed at the front tire and shot! "Bang!" The tire went flat. "Got his ass now!"

The back tires burned rubber furiously and spat salt and sand into the air! A red light on the dash lit up and indicated a flat. Then, the tire re-inflated.

"What the hell?" The agent took aim again. "Really? Tires that re-inflate!"

Elliot let off the brake, jerked the steering wheel to the left, and took off!

"Blast him!" The agents shot and the rounds ricocheted off the car!

One doughnut, two doughnuts, three doughnuts, and then he let go of the wheel just as the car was aimed at the exit lane! The car roared toward the exit!

The hail of bullets hit the concrete parking deck, other cars, and the metal door to the lift! The agents fired shot after shot! Two punctured the Audi's skin near the rear door, but that was it.

Elliot raced to the exit, jerked the wheel to the right, and then went down the circular sloped ramp to the ground level.

"Call it in!" The agents ran back to the exit door, hurried down three flights of steps, and rushed to get back to their SUV. "Echo four, he's headed out!"

"Echo four, copy. Drone is up and headed your way." The dispatcher said.

The Audi skidded past the valet stand and then skidded around the corner out of the garage. The black SUV was on his right and Elliot jammed both feet on the brake pedal! The Audi skidded to a stop. The passenger window went down, he pulled his Sig Sauer out, and paused. "Four minutes." A few people walked by and looked at the big SUV. "Excuse me." He said.

They passersby paid him no mind. So, he tapped the horn. "Excuse me, please move!"

An older, distinguished Frenchman and his wife looked at him. "Can you not be so rude!" The disgruntled man's accent was thick.

"No, I can't." Elliot brought the Sig up and aimed at the SUV's tire. "Move your ass!"

The Frenchman and his wife ducked for cover! People screamed and ran for cover!

"Bang!" He shot out the front tire and then, he leaned up on the center console, aimed at the other front tire, and shot. "Thanks!" He sat back down and then floored the Audi! The wheels ripped up the pavement and smoke billowed from the back of the car!

"Damn Americans!" The man shouted.

His wife tried to comfort him. "Darling, it's fine. Let's just go!"

The two agents leapt from the parking garage door and ran toward their SUV.

"What the hell?" The man looked at the two agents. "This isn't a western!"

The agents ran past the man and stopped. "Damn-it!" They looked at the tires and then stomped around in anger. "Don't suppose we have auto-inflate?"

The Frenchman went to say something and then his wife pointed at the agent's; "They have guns, mon cher." She gulped in fear. "Perhaps, it's best to just go."

"Oui." He got her by the hand and they hurried off.

Elliot sped down the mountain and then whipped around the corner onto the main road that went along the Goldcoast of Lake Zurich. "Can't be on the ferry yet."

The bus was at the ferry and waited behind several other cars to board. The guide got the mic in hand. "So, you can use this time to take pictures of our beautiful Lake Zurich and enjoy the crossing." He looked ahead and then back at the tourists. "You're welcome to exit the bus once on the ferry and go to the second level. Please, please be careful of other cars and where you're at, thank you."

Elliot raced down Seestrasse! The red Audi flew past a car, past a truck, and then past several cars at once. "Move!" The horn blared!

Marco and his buddy waited in a car just a couple cars behind the bus.

The ferry agent raised a flag that the ferry approached.

The captain pulled the cord and blew the horn several times. Then, the ferry docked and was tied off. The ferry's ramp came down and the cars drove off.

There were lights at the ferry stop for the traffic that waited to board.

Elliot looked up the road and saw the bus. "Okay, what to do?" He swung out into the opposing lane to avoid a postal truck! "Damn!"

Oncoming traffic flashed their headlights and honked their horns!

"Sorry!" Elliot shouted and swerved back to the right.

The light turned green and cars drove aboard the ferry.

Elliot jerked around another car and then whipped into the parking lot. "Have to stop the SVR from getting to her."

Marco pushed his sunglasses up the bridge of his nose, slowly pulled ahead and then stopped.

The red Audi skidded into the ferry lane, drove right up to the black BMW, and hit the rear of it!

The BMW lurched forward and then back. Marco's face turned an ashen red. "What the hell!" He jammed the gear into park, got out, and looked at the driver. "Elliot!" He sneered.

The ferrymen looked on and wondered what to do. Other cars got in the opposing lane, drove around them, and onto the ferry.

Elliot got out. "Hey, Marco."

"You won't stop us." Marco thought and then looked at the ferry gate. "Don't close!"

His buddy yelled at him to get in the car! "Marco!"

Marco turned, got back in the car, and slammed the door shut. He pulled ahead.

Elliot put the car in drive, revved the motor, and then rammed them again!

The jolt knocked Marco's sunglasses from his face and cracked the lenses! "Idiot!"

Elliot got out, ran to the driver's door, and smashed the glass with the butt of his gun! The glass shattered and he punched Marco!

"Marco, don't!" His buddy said.

The ferry agent called the police and the captain of the ferry radioed the trouble to the authorities.

Marco got out and brought his fists up! He swung over and over! "You going to pay now for that bullshit!" He spat. "Broke my new sunglasses!"

"Too bad." Elliot swatted the punches away from him and then he ducked and shifted!

"Get in the damn car, Marco!" His buddy yelled at the top of his lungs.

Elliot looked at the ferry. "You suck at boxing." He ran toward the ferry.

Marco ran after him and tackled him right at the gate to the ferry.

The agent hurriedly closed the gate, raised the flag, and cleared the ferry!

The up and down wail of Zurich's police force screamed some distance from them.

Elliot kicked, then punched, then blocked and then …

Marco landed a heavy blow to Elliot's cheek! "Ah!"

Elliot spun around, threw his hands to block, and then kicked!

The ferry's engines roared to life and water burst out from the propellers!

Jan, Mary, and Aaron were on the top deck and at the stern.

Aaron smiled, "so nice and peaceful."

Mary looked up Seestrasse. "Except for the sirens."

"No kidding." Jan said.

Marco kneed Elliot in the chest over and over! "You stupid American!"

Marco's buddy shook his head and got on his phone.
Elliot blocked Marco's knee and spun out from him.

Marco tried to grab him, but couldn't with Elliot's arms blocking him.

Then, Elliot pulled a short blade Victorinox Army knife out and stabbed Marco's calf!

"Ah!" Marco yelled and grasped his calf. "You pig!"

Elliot got to his feet and then high kicked Marco in the chin!

There was a pause and the two men stopped. Each man locked his eyes with the other and rage came over them.

"Going to beat you to death!" Marco said and rubbed the stab wound. "Damn it."

Elliot looked at the stern of the ferry and waved at Jan, Aaron, and Mary. "Hey guys!"

"Oh my God." Jan said. "Look!" She pointed at Elliot. "It's that guy!" Mary looked and her eyes widened. "Holy …"

"Shit." Aaron said. "What's with that guy?"

Elliot waved at them. "How's it going?"

Marco saw his chance! He bent at the waist, charged Elliot, scooped him up, and then ran with him toward the seawall.   "Ah!"

"Stoy!" Marco's buddy yelled in Russian and ran after them, "Stoy!"

"Is he straight or gay?" Aaron asked and videoed the fight. "Get a million hits off this fight."

"Why is he here?" Jan asked and tapped record on her tablet.

"Maybe he's after you." Mary said and focused on the two men headed for the seawall.

"Oh god." Jan said. "Stop! I have enough love to go around!"

Elliot turned his head and saw the seawall. Blow after blow, he punched Marco's back and head furiously to get him to stop or they were going to go over the wall and into the icy waters!

"Oh, this is going to be good." Mary said. "Sinners!"

Just then, Marco's rage eased after he saw the very top edge of the seawall, but it was too late. Slam! They hit the wall and went head over heels into Lake Zurich!

"Holy ..." Aaron held his phone up.

Mary shook her head. "Shit."

Jan looked at Mary with wide eyes. "Mary, language."

Elliot bobbed up, got his bearings, and shook off the sudden chill from the icy waters.

Marco came up and shook his head to get his bearings, but it was too late.

Elliot was right there, raised his fist, and dead slammed his cold knuckles right into Marco's face!

"Ah!" Marco yelped; he tried to shake off the punch and then threw a blind punch! His fist slammed the water.

They bobbed up and down with the waves.

The captain slowed the ferry for a moment. "Idiots." With the mic in hand, he radioed an update.

Three Zurich police cars raced into the ferry lot and skidded to a stop!

Elliot inhaled deep to raise his body up enough to throw another blow. Then, he drew back and waited.

Marco shook his head again and things were sideways, blurry.

"Marco." Elliot said.

Marco turned, the wave passed, and he was at eye level with Elliot's fist. "What the …"

Wham! The punch slammed into his face and there was a deafening crack!

Marco was out and bobbed with the next wave.

Jan, Mary, and Aaron looked on in a stunned gaze.

Aaron shook his head. "I've been in a few fights." He lowered his phone. "That guy is deadly."

Elliot shook his hand out. "Damn it." His knuckles were bloody and bruised.

Jan looked waved at Elliot. "That water must be freezing." She shouted, "Are you okay?"

The police rushed to the seawall with a life preserver.

"You're supposed to say Polo when someone says Marco." Elliot spat the lake water from his mouth, got ahold of Marco in a lifeguard carry, and swam back with him to the seawall. "Oh yeah!" He shouted back to Jan, "my teammate … we water fight! It's an exercise thing!"

The guide walked up and looked at the two men. "Oh, it's not uncommon for a swim in the lake during winter."

"No?" Aaron looked at him.

"It revives the senses and enlivens the soul." The guide smiled.

"Uh-huh." Aaron said.

The captain blew the horn twice and pushed the engine throttles ahead.

Two police boats approached; their blue lights flashed and their sirens wailed.

"All clear." The captain said and the ferry sailed to the other side of Lake Zurich.

Elliot treaded water and one of the policeboats got alongside him. The officers pulled him and Marco aboard. Then, they wrapped them in blankets.

Mary looked at Aaron. "Should we be concerned?"

"I don't know." Aaron looked at Elliot and Elliot winked at him. "Maybe."

"What did they really fight about?" Jan asked and stopped recording.

Mary put her arm around Jan. "It was over a woman."

"That gal from Petite Venise?" Jan smiled.

"No, you." Mary held her camera up. "Selfie."

Aaron, Jan, and Mary smiled at the camera with Lake Zurich and the city of Zurich in the back ground.

Mary pressed the button several times and then looked at the pictures on her screen. "Wow."

"No kidding, very nice." Aaron said.

"Send me those.' Jan said.

"So, now that the fight is over, we're off to the cable car ride, then to Zurich, and home." Aaron said. "Tomorrow it's off to …"

"Schitt-horn." Mary exclaimed.

"Mary!" Jan shook her head. "Shame on you."

"Really, Mrs. Catholic." His hand went up. "Talk to the hand."

"Ladies and gentlemen with the Zurich tour, please return to the bus." The captain announced.

Jan looked at the stern, back at the Goldcoast of Lake Zurich. "Wonder what happened to that guy."

"Your love is probably under arrest and on his way to a Zurich jail." Aaron hoped.

Elliot shook hands with several of the Zurich police and a senior policeman in a suit. "Thank you, Stephan."

"It's not a problem; we remember your contribution." Stephan nodded.

"And what about them?" Elliot looked at Marco's bloodied face and his thug who were in handcuffs.

Marco locked eyes with Elliot and spat blood on the ground. "I don't forget you."

Elliot smiled and turned his attention back to Stephan.

"We hold them until Moscow sends word to release them." He smiled. "If they find out tomorrow, they will be out in a day or so."

"So, I've got about twenty-four hours." Elliot looked back.

"Where the hell are they?" Natalya demanded. The driver looked at her in the rearview mirror. "Word is that there was an incident by the ferry."

She gritted her teeth and slammed her fist on the seat's headrest in front of her. "Damn him!" Her phone vibrated and rung; it was Savarine. She let out a frustrated sigh and her skin warmed. "Marco, you idiot." Then, she swiped the face of the phone. "I'm here."

Savarine talked and chose her words carefully. "We shall speak in our native tongue, English." She waited. "I hear that we are in the open."

"Marco …"

"Don't." Her word was firm, permanent. "You chose to keep that team."

"Yes," she pressed her fingers against the bridge of her nose. "I'm still active and the ferry will be here shortly."

"The beasts are involved; it's no longer just one man." Savarine sighed softly, easily. "The gloves are off."

"I understand." Her finger pressed the window button and the window went down to let the cool air in. She inhaled deeply.

"In twenty-four hours, the matter must be resolved." Savarine demanded.

"Yes." She looked at her driver and nodded. Then, she looked at her watch; it was nearly five.

Savarine looked away from her window that faced the square in St. Petersburg. "No incident tonight, Natalya. Tomorrow, they go to Schilthorn; it's remote and we have friends nearby."

"Yes." She pointed toward Zurich.

The driver left the parking lot of the cable car ride. He turned onto the local road and drove down to the main highway back to Zurich.

"They go there for the day." Savarine, a voluptuous brunette with shapely legs, picked up a dagger and brought it up to her heart. "Our friends will be on the mountain and get it back. You will wait for them to bring it to you, and then you come home."
"Yes."

The driver sped down the main highway.

"Tell me when you have it." Savarine tapped the end of the blade against her breast.

"Yes."

Savarine ended the call and looked at a Russian General who had two armed guards with him.

The general dipped his chin and his eyes bulged. "A failure in any of this is a reflection of your unit." He turned and left her office.

Savarine lit a cigarette, drew in, and then gently exhaled. The white cloud hung in front of her like clouds that shaded a snow-capped mountain top from the burning sun. "We must get that tablet."

Chapter Fourteen: Try to Rob an Old Lady!

Elliot showered at a safe house. The bruises were dark and covered the side of his chest; he cringed as he washed. The bruise to the side of his face wasn't too bad, somewhat bluish. "Damn Marco." The water streamed down his face, his chest, his torso, and his legs until it finally took the soap and some of the pain into the drain. The hot water massaged his strained muscles and the steam rose up around him.

The two agents who shot at Elliot waited while the repairman replaced the tires on their SUV.

One of the agent's phone buzzed. "This is Bill."

"There are other players on the board now." Beth said. "John's new, so keep him in line."

"Clock's ticking." Bill looked at John and he motioned with his hand for him to get something.

John got a tablet and held it up.

Bill nodded. "We've got the address."

Beth sighed. "You have to get the tablet before the other interested party does."

"Use of force?" Bill asked.

John looked on the tablet and mouthed the words, "drone's up."

There was silence as the repairman finished with the tire.

"Clean." She huffed. "The last thing I need is for an international incident on the news."

"I understand." His finger spun around.

John hopped in the SUV, got it started, and set the tablet in a cradle.

"Don't lose sight of what's involved." Beth said and ended the call.

Bill tucked his phone, got in the SUV, and tapped the screen. "We get the device, clean."

Jan, Aaron, and Mary slept on the way back to Zurich's city centre.

Bill and his buddy were on their way down the mountain back to Zurich too.

It was after six and darkness swallowed the city whole.

Elliot, dressed in a tank top and jeans, looked at a tablet. The Bluetooth keyboard sat in front of him and his fingers typed away. "So, where are they?" The software ran multiple lines of code, a hack program that would give him access to the SEAOPS drone.

The tour bus slowed and made the turn into the tour bus parking lot.

"So, ladies and gentleman, welcome back to the city centre in Zurich. We drop you back at the station and thank you so much for joining us today." The driver slowed and then stopped in a parking space. The engine sputtered and then stopped. "We say in our language, gute nacht und frohe Weihnachten which translates to good night and Merry Christmas."

The door opened and people slowly got up the steam to exit the bus.

"We're here." Aaron said and touched Jan's shoulder. "Hey."

Jan snapped too and sat up. "Oh."

"Time to go missy." He smiled and helped her with her things. "We'll rest and then go to eat." They got off the bus and made their way to the tram stop.

Elliot was on his phone and smiled. "Yeah, probably two agents, Hans."

Hans chuckled. "You don't believe this, but that apartment was robbed, and the owner beaten earlier."

"What?" Elliot thought about it and then said. "Our friends at the ferry today or SEAOPS?"

"I don't know, either is possible." He cleared his throat. "Life here is fun."

Elliot chuckled. "It is." He looked at the live video feed above the apartment from the drone. "I'm into their drone." His finger tapped a few keys. "They're on their way home now."

"It's the holidays, such a good time to be in Zurich." Hans said.

"It is." The drone circled and then flew toward the tram. Elliot tapped a key to zoom in.

"I have good people who love this kind of thing." Hans laughed again. "When you retire, my heart will break."

"That so?" Elliot studied the tram as it wound its way along the strasse.

"Yah, it's so. There will be no more fun with spy work and fights." He huffed.

"I'll come back with a friend of mine; she'd love to meet you." The tram stopped.

"A beautiful woman, okay." Hans laughed. "I know of some."

"She's beautiful, but not in the way you think." The drone hovered over the stop and three Americans got off. "Hey, it's time."

"My people are within a block." He sighed. "Ah, enough fun for tonight."

"I'm grateful, Hans." Elliot grinned.

"Ja, you stop by for some Gschwellti with your lady friend." Hans searched for some final words. "Be careful."

"I will. I don't want to miss out on your wife's jacket potatoes." Elliot looked at the time; it was just after seven. "Until we meet again."

"Until we meet again." Hans tapped the red radial on his phone.

Elliot's phone screen brightened, "call ended".

Bill pointed at a side street. "Go down here and park over there." He checked the tablet. "It's a second-floor apartment on the corner."

"Got it." John said. He pulled into a space and stopped.

Jan, Aaron, and Mary kicked off their shoes and collapsed on their beds.

Mary stared at the ceiling. "The tour was great, but way too long."

"Yeah, eight hours plus driving is too much." Aaron said.

Mary laughed, "And it's good that we have another tour that long tomorrow."

"Shh." Aaron shook his head.

"The fight scene was the highlight." Jan said.

"Uh, I don't think that was part of the tour." Mary said and closed her eyes.

"No, but it added to the fun." Jan said.

"Yeah, but …" then he stopped and realized it was better to say nothing about the man who had been in France and, now, was in Switzerland.

"But what?" Jan asked.

"But we have dinner reservations at Zeughauskeller at eight or so." The screen on his phone was bright.

"Oh, let's rest." Jan said and turned on her side. "An hour at least."

"We have time." He got up and turned the light off. "Peace and quiet for one hour."

"One hour." Mary said.

Bill looked at John. "Use of force is clean."

"Alright." The silencer screwed onto the semi-automatic pistol easily. "Make it look like a robbery."

"Yeah, something simple. No terrorist links." Bill had a knife in hand. "Knock, when they open the door, we push in and take it."

"Sounds good to me." John got his jacket open and looked at a knife and a gun. "I'm ready."

"Good deal." Bill's watch glowed in the darkness. "Seven-thirty."

"It's a white tablet … right?" John checked their surroundings.

"Yeah, scan it though to be sure." Bill handed him a small scanner. "Whoever gets it first."

"All three, right?" His brow went up.

"Yeah, it sucks, but tourist get killed all the time." Bill pursed his lips.

John smiled. "Collateral damage. Besides, Elliot brought them into it, not us."

Bill looked up and thought. "Yeah, roger that."

Jan, Aaron, and Mary slept soundly.

Bill and John walked up the alley dressed in long coats and hats. Bill stopped and put his hand up. "The main door is broken, so we can walk up. They have the end door to the left." An alley cat meowed at them. He drew his pistol and pointed it at the cat.

"Dude, don't shoot the cat." John knelt and the cat came over. The cat hunched his back with each stroke from John's hand. "See, nice kitty."

Bill spat at it.

The cat hissed and, in a swift and deadly swipe, clawed John's hand! He shot the cat! "Damn thing!" The silencer muffled the sound.

Bill laughed. "Thought you liked cats?"

"Until it clawed me, jerkoff." He shook his bloodied hand. "Damn, clawed the shit out of me."

"Really man." He handed him a small cloth. "Keep it."

"Give me a sec." The blood dripped from his hand down his fingers. He put his gun in his other hand and put pressure on the cut to slow the bleeding. "My gun hand, man."

"Are you going to bleed out right here." Bill got his mini-flashlight out. "Jesus, let me see."

A beautiful police woman knocked on the door to the apartment.

"I got it." Mary looked through the peep hole. "Oh, it's the police."

Aaron stepped into the hallway.

Mary turned the doorknob and opened the door.

"Guten abend." Her smile was warm, friendly and her hands were up, cupped together at her chest.

"Uh, American?" Mary asked.

"You mean English, does she speak English." Aaron looked past Mary at the officer. "Sprichst du Englisch?"

"Yes, of course." She laughed. "I'm with the Zurich police, Officer Christina Landau. There was a burglary earlier here. In fact, the apartment owner, Michael Haalvast, was injured." She waited for them to take in the shock of the crime.

"What!" Jan said and clutched her tablet to her chest. "Oh my God."

"When?" Mary asked.

"Earlier." She looked past Mary at Aaron. "The owner will be alright, but he is in the hospital."

"How'd they get in?" Aaron asked.

"Seems that they broke in and were here when he came to check the apartment." She lowered her hands.

"We never heard." Aaron put his arm around Jan. "It's alright."

"He must've been here to look at the heat." Mary said.

She stepped in. "He asked us to stop and talk with you as he is under care." She rested her hands on her hips.

Mary, "Is he going to be alright?"

"Yes, he will be … alright." She nodded.

"I thought Zurich is safer than most cities in Europe." Mary said.

"We are." She got a card from her pocket and handed it to Mary. "This kind of crime is very unusual for here."

Mary got the card.

"You call #117 for police." She tapped the card. "We are in the neighborhood as a precaution."

"Good." Jan said.

"We were just about to leave for dinner." Aaron looked at his watch.

"Ja, it's no problem. We will be nearby and try not to let it ruin your holiday." She nodded. "Well, good night and enjoy your dinner."

"Good night, thank you." Jan said. "Enjoy how? Robberies and fights."

Mary closed the door, looked at the locks, and turned the deadbolt. "Sinners."

Bill looked at John's hand and shook his head. "She will fire us if we don't get this done. You get taken down by an alley cat."

"I'm not down." He held his hand up to the light. "See, it stopped. Must've got a vein."

Bill looked at him. "Yeah, cat knew where to strike."

John rolled his eyes and gritted his teeth so he wouldn't tell Bill to go piss himself.

"Let's get this done. They've got dinner reservations at eight." The face of his watch was bright. "C'mon."

"It's 1930 hours. What if they're gone?" John shook his clawed hand and got his gun back in hand.

"Then, we wait." Bill said and walked to the corner.

"Wow, it's already ten to eight." Aaron said in a rush.

"How far is it?" Jan asked and got her coat.

Officer Landau went down the steps to the street, turned, and walked across the corner to a waiting undercover car. She got in the front passenger seat with two other police officers, another woman and a man. She spoke in German. "They leave for dinner now."

Just then, Aaron came out and looked up and down the street. He looked at the entrance to the apartment and nodded. "C'mon, it's fine."

Mary and Jan came out and their eyes darted all around them.

"Brr." Jan clutched her tablet and had her purse tucked to her side. "Been robbed already too."

"It's cold." Mary held her small bible up. "In Jesus name, keep us safe Lord."

"It is cold." Aaron laughed. "We're okay. Criminals rarely return to the same place."

"Where have I heard that?" Jan said.

"Lightening doesn't strike the same place twice." Mary said.

"So, what … like criminal lightening?" Jan asked.

"Let's hurry. The tram's coming." Aaron looked up the street.

They walked past the police in their car.

Bill and John stood at the corner to the apartment, one block up from the police who watched the place. "Go across and check it out."

The tram rolled to a stop. Mary, Jan, and Aaron got on and took a seat. "Wow, hardly anyone on." He said.

"Hope we don't get robbed." Jan said.

Mary rubbed Jan's shoulder. "Jan, you know I can fight."
Jan laughed, "I'm so terrible. I forgot about what you did in Colmar."

"See, we're safe. Mary will bust a bad guy up and … she's got Jesus on her side." His brow went up and he nodded.

John walked slowly by the apartment and then paused in the shadows of a doorway. His ear piece was in and he pressed the button for his mic. "Looks clear, but the lights are off."

The light from Bill's watch lit his face up. "It's nearly 2000 hours."

"Let's just go in and search for it." John said.

"No, Beth said clean. We're not going to tear the place apart." He looked around at each thing in his field of view: the cars, the doorways, the windows, and the streets. "Fall back."

John stepped out and turned back the way he came.

They met in the alley and then went back to the SUV.

Bill shook his head. "We'll get something to eat and come back at 2200."

"Alright." John looked up. "What about the satellite?"

"Out of range to task it." Bill said. "Drone."

Aaron, Jan, and Mary sat at a long, picnic like table with other people at the restaurant.

"Hi," Mary's jovial spirit lit up at the prospect of different people.

"Hello, I'm Jahn." The young man said and extended his hand. "That's my wife, Elly."

"Hi, I'm Mary, that's Aaron, and that's Jan." She pointed at each of them.

"Hey." Aaron waved and was too far to shake his hand.

Jan raised her tablet and took a picture. "Hi!" The flash blinded everyone!

Jahn, "Ah!" He rubbed his eyes.

"She talks through her tablet; she's just funny that way." Aaron laughed.

"Okay, then." Jahn said.

Dinner was a traditional Swiss meal with Alplermagronen—gratin with potatoes, cheese fondue,

And Rosti (fritters). There was beer, talk, wine, talk and more wine and beer with lots of good food as the night went on.

Elliot sat at the bar and drank beer with his schnitzel. He kept a low profile and an eye on Jan.

The bartender, a heavy-set man, walked up and smiled. "You are good?"

Elliot's smile was heartfelt; Jan, Mary, and Aaron laughed with their new friends.

The bartender looked over and smirked. "Sometimes, it's good to be just alone with your thoughts and food."

Elliot turned to him and his smile faded. "Sometimes."

The bartender walked away.

Elliot's attention turned back to the group at table twenty-four. "Not all the time." His phone buzzed and he looked at the screen. There was a text from "Blue Moon", "Nearly Christmas!" His thumbs tapped a reply, "Yep, just a few days, Merry Christmas Mom."

The Zurich police kept low in their car. Officer Landau pressed her mic button. "Clear, twenty-one thirty."

"Wow, it's nearly ten." Aaron said.

"You're not giving up already!" Jan bellowed. "Oops." She spilled a little wine.

"Jan, don't stop now." Mary laughed and spit up beer through her nose. "Sinner!"

The people at the table and other people nearby laughed at the sight of beer coming from her nose!

"Any word?" John asked Bill and looked his hand over. "Better not get a disease."

Bill chuckled. "Better not." The phablet on the center console lit up. "Finally."

"They're on the move?" John studied the feed from the drone.

"2300." Bill checked his pistol. "Be glad when this is done."

Aaron stopped at a jewelry store with beautifully decorated windows full of Christmas ornaments and expensive jewelry. "Cuckoo clocks, Swiss chocolate, and Swiss watches."

"Huh?" Jan stumbled and Mary caught her. "Oops." A belch erupted from her mouth and then a series of uninterrupted farts blew through her jeans. "Wow." She fanned her nose.

"Cheese and rice, Jan … what a stench!" Mary laughed and fanned her face. "Buy one."

"Pretty raw, Jan." Aaron studied the price tag and the numbers were blurry. "Damn eyes won't focus. Looks like fourteen hundred bucks."

"Oh, not that much." Mary got Jan to lean against the building. "Stay … and no more farting."

Jan laughed, "bark!" Then, her cheeks blew up as she held her breath and farted. "Sorry." She looked up. "Pretty lights."

Christmas lights hung from wires above and glowed in blues, reds, and gold; the luminescent colors floated on the buildings around them and on passersby. Snow drifted past in swirls and the flakes rode the wind up and then down.

"Well, I'm not as drunk as you two." Mary studied the watch and the price tag. "Good Lord!"

"What?" Aaron looked over her shoulder.

Elliot stood in the shadows just a block away and smiled.

"It's $14,000.00 dollars." Mary turned and looked at Aaron. "Ouch."

"No kidding." He shook his head.

"I'll buy it for you." Jan said and hiccupped. "C'mon."

"No thanks sugar-mama." The watch face was steel with a skeleton design. "It's neat. You can see the movement." He got his arm around Jan. "Oh well, in another life."

Elliot walked up, looked at the watch, and then followed them.

"Snows coming down hard." The cool flakes landed gently on Jan's face and soothed her. "Feels so good."

Aaron looked up; the flakes were so white and looked like puffs of shredded tissue against the dark clouds. "This is so nice."

"Lucky us." Mary said. "Flakes look so neat just drifting over our heads."

The wind whooshed past them and that was all the noise to be had.

"We are lucky." His arm flopped around Jan and his hand was on Mary's shoulder.

Bill looked at John. "Now, a little luck. We get this done and then head home."

"Get my hand looked at." John studied the gash.

"Damn, enough about your hand; it's not like a zombie apocalypse and the cat's a carrier of the plague." Bill smacked John on the shoulder.

"You serious?" John was confused.

Bill stopped. "Focus." Then, he turned and marched off with John in tow.

Mary got off the tram first and then she helped Aaron with Jan.

"C'mon alcoholic." Aaron laughed.

"I'm not a mal-choloic." Jan stumbled and laughed.

"Right." Mary got her by the arm. "We're nearly home, just another block."

Bill and John rounded the corner to the street where Aaron and Mary fought keep Jan upright. Bill looked through a small, single lens scope. "Alright, they're coming."

Officer Landau looked at her partners. "It's time. Kill the lights."

The officers readied themselves to get out of the car and the driver flicked a switch. "No dome or courtesy lights."

"Good." She replied and eased her door open.

Just then, Mary, Jan, and Aaron walked slowly across the street.

Bill eased the slide back and looked at the pistol's chamber.

John whispered. "I'm surprised she authorized a kill."

"Got something to do with anyone who's been in the company of that tablet." He locked eyes with John

John tapped Bill's arm. "Uh, we'll be in the company of it."

"We're on the in though." He smiled. "Chill out, they won't kill us." Then, his smile faded.

"How far is it?" Jan asked. "I have to pee."

"Another five steps to the door, then up half a flight of stairs and …" Aaron said and looked around.

Jan smacked him. "Can't you just say five minutes?"

Mary laughed. "She's right."

Elliot was on the other side of the strasse now and pressed the button on his mic. "In two."

Jan, Mary, and Aaron stood at the exterior door to the apartment.

Bill and John pulled masks on.

Jan suddenly stood erect. "Where's my tablet?"

"I've got it missy." Aaron held it up.

Bill and John shot around the corner and pointed their guns.

"Ah!" Jan yelled.

Bill pointed his pistol at Jan's face. "Shut up!"

"Ah!" Mary turned and held Jan. "I thought you said lightening never strikes twice!"

"Hey, just shut the hell up and give me that tablet." Bill held his hand out.

"Huh?" Aaron had the tablet in his hand next to Jan.

"No!" Jan grabbed it from Aaron and tucked it into her bosom.

Bill leveled the barrel at Jan's head. "Then, I'm going to kill you and take it anyway."

In the next second, sirens blared! Four Zurich police cars raced up and then skidded to a stop! Blue lights danced all over the buildings and an army of Zurich's finest leapt out with their guns and machineguns drawn! "Halt!" "Polizei!"

Office Landau and her team ran up! "Halt!" "Polizei!"

Other police officers moved in! "Halt! Drop your weapons!"

Bill turned and pointed his gun at them.

John was stuck like a deer who stared at oncoming headlights.

"What the …" Bill said. The blue strobe lights and headlights partially blinded him. His hand went up naturally to cover his eyes.

Officer Landau was within a foot of him and leveled her semi-automatic pistol at his head. "You drop the gun or I drop you."

"Dude, what do we do?" John asked and slowly raised his hands.

Bill smirked. "Chill." He lowered his hand to his coat and slowly reached in.

The officers yelled! "Halt!" "Halt!"

Officer Landau pressed the barrel against Bill's temple. "You don't do that!"

"Okay, okay." Bill said. "I was going to get my ID."

Officers rushed in! They grabbed Bill's gun and John's gun, jerked them around, and then slammed them on the ground!

"You are under arrest!" Officer Landau looked at the terrified threesome. "I told you, it's not a problem." She smiled. "Deep breath to calm down."

Jan looked at her pants. "Damn it, I think I just peed myself."

"Ah." Mary said. "Let's get inside."

The officers tore the masks from the two men, got their coats opened, and searched them.

Elliot watched from the shadows across the strasse.

Bill's head was pressed down on the stone-cold sidewalk, but he managed to turn and looked across the strasse. He studied the shadow of a man. "Son of a ..."

Elliot nodded at him.

Bill's face contorted in anger and his teeth ground together. "Elliot."

An officer pulled Bill's hands behind him and put cuffs on him.

Another officer had John's hands in cuffs, "Easy on my hand man! Don't you see the gash?"

Aaron looked up and locked eyes with Elliot. "What the hell is he doing here?"

"Who?" Mary asked and loosened her grip on Jan.

Elliot slid back and disappeared into the darkness.

Aaron sighed. "Nothing, never mind."

"Who was it?" Mary insisted.

Jan swiped the screen to her tablet, tapped the camera icon, and tapped the flash button to turn it on. "Try to rob me you rat bastards." She tapped the photo icon repeatedly!

Bill and John were blinded by the repeated flashes.

"Jan!" Aaron got hold of her. "C'mon dear, you need to get inside where it's safe."

Mary laughed and then knelt by the two men. She tapped Bill on his shoulder. "I'd have kicked both your asses." With her palm sized bible in hand, she held it up, and smacked the hell out of Bill's head and then she smacked John. "Sinners!"

"Damn!" John turned and tried to bite her, but an officer knelt on him. "What the hell bitch!"

"How dare you!" Mary's face turned red and anger surged through her muscles. "Filthy sinner!"

"Kick his ass, Mary!" Jan shouted and fell against the door frame with Aaron.

"No, no, no." Aaron left Jan and got Mary by the arm. "C'mon, the police are here."

"Sinners!" She kicked at them. "You're going to hell!"

"Yeah!" Jan yelled. "Try to rob an old lady!"

Officer Landau helped Jan inside. "You were so brave." She smiled and hugged Jan.

"I am." Jan said. "Hey, what's the name of the cop who was next to you?"

"Ah, Frederick." Her brow bobbed up and down. "He's cute."

"Yeah." Jan said.

"Jan!" Mary said.

"They don't get paid much." Jan's smile was sly. "Do they?"

Officer Landau laughed. "In fact, we are paid quite well and we drive BMW's, so it's very nice."

"That's too bad." Jan said.

They stood at the door to the apartment. "Okay, enough crazy shit for tonight." Aaron got the key in the lock, wiggled it around, and they went in.

Mary tripped and landed on officer Landau. "I'm not drunk, sorry."

Officer Landau cringed from the smell of alcohol. "No problem."

They got Jan to the bathroom and shut her in.

Jan spoke loudly, "I don't have to pee now."

"Oh God." Aaron looked at officer Landau. "Thank you very much."

"Yes, happy we caught them." She tapped her shoulder mic and spoke in German. "One fifty will be clear in five."

"I'm curious why they came back." Aaron crossed his arms.

"Ah, it's nothing to worry about." She looked at Mary. "It's good that they've been caught."

"Yes, it is and thank you." Mary got her camera and stood next to officer Landau. "Hey, let's do a selfie."

"Mary." Aaron shook his head.

"This once, it's alright." Landau said.

Jan moaned from the bathroom. "I want a selfie with that hot cop!"

Mary snapped the picture. "Merry Christmas."

"Yes, Merry Christmas to all of you." Landau and Mary hugged.

Aaron shook her hand and then Landau left.

"What a night." Aaron caught his breath. "We have that tour tomorrow too."

"What time?" Mary asked.

"Ten to five." A heavy sigh bursts through his lips. "Another long day."

"Is someone going to help me get off this damn toilet?" Jan shouted.

Mary and Aaron looked at each other and laughed. "We're coming."

On the street and a block away, Elliot talked to Landau. "I'm grateful."

"You should be." She extended her hand. "You owe me schnitzel."

He smiled. "I do." Then, they embraced. "Merry Christmas."

Aaron pulled the curtains apart and looked up the street. There was officer Landau near the very edge of an alley and a man in her embrace.

Chapter Fifteen: Trip to Schilthorn

The next morning at six, Jan took a hot shower while Mary did her hair and makeup. Aaron drank an espresso and rubbed the sleep from his eyes.

"What a night." Then, he rubbed his temples. "Ouch."

Jan's towel was wrapped tight around her. "Next!" She walked to her room and shut the door.

"Aaron?" Mary said.

"You going in or not?" His towel rested in his hand and his robe covered the rest.

"No, showered last night." Mary grinned. "Be ready in five."

"Okay."
They were dressed by seven and stood at the door to the apartment.

Aaron hesitated and had his ear near the door. "I'm worried about opening the damn door."
"Sinners!" Mary shouted at the door.

"Yes, that helped." He shook his head, got the doorknob in hand, and turned it.

"Let's go." Jan said and had her tablet firmly in hand. "You know it's funny that one guy stole my tablet and gave it back."

"After I ran him down." He descended the stairs.

"Yeah, and then the robbers last night wanted it." She got ahold of the handrail and slowly made her way down.

"She's right Aaron." Mary said. "It's odd."

"Maybe tablets are a hot item." The thought that anything he just said might be true made him grit his teeth. It was unlikely that the tablet was a hot item; it was more likely something else.

"I can hear your teeth." Mary said.

They walked out and pulled at their coats and scarves.

"Kind of artic." He said and pointed up the road. "We've got a half an hour for coffee.

"Here or at the station?" Jan asked.

"Let's go to the station." Mary said.

Unbeknownst to them, an audience watched them: the Zurich police, Elliot, and the Russians.

Elliot looked through a scope from two blocks away. Natalya's thugs, just the two of them, sat in a car at the end of the street which was nearly three blocks away. From the other end of the street, two new US agents with SEAOPS, a woman called Renne, and her partner, Sam, watched the threesome head toward them. "Echo four alpha, they're on the move." Renne's crew cut resembled Sam's and the only way to tell them apart was Sam's gray hair. "I understand."

"Understand what?" Sam asked.

"We're not to get arrested by Zurich police." She made like her hand was a gun and held it to her temple.

Sam chuckled. "They were amateurs." He looked at the street. "And the other agent?"

"Elliot?" She pondered. "Have to get a pic." Then she looked at the three Americans. "So, the grandma has the tablet."

"I'll get a message to Beth and get a pic of Elliot." Sam said.

The Russian driver looked at his partner and shook his head. "All this for them." Then, his phone vibrated. "Da." An aggravate sigh pushed through his lips. He spoke Russian. "Natalya …" His eyes moved around the car for something to occupy his mind while he was lectured. "Elliot is a target too."

His buddy looked at him and checked his pistol. "It's good."

He swiped and ended the call. "No, it adds. The Americans have more assets involved now."

"Us, Elliot, and the Americans are involved to get one woman." He shook his head. "So stupid."

The driver smacked him. "Not stupid, Yuri." The engine roared to life and he put the BMW in drive. "We go to the station."

"Sorry, not stupid."

The sound of the engine echoed up the street. Elliot turned his scope and looked at the car. "Natalya's boys." The scope went out of focus just as the car whipped around the corner.

Aaron, Mary, and Jan sat at a café.

"Love these drinks." Jan sipped her coffee.

"Me too." Mary said and admired the view. "It's such a beautiful city."

"It is." The passersby paid no mind to the three Americans who people watched.

In Zurich's Hauptbahnhof, Natalya sipped on an espresso too. The Christmas market was full of life with many travelers. Marco walked up and sat down. "They are clueless that their lives could be extinguished in the moment."

Marco spoke in Russian. "Consular General said I have until tomorrow to leave Switzerland."

"Because you are an idiot." Her eyes locked with his. "You let him beat you."

"I don't swim well." He shoved himself back into the chair and threw his hands up.

"You don't think!" She said. Then, she sat up and leaned over to him. "I told you to stay with the tablet."

"Yeah, but he smashed the window." Marco's face warmed.

"And then your balls gave you orders to fight him, not your brain." She gently smacked his head. "You are a good lover, but a stupid man."

"Ha, whatever." He sneered at her. "I am no stupid."

Yuri and his buddy walked up and waited.

Several Zurich military members walked by with their machineguns in hand, ready to fight.

Marco looked at the men and shook his head.

Natalya dipped her head and her men sat down. "You do nothing without my okay … Yuri? Dimitri?"
"Okay." They said in unison.

"We leave for Schilthorn and then I give you the rest of your orders." She stood, pulled on her coat, then she got her scarf and swung it around her neck. The three men got up and waited for her to move.

Officer Landau was dressed in civilian clothes and stood near a Christmas market stand not far from Natalya. She nodded at another police officer and then they trailed the Russians. "One fifty is in play."

Jan and Mary laughed as they made their way along the strasse to the tour bus.

Aaron shook his head. They crossed the street to the busses. "You two merry maids need to get on bus forty-seven."

"Oh, whatever!" Mary shouted. "Sinner!" Her bible was over her head and went around in circles.

"Does it cast spells when you twirl it?" He asked.

"No, it's not a spell book! It's the bible … you sinner!" She pointed at a white placard, "forty-seven!"

"Jesus, it's like you two are drunk again." Aaron sighed, then he laughed at them. "Let's go."

"Let's go!" Jan shouted, stopped, and took a picture. "After last night, who knows what will happen next."

Mary laughed. "Yeah, so we better live for the moment."

At the Zurich train station. Natalya pointed at the tourist bus parking lot. "Forty-seven. We will follow it."

Marco lifted his chin and stood tall; he felt he knew something that she didn't and he was proud. "The bus will not go to Murren."

"What?" She turned and faced him.

"There are no cars in Murren, no busses either." He grinned.

"Yes, Murren is car free." She shook her head. "That's why we will go to Lauterbrunnen and the three of you will take the cableway to Grütschalp."

He tucked his chin and his pride or more like his ego came down a notch. "Da."

"And then?" She asked.

"We get the tablet." Now, he was a puppy to be coddled.

"No, you take the train to Murren from Grütschalp and then up to Schilthorn you use the cable car." She ran her hand down his face. Then, her hand slid behind his head and gripped his neck. She pulled him close, lower.

"I heard you." His eyes looked away.

She pressed her lips to his and their noses rubbed together. "And that is why I love you."

His eyes closed and he kissed her. "I try to do right."

"Natalya." Yuri dipped his head toward the bus, number forty-seven. "It's leaving."

She looked at the bus.

He looked at the bus. "The car."

Her phone rang, "Natalya." She answered and looked at the ground.

"It's Savarine."

Yuri walked over and opened the front door to the BMW. She got in and the boys got in the back.

Officer Landau held her mic close to her mouth. "Handoff, Elliot."

Elliot pulled around the corner which was a block away from the tour busses. The front of his red Audi was damaged. "Thanks."

Aaron, Mary, and Jan had their seats together.

Aaron looked around and Mary watched him curiously.

"What … who are you looking for?" She asked.

"Nobody. You know me, have to see what's going on around me." He said. "Especially after last night."

Mary got her camera and took pictures. "Alright."

"Guten morgen, meine damen und herren, I'm Gunter and I am your guide for our journey to Schilthorn. It's a beautiful day and so fortunate to have it so nice." His wire frame glasses sat just near the end of his nose and his chin whiskers were salt and pepper, a thin man who knew all about his country.

The bus wound its way through the city centre and up the street toward the highway.

"So, we leave Zurich's city centre and get on the road to Lauterbrunnen." The bus rolled onto the highway and picked up speed.

Aaron, Mary, and Jan chatted amongst themselves.

Behind the bus and a mile or so back, the Russians followed them in a black BMW. Further back from the Russians, Elliot followed them.

Renne and Sam, the SEAEOPS agents, took a different route to try get ahead of the bus. Renne was on the phone and looked at her reflection in the SUV window. "Yes, ma'am."

Beth, the director of SEAOPS, was on a jet headed to Zurich. "I'll be there in two hours."

Renne looked at her partner who had his eyes on the road. "Inbound."

Savarine, SVR-RF director, was on a jet headed to Zurich. "Natalya, no mistakes. I'll be there in a couple of hours."

Natalya bit at her lip. "No, no mistakes." She turned and looked at Marco. "Not one." Then, she swiped and hung up the call.

"We will be in Lauterbrunnen in one hour thirty minutes." The guide said.

The bus wound its way through the mountains and then into valleys with beautiful villages that took a tourist back in time. They passed through Lucerne and then continued south to Lauterbrunnen. The snowcapped mountains glistened and the valleys were easy on the eyes with their green grass.

"Aaron's sleeping." Mary said and tapped Jan's arm. "Never mind, both of you are asleep … sinners." The bus rode like a ship on the ocean with each hump in the road the front of the bus bobbed up and then down as the wave rolled under it. Mary knelt next to the tour guide. "Hello."

"Ah, how can I help?"

"How long before we get to Lauter …" Mary searched for the rest of the word.

He sat up and smiled. "Lauterbrunnen, yes, it's about an hour or so from here."

"Okay, thanks." The front of the bus went up and Mary lost her balance. "Oops." She landed on this dirty old man who opened his eyes to find a petite brunette against his chest. "Sorry."

"Not me, I like." He smiled and winked.

She got her balance and cleared her throat. Then, she made her way back to her seat and mumbled, "sinner, big sinner."

Elliot looked at the map on his video display. There was a blip for the bus that traveled about a kilometer ahead of him. Between him and the bus were the Russians.

Renne and Sam looked at each other and then at the map on the center display. "We're running about twenty minutes behind them." She said.

A frustrated sigh seeped through Sam's lips. "Call for a chopper?"

"No, let's just take it up a notch when we can." A swipe and her phone came to life. "I'll look for alternates."

Beth, head of SEAOPS, got off a jet and was greeted by Swiss Security Services. "Beth Freidman." She looked at the chopper. "That for me?"

"Hans Dietrichite ... ja, it's there and ready for you." He pointed and walked with her. "Uh, what does SEAOPS stand for, if I may know?"

She hurried to the door, set her things inside, and climbed in. "Strategic Enforcement Abroad operations."

"But you have the CIA abroad." He reached for the door to close it.

The chopper's engine wound up and the blades turned faster and faster.

Beth shook the man's hand. "We do." She got ahold of the door and pulled it closed.

The pilot throttled the engine, pulled up on the stick, and the chopper gently lifted into the air.

An agent walked up and put his hand on Han's shoulder. "They don't even take time to have a coffee or polite conversation."

"Nein, they are always on the clock and she said that SEAOPS stands for …" Hans laughed. "Who cares, let's go for coffee."

Aaron turned and then his eyes slowly opened. The rumble of the diesel motor hummed along as the bus went down the road to Lauterbrunnen.

Mary was on her phone and Jan was fast asleep.

"All good?" He asked Mary.

"Oh, yeah. Well, the bus bobbed up and I fell on this man's lap, a dirty old man." She rolled her eyes.

"You kick his butt?" He laughed.

"No, no need." She set her phone in her lap. "Guide said we're about an hour or so from Lauter … whatever it is."

"Yeah." He looked at the passing landscape. "Beautiful countryside."

"It is." She looked past him.

"We visit Lauterbrunnen and then we have to catch a cable train or something." He looked at his phone. "We're going to be wiped out after this tour."

"We get some lunch and then a nice dinner, it'll be alright." She looked at Jan.

"She asleep?"

"Since the bus left Zurich." Mary rolled her eyes.

"Oh well." He smiled softly. "To each their own."

"Hey." She touched his arm.

"Yeah?" He turned in his seat to face her.

"You didn't say so, but what is really going on with her tablet?" She inched up to be closer.

He sighed. "To be honest …" Hesitation kicked in and he wondered what, if anything, should he say.

"The whole thing is weird. I don't know what's up, but it is odd that the one guy stole it and gave it back. Then, those two nutcases show up at our apartment and they want it."

"Maybe, she's a spy." She pondered. "Oh, and the apartment got broke into."

"She's a fool for a spy." He shook his head. "Yeah, I forgot about the apartment, but I don't think Jan is a secret agent."

"Maybe it's three fools for spies and she's using us." Mary looked around and caught the eye of the dirty old man! "Good Lord, that dirty old man is looking at me."

Aaron got up and put the evil eye on him. "What are you looking at?"

The dirty old man sat up. "You." Then, he winked and had a toothy smile.

Aaron sat back down and pushed back in the seat. "God, he's tri-sexual."

"What is that?" Mary's tongue hung out in disgust.

"He'll try anything, dirt bag." Aaron peeped over the seatback in front of him. "He's turned around."

"When we get off the bus, I'll walk up and smile at him and then …" She balled her fist.

"You'll yank him over you and into the air." They laughed.

"Why not." She shook her head. "Well, I hope that no one else is going to try and take that tablet from her."

Aaron thought about it and wondered. "Me too." He laughed to himself. "Maybe, I'll say take the damn thing and get her a newer one!"

The bus slowed and then went through a roundabout onto another road.

"Ah, Lauterbrunnen, fifty-six kilometers." The bus zipped right past the sign.

"Good, I'm ready to get off this thing and use the restroom." Mary leaned over to her side and looked up the aisle.

"There's a bathroom in the center of the bus." He sat up and pointed.

"God, no … I'm not using that." She stuck her tongue out. "Gross."

"Okay." He sat back and looked out the window. "I'm going to close my eyes for a little while."

"Who sleeps on a bus, yuck." Her phone lit up and she scrolled through things to do.

It wasn't long before the bus slowed to a crawl and then made a roundabout into the city of Lauterbrunnen. Houses dotted the strasse and shops were decorated with Christmas ornaments that hung on their storefronts and on benches and chairs on the sidewalk.

"So, ladies and gentlemen, we have arrived in Lauterbrunnen and will come to a stop in a few minutes at the cableway." Gunter looked around and then pointed for the driver's sake. "Ja, just there."

Elliot drove past, looked at the bus, and smiled.

Beth was on her phone and looked at the landing pad for the helicopter. "Yep, I'm here."

Renne looked at Sam, "She's there." Her teeth sank into her bottom lip. "We're about fifteen minutes out, ma'am."

"That so?" Beth looked at her watch. "Alright."

Savarine's plane touched down at a private airport not far from Lauterbrunnen. There was just one man, a stocky - bearded man with shadows under his eyes and sullen cheeks, who waited for her. He nodded, got the door to their BMW, and she got in.

Savarine had a small case and purse. She smiled politely. "Time Lev?"

He spoke in Russian. "We are thirty minutes away." The engine roared to life, the tires spun out, and cast dirt and rock into the air. Then, they flew through the gate headed toward the highway.

Natalya and her boys sat in a parking lot nearby. She turned to Marco, "You take the cableway to Grütschalp, then, change to the train to Murren and from there to Schilthorn." She looked at Marco in the rearview mirror.

"And the tablet?" Marco asked.

"You corner her, use force, and take it." Natalya turned to face them. "If any of her friends or anyone else gets involved, put them down."

"Why not just take it now?" Yuri asked.

A frustrated sigh pushed through her lips. "We have people in Murren that will take it from you." She got her compact out and looked herself over. "The Director doesn't want them to have any time to get help. On the mountain, we will jam electronics so no one can get a call out." She put her compact away. "Down here, we can't jam a whole city and people will take pictures, video etc."

Marco looked at his phone. "But they can video or take pictures with jam or not."

She turned to him. "Yes, but they won't be able to send it anywhere." She puckered her lips and blew him a kiss. Then, she turned and looked at the bus. "By the time you are in Murren, it will be over and then we go home."

"Da." Marco said.

She looked at Yuri and then the thug stocky runt with them. "What are you waiting for?"

They got out and went to the ticket booth where a bunch of tourists waited with Gunter. "Please move up!" Gunter waved his hand and had a rod with an orange flag in his other hand. "Yes, come ahead from Zurich!"

The group moved forward. Jan took pictures with her tablet while Mary people watched.

"C'mon." Aaron said and tugged on Jan's jacket. "Lots of opportunities to take pictures."

"I know." She tucked the tablet to her side and then looked around.

Marco, Yuri, and the runt moved up to the ticket booth, got their tickets, and then went to the cable car line.

"Please board." Gunter counted his group as they boarded.

"This is neat." Mary took pictures.

Jan had her tablet up and videoed. The tablet hung in the air and panned the interior of the car.

Marco smiled when the tablet got to him and then he waved.

Yuri bumped him. "What the hell you doing?"

"We will take it … so I have a nice video for me."

Jan lowered the tablet, tapped the red icon to stop recording, and then she pondered about what she saw when she videoed. She looked around the car and then locked eyes with Marco. "Okay."

The cable-car pulled out of the station.

"Oh," Jan said and got a firm grip on the pole in front of her.

Aaron smiled, "yeah, you better hang on."

Just as the car left the station, Beth, Renne, and Sam raced up with their SUV and skidded to a stop near the cable car station. Beth looked at the crowd. "See if they've left."

Renne got out and Sam looked for a place to park.

Elliot donned a moustache, a gray wig, and some skin enhancements that looked like wrinkles around his eyes. There was a cane at his side and he limped to the ticket line. "Behinderung."

A woman touched her husbands' arm. "Honey, let him by."

"Ja, danke. behinderung." Elliot was hunched over.

"What?" Her husband looked around.

"Behinderung, means he's handicapped." She smiled. "Bitte." She motioned with her hand for him to pass.

"Danke, danke." Elliot barely raised his hand and waved. "Danke." He got a ticket and got on the next car up.

Her husband nodded at Elliot. "Looks in worse shape than your mother."

She smacked him.

Renne came back and had tickets. "They're on the way to Murren by now."

"Get on the next car with Sam and get that tablet." She shook her head. "We're here and already two steps behind." Her face warmed and her soft cheeks turned an ash red. "Now!"

Sam and Renne rushed off and got in line for the next car.

Gunter had a clicker and pressed it. "Click-click!" He looked the group over. "So, if you are with the tour from Zurich, please to get off when we stop, and go to the train to Murren." The orange flag waved back and forth. "Or just follow the orange flag."

A short time passed and the cable car came to a stop at Grütschalp.

Gunter waved his hand and tapped his clicker. "Okay, we go from here to the train to Murren." He counted as the tour group disembarked.

Marco stopped and looked him over.

"Are you enjoying the tour?" Gunter looked up at Marco.

Marco frowned, "no." Then, he bent at the waist and was face to face with Gunter. "But, I'm not on your tour."

Gunter had a gulp stuck in his throat and swallowed hard to get it to pass. "Ah, okay."

Marco and his buddies walked past and waited for the doors to open to the train to Murren.

"We're boarding a train from here!" Gunter's voice was shaky. "Please stand by the doors."

Aaron looked at Jan and Mary, "this is pretty awesome."

"It is." Mary said. "Beats hanging out in town."

"I love it." Jan said.

Savarine's driver pulled up and parked near the station. Natalya walked down the cobblestone path toward Savarine. Lev got out and got the back door open for Natalya. Their eyes met and then she sat down with Savarine.

Lev slowly closed the door, got a cigarette from his jacket, and lit up.

"So, the SEAOPS director is here too." Savarine sighed and was frustrated. "It's getting too big."

"Who is that?" Natalya handed Savarine a palm device.

"Her name is Beth and she was Elliot's handler." She sat up and looked up and down the road. "Have we seen Elliot?"

"No, but he must be nearby." Natalya grinned. "We are ready."

"Are we?" Savarine's grin faded. "I wonder."

"Wonder?" Natalya was puzzled

5341.

Sam and Renne boarded the car with Elliot. She looked around. "I've never met Elliot."

Sam looked around too, got his phone out, and brought up a picture of him. "That's him."

"Kind of handsome." She said. "He's a target too."

"Anyone who is in the way." Sam's eyes scanned the crowded cable car to Grütschalp.

Elliot stood near the back and sized up the tourist. Were any of them Russian spies? He eased his way through the crowd, "bitte."

People admired the old man with a cane who had made his way onto the car and was headed up the mountain with them.

"Do you speak English?" A teenage girl asked.

Elliot smiled. "Ja, little." He pinched his fingers together.

The train with Aaron, Jan, and Mary moved quickly toward Murren. The tracks were covered with snow and the driver didn't seem to mind that the dark lines of the tracks faded to white.

"This is so cool." Aaron said and snapped a bunch of pictures of his own.

"You don't usually take pictures." Mary said.

"Ah, I've been to Switzerland before, but not here." He looked at the mountains. "This is beautiful."   Jan turned once to glance at the thugs who stood nearby. An uneasy feeling came over her and she edged up and past Aaron. "Sorry, I want to get near the driver so I can get some pictures."

"Video the train going up." Aaron said.

"Yeah, it's a lot better than high speed rail." Mary said.

"I know." Jan got her tablet and the screen flickered. "Damn thing."

"Uh-oh, I forgot to look at it." He leaned over her. "Sorry."

The flicker went away and Jan tapped the record button. Then, she faced it toward the front. "It's alright. We've had a lot happen."

"No kidding." Mary said.

Marco looked at the tablet and then looked at Yuri. "I should just grab it and get off at Murren."

Yuri shrugged his shoulders. "I thought that's what we were to do."

"Idiot." Marco raised his hand to hit him.

Several tourists looked on and their expressions turned to worry.

"No, it's just I'm joking with him." Marco said and lowered his hands. A few minutes passed and he leaned over to Yuri. "They will jam the station at Schilthorn and then we take the tablet."

"So, we wait." Yuri said and looked at the runt.

The runt shrugged his shoulders.

The cable car arrived at Grütschalp with Elliot and the two SEAOPS agents. Now, he just had to wait for the train to Murren.

Gunter pressed his clicker.

Mary huffed, "he presses that much more and I'm going to flip him."

"Ladies and gentlemen, we will arrive at Murren shortly. Please be sure to have your things and go to the cable car to Schilthorn. This is our final leg for this journey and you will have the most fantastic views from the top." Gunter spoke with the train driver. "We have a walk to the cable car, so please stay together, thank you." He waved the orange flag and pressed the clicker. "Click-click!"

"Okay, that's it." Mary face warmed and her soft skin turned to an ashen red.

"Mary!" Aaron got her by the arm and gently eased her back. "It's all good." His hand fell back to his side. "He's a nice, gentle man."

"I'll click him." She ground her fist into her other hand.

"Be a good Catholic." Jan said.

"I'm trying." She looked at Gunter and he smiled back at her. She smiled and mumbled the words, "sinner clicker."

Aaron laughed.

"Good Lord, not everyone is a sinner." Jan said.

The train slowed and the driver blew the horn.

"I don't see any streets that cross the tracks up here." Mary said.

"No, probably did it for fun." Aaron's brow went up and down. "Fun."

"What is it with people and noise?" Mary huffed.

The train slowed to a few kilometers per hour.

Savarine was on her phone. "At Murren? Good, and the drone?"

Natalya pulled a gun from her purse, checked the ammo, and then put it back.

"Good," Savarine swiped the face of her phone. "The drone is ready." She moved in her seat. "Let's find a café."

Beth looked at the sky and winked. Her phone was in her hand and her thumbs tapped away at the keyboard. "My drone can dance too, Savarine." Then, she got a reply. "Drone is up."

Sam and Renne rushed to the train to Murren.

Elliot was on board with them and looked them over. "Wow, amateurs." He limped to a corner and leaned against the glass.

Renne's phablet vibrated. She looked at the screen, tapped an icon, and had a live feed from Schilthorn. "We're live."

Sam looked at the screen. "Good, we change at Murren and then to Schilthorn."

Renne nodded and put her phone away.

The Zurich tour group made their way to the cable car for the final ascent to Schilthorn. Gunter held his orange flag in the air and waved it. "This way please!"

Mary, Aaron, and Jan followed the group, but every once in a while, Jan stopped to take a picture of the mountains.

"You want me to take your picture?" Marco asked.

Jan's eyes widened. "Uh …" The group passed by and she was at the tail end.

Aaron looked back and then went back for her. "C'mon Jan." He looked at the tattooed giant by her. "She's not your type." They walked away. "I can't believe you tried to pick him up." Then, Aaron gasped and swallowed hard.

Jan looked at him. "What's wrong?"

"Nothing." He glanced back at Marco and realized it was the man from the fight near the ferry.

"He offered to take my picture." She said.

Yuri sneered at Aaron. "Should have just took it and knocked her boyfriend out."

Marco grabbed Yuri by his jacket. "I will knock you out."

There was a large sign on the cable car station, "MURREN 1638 m 5374ft".

"C'mon." Aaron pulled on Jan and Mary. "Hey, take our picture please." He asked a teenager.

The teenage boy got Aaron's phone and held it up. "Ja, smile."

They smiled and then Jan handed her tablet over, "with my tablet please?"

"Ja, no problem." He got ahold of the tablet and turned it around.

"I help." Marco towered over the boy.

"No, she asked me." The boy defended himself.

Yuri stepped up. "How are old you?"

Aaron stepped up and studied the men. "Guys, what's the problem?"

"Seventeen." The boy shook his head at the giant.

Yuri whispered. "Do you want to live to eighteen?"

"The kids got it." Aaron said and stood next to the boy. "Thanks though."

Marco tapped Yuri and they walked away.

Mary sized up Marco. "Sinner, big sinner." Then, her eyes widened. "Aaron."

Her expression was an easy read. "Yes, it's him." Aaron dipped his head.

The boy took their pictures just as the cable car slid into the station.

Gunter shouted, "Okay, with the Zurich group you get on please."

Marco, Yuri, and the runt stood with the group.

The guard at the gate looked at Gunter. "Who is your group?"
Gunter looked the three thugs over and shook his head. "Not them."

"You there, please step back. We are just boarding this tour group and, after, if there is space, you may board." He put his hand up and in Marco's face.

Marco sneered and made a bite like he was about to eat the guard's hand. "Idiot."

Aaron, Mary, and Jan made their way to the back of the car and the rest of the group boarded. A few moments passed while Gunter counted. "Ja, all good."

The guard closed the gate.

"Hey!" Marco yelled. "We are going too."

"Nein." The guard had his radio in hand. "You don't go unless I say."

Another guard walked over. "What's the problem?"

Yuri jerked on Marco's sleeve and pulled him back. "Not here." He got between the guards and Marco. "He has misunderstood, no worries." They stood their ground.

"The next car you can go." The guard said flatly and sized up Marco. He took a deep breath and his chest blew up. "Stay back, danke."

The cable car moved from the station and then headed up the mountain to Schilthorn.

Mary looked at Marco and whispered to Aaron. "It is him."

"Yeah, but what does that mean." Aaron said. "So, he got in a fight with that other goofball."

"Oh, look at the views." Jan said and videoed with her tablet.

Mary whispered, "tell Jan?"

"Wow, this was worth the drive." Aaron videoed and leaned over to Mary. "No."

"Okay." Mary laughed the matter off. "You two slept the whole time on the bus."

The next train arrived at Murren. Renne, Sam, and Elliot got off the train and headed to the cable car.

Elliot kept up the disguise and limped along with his cane in hand. "Ja."

Renne and Sam hurried to the cable car station.

Skiers, tourists, and locals waited in the station. The car with Jan, Aaron, and Mary was halfway up the mountain to Schilthorn.

Elliot walked in the station and went to a vending machine. He studied the reflection of everyone in the glass. In the corner of the station near a ticket machine were two Russian agents. To the left and down the hallway, another two Russian agents waited. To his surprise, there were two more

SEAOPS agents with their phablets in hand; they scanned the faces of passersby. "Two other agents, why?"

Renne and Sam didn't pay any mind to the other two SEAOPS agents.

Elliot was curious about this game; it had changed and the odds of success were less. "She's got agent's piggy backing other agents." He mumbled and got his phone out. Then, he leaned on a counter, held his phone up, and did a facial scan of the other two SEAOPS agents. One glance at his phone and the dynamic face scanner ran its recognition program. He looked at Renne and Sam. "Either one of them is the mole or someone else is." The recognition software beeped and Elliot looked at the screen. "FILE NOT FOUND", he sighed in frustration and then he tapped the next button. The other agent had "FILE NOT FOUND". "Private contractors Beth, really?" He shook his head, turned to the doors, and waited to board the cable car.

"Meine Damen und Herren, das Auto ist da, bitte seien Sie bereit, an Bord zu gehen." The guard didn't look at the Russians: Yuri, Marco, and the stocky runt trailed behind them to the gate.

One of the Russians in the corner locked eyes with Marco. Marco gently dipped his head and boarded the car.

Elliot got to the doors and bumped into Renne, "wie bitte."

"Oh," she moved to the side and let him by.

"Danke, danke." Elliot said, stole her phone, and nodded with each word as he moved to the back of the car. Just about everyone else pressed to the front for a good view.

Renne and Sam stood near the door.

Marco, Yuri, and the runt were just behind the teens with skies near the front and to the left. Marco looked around the car and studied Renne. "Dayk shpion yest."

Yuri laughed and fought the urge to look. "A dyke as a spy." He shook his head.

"Da." The runt said. "I will change her."

Marco smacked the runts head, "enough."

Their cable car waited until the return of the other one. "Ladies and gentlemen, we will leave shortly, thank you."

At Schilthorn, the car slowed as it approached the station. Aaron, Mary, and Jan waited anxiously.

"Wow," Jan said and pointed. "Look at that!" Her tablet was up and she videoed the arrival. "Nine thousand feet up?"

"Yes, so take nice easy breaths." Aaron said.

"Ladies and gentlemen, please." Gunter said and pressed his clicker. "Click-CLICK!"

Mary jerked her head around and balled her fist. "I'm so close to clicking him!"

"We're nearly off.' Aaron stood right next to her.

"The air is so much thinner here." Gunter looked at each of the tourist. "Please, you may feel lightheaded, so sit down and just breathe easy. We are nearly at the summit and this is some nine thousand feet up or nearly two miles above sea level." He went to the doors as the car came into the station. "If you don't feel well, please tell an attendant or ask someone for help, thank you."

The doors opened and the crowed eased through the doors into Schilthorn.

"I love it." Jan said and walked to a corner where she could take pictures. "Look at the Christmas decorations!"

Mary got her camera in hand and zoomed in with her super telephoto lens.

"This is where they filmed the James Bond movie, 'On Her Majesty's Secret Service!'" Aaron exclaimed. "Wow, this is awesome."

Christmas decorations adorned the lobby and beautiful colored lights hung all around the exterior. Holiday music played in the background while tourist looked and pointed at the majestic mountains that surrounded them. Tourists sat at tables on the patio at Schilthorn and sipped on espressos or cappuccinos and had pastries. However, three American tourists were on the verge of an international incident.

Mary and Jan wandered around the lobby and Aaron went upstairs to look at the Piz Gloria restaurant.

The cable car was loaded and headed back to Murren.

The other car with Marco, Yuri, the runt, Renne, Sam, and Elliot was on its way up to Schilthorn.

Beth went to a local café, sat down, and got her phone out. "Ryan, Sal … you two are my eyes and ears now."

Savarine and Natalya sat across from Beth and neither knew their counter agent was nearby.

Beth sent a few texts and ordered an espresso. Her bodyguard sat down and listened to his earpiece.

The Russian agents at Murren heard that it was to happen soon. "Da," the thug waved at the other two Russians to come to him. "The drone is overhead and jamming all signals."

At Murren, Ryan and Sal, SEAOPS agents, eyed the Russians with disdain. "Damn Ruskies."

Sal looked him over. "Think that's a word from the 1990's."

"Maybe." Ryan looked at the exits. "This thing's going to go down here."

"Probably." Sal had his pistol at his back and tucked in his waistline. "I'm ready."

The Russian thug looked at the Americans. "Yankees, they will not get in our way. We play a game they like, football." He tapped the thug next to him. "We get tablet, you take and fake to Vladislav and then go out to our man on snowmobile."

Aaron found Mary and Jan. "Hey, let's get lunch and then walk around."

"Alright." Jan said. "Isn't it early though?"

"Nearly eleven, but by noon everybody else will be hungry." He smiled.

"Yeah, yeah." Mary said. "We can have our pictures after."
They sat down to lunch and had drinks.

"Sir?"

"Gin martini …"

"Shaken or stirred?" The server asked.

"Shaken." Aaron smiled and sat back in his chair. "Get my Bond thing going."
"Ha, you wouldn't know a spy if you saw one." Mary said.

"He would, because he worked for N.A.T.O." Jan patted his shoulder.

"Worked with not for." Aaron nodded at her. "It's nice that you remember."

"I'll get your drinks and be back shortly." The server walked off.

Five minutes away, the other cable car approached the station to Schilthorn with a mix of tourist, spies, and locals.

The car slowed and then eased up into the cradle where it locked into place. People exited. Renne and Sam walked out, went to the side, and stood.

Marco, Yuri, and the runt looked up the hallway and went to the center of the building. "Find them." Marco said.

"Shit." Renne said. "My phone."

"What?" Sam looked at her and then around them.

Elliot limped out and went straight to the bathroom. "Ja, danke."

Sam looked at the old man who limped toward the WC. "Son of a bitch, that old man got you."

"What?" Renne turned. "He picked my pocket." She reached for her pistol.

"No." Sam pushed her arm back. "I'll do it."

Elliot went to the end of the bathroom, got the door open to a stall, and hung his cane on the hook on the back of the door.

Sam opened the door and looked in the bathroom. Then, he edged his gun from his side and held it low while he checked the stalls.

Elliot bobbed and tilted as he made like he was taking a piss.

Sam looked at the open door and the cane that hung from the hook. "Got you."

Elliot whistled gently and fought to keep his balance. "Ja, danke, danke."

"Hey." Sam said.

"Ja?"

"You got something that belongs to my friend." His gun was aimed at the ground, but he was ready to point and shoot.

"Nein."

"Bullshit, you speak English." He stepped closer and slowly brought his gun up.

"So do cows, but they don't bitch about it." Elliot turned, got his cane, and emerged from the stall.

"What the hell is your game old man?" Sam said and brought his gun up where the barrel centered on Elliot's chest. "Just give me the damn phone."

"Ja, no problem." Elliot pulled the phone from his coat pocket, held it up, and then tossed it in the air.

"Hey!" The phone flew up and then down toward Sam.

Elliot watched Sam's eyes. Sam looked away for a second and Elliot struck! He turned his cane, let the end drop so that the hook was up, and swung! The curved end of the cane slammed on Sam's hand! His gun flew out of his hand and down the tile floor under a stall door.

"Ah!" Sam yelped.

Renne looked at the WC door. She pondered and then slowly made her way to the bathroom.

Elliot turned, ducked, and swung the cane again! This time, the solid wood cane struck the side of Sam's knee!

"Ah!" Sam fell to the floor. He flipped, turned, and kicked Elliot's legs out from under him.

Elliot's wig flew off. "Nice kick!" He hunched his back, kicked up, and was back on his feet.

Sam was up too and threw punch after punch! "Hit me with that cane again and I'll show you another kick." He wiped the sweat from his face.

Elliot blocked, swung, and punched Sam!

The fight was brutal!

Sam got ahold of Elliot and threw him on top of a sink! The sank shattered under the force of Elliot's body. "Old man my ass!"

Elliot caught his breath and cringed from the body slam. "Damn-it!"

Then, Sam kicked him in the chest, drew his leg back for another strike, and waited. "C'mon!"

"Ah! You dirty ..." Elliot's lungs blasted breath in and out like a bellows! He grabbed the steel pipe under the sink and yanked it loose! He swung the metal pipe and smashed it against Sam's shin!

Sam collapsed! "You dirty prick!" He struggled to catch his breath.

Bloodied and bruised, his clothes torn and filthy, Elliot got up and stood over Sam. "Who's the mole?"

Sam looked at Elliot and rubbed his shin. "What mole?" He shook his head slowly to get his bearings and find his gun. "You're the damn mole!"

"No, it's not me." He fought to keep his breath.

"Oh, bullshit … you went rogue." His gun was in a stall a few feet away.

"Don't do it, Sam." Elliot raised the pipe. "You won't get it."

Renne drew her gun, put a silencer on it, and stood by the door. The door flung open and Renne stood there with her gun aimed at the center of the bathroom. "Drop it!"

"Shoot him!" Sam leapt for his gun.

Elliot swung, knocked Sam out, and then ducked into a stall.

"Pop! Pop! Pop!" Renne moved to the wall and aimed at the stall. "Give it up, Elliot!"

"Why?" Sam's gun was a few feet from him. "I'm not the mole."

"You're not SEAOPS either." She knelt to get a shot, but Sam's body was in the way. "You don't have a chance."

"There's always a chance." Elliot pulled the disguise from his face. "There's always a choice too."

"Right," she took a step to get a shot at him. "Like you just chose to hurt Sam."

"I didn't kill him." He laid flat and there was Sam's gun within arm's reach. "She's an innocent."

Renne breathed slowly, calmly. "You brought her into the game." She exhaled softly, brought her aim just to the side of Sam and looked for Elliot's hand. "You're going to lose some fingers."

"She's a grandma." He looked at the butt of the gun and inched toward it.

Two teens walked into the bathroom and stopped.

Renne turned for a second and everyone, but Elliot, froze.

Elliot shoved himself up, got the gun, and slid back behind Sam's body.

"Terrorist." The boy said.

"Don't shoot us, please." The other boy said.

"You're going to blow this out of proportion, Renne." He edged up by the door, pointed the gun at her side, and caught his breath. "Renne?"

She looked at the two boys; they trembled and their faces were as pale as snow. "Get out."

The boys couldn't move. "You'll shoot us."

"No, I won't. Get out." She looked at them and they didn't move. "Now!" She aimed to the side of the boys shot. "Pop!"

The boys turned and slipped on the tile floor as they rushed to get the hell out of the bathroom!

"Great work, Renne." Elliot inhaled, held it, and then slowly exhaled. She turned back to Elliot. "Throw the gun out."

"I can't do that." He peeped through the space just over Sam's hip and the stall wall.

"Do it or die." Renne focused on her aim.

"I've got to get to her before the Russians do." He looked at the mirrors along the wall and saw Renne. "Let me fix this and help her."

Jan looked at the ice cream sundae. "Oh, gosh that was good."

"A salad and then chocolate ice cream." Aaron shook his head. "Like a kid."

Mary took a bite of her "Bond" Cheese cake with "007 – BOND" written in frosting across it. "I'm a kid too."

Two teens ran from the bathroom into the lobby. "Help!"

Aaron looked at the lobby, but the crowd was loud. "What's that about?"

Mary looked over and then shook her head. "Two kids. Probably broke something."

"I'm going to go see what's up." He stood and got the check. "My treat."

"Thank you!" Jan said.

"Yeah, thanks Aaron." Mary winked.

"Merry Christmas."

"Merry Christmas!" The ladies said.

"I have to get to her, Renne." He edged up to get a clean shot. "It's my fault and I'm going to fix it, but if it means I have to shoot you to do it, I will."

"Then, you better not miss." She looked for a shot.

"Bang!" Smoke drifted into the air.

The bullet went through her hip and hit the tile wall.

"Ah!" She yelled, fell to the floor, and gripped her side.

Elliot leapt from his place and ran to her.

She turned to shoot him, but it was too late!
He snatched her gun just as she came around with it. "No," he tucked it to his back side.

"So, it is you." She paled quickly and her pupils widened.

"No, it's not me." He got her gun and tucked it to his backside. Then, he got some paper towels and put pressure on the wound. "It's through and through, no arteries. You'll be fine."

A puzzled look came over her. "If not you, then who?"

"I don't know." He thought for a moment. "Who were the other two SEAOPS agents at Murren?"

She looked away and nearly passed out.

"Renne!"

"Yeah," she fought to keep her eyes open.
"The other agents."

"Don't know. Beth sent me and …" She passed out.

"Sorry." He splashed his face with water, dried himself off with a towel, and then got Renne's phone. Her finger rested on the fingerprint ID scanner. The phone unlocked. "Code red, agent down, Renne at Schilthorn." He waited for a response and then saw, "NO SIGNAL." He checked her wound and then went to the door. "Jamming the place, damn-it." He fixed his disguise and got his wig on.

An elderly unarmed guard slowly opened the door. "Hello."
Elliot pulled the door open and the man nearly fell in! "Yeah."
"Someone said there is a woman with a gun?" He looked frightened of his own shadow.

"Yeah, she's been shot." Elliot pulled him in and shut the door. "Stay here with her." He rushed out, went to the cable car station, grabbed a landline, and called. "Shots fired, someone's been shot." Then, he set the phone on the shelf.

Marco walked up to Mary and Jan and hovered over the table. "You should have let me take your picture."

Mary and Jan turned suddenly.

Aaron walked around the landing outside.

"What?" Jan asked.

"Give me the tablet." Marco said.

Yuri stood by the entrance to the restaurant.

The runt stood by Mary. "Give it to him or we take it."

"I don't want my picture taken, thank you." Jan said and moved the tablet from the table to her side.

The server came back and confronted the men. "What's going on?"

Marco grabbed the young man, lifted him up, and tossed him into some tables and chairs!

People were in shock! Everyone looked on and didn't move.

Mary got a dinner plate in hand, slowly slid her chair out, stood, and smashed the plate in the face of the runt.

"Ah!" The runt threw his hands up to cover his face and blood dripped from the cuts.

"What the hell!" Marco said.

Jan tucked the tablet under her arm, got her purse, and got up. "Help!" She screamed.

Marco reached for the tablet and Mary hard kicked him on the side of his knee!

"Ah!" His knee gave out and he dropped to his side. "You American bitch!" He swung and missed.

"How dare you!" Mary grabbed another plate and smashed it against his head. "Sinner!"

The glass shattered and cut Marco's face up.

"Ah!" He reeled from the pain and fell to the ground. Blood oozed from the cuts to his face.

Mary snatched her bag with her bible in it and jumped up. "Get your coat!" They got their coats and bags and then ran toward the exit!

Screams erupted! Jan and Mary jogged as fast as their legs would let them! Jan had her tablet tucked neatly under her arm and Mary had her old school camera strap in her hand.

"So rude!" Mary said as they made their way toward the doors.

"I got you!" Yuri pulled his gun. "Give me the tablet!"

Mary and Jan stopped right in front of Yuri.

From behind, the runt ran toward them.

"Give it to me!" Yuri demanded.

"Jan, give it to him." Mary winked and tightened her grip on her camera strap.

Jan got the tablet and held it up.

Yuri reached for it.

Mary drew back and swung her camera against Yuri's head! The impact broke the 28-200 zoom right off her Canon EOS and knocked him out. "I'll show you who's a bitch."

Jan's eyes widened. "Mary!"

"Please forgive me oh Lord." She looked up and then back at Jan. "Run!"

"I got you!" The runt said.

Mary looked at Jan. "Look out."

Jan stepped to the side.

The runt ran up with his hands out to choke Mary!

Mary grabbed his hands, fell back, and yanked him onto her feet. Then, she shoved her feet up and flipped him over her! "Ha!"

The runt landed on the concrete floor and was in dire agony. "Ah, my back."

"You have got to teach me how to do that." Jan said.

"I will." Mary looked at Marco's bloody face. "Oh god!"

Marco rushed toward them. "Give me that damn tablet!"

"Run!" Mary yelled and turned to Marco. "Sinner!"

The girls rushed out of the restaurant and toward the steps.

Aaron looked at the lobby and watched as two men chased after or looked like they chased after Mary and Jan. "What the hell is going on?"

Marco got hold of Yuri and got him up. "Go!"

The runt was down for the count of ten. Marco hunched over him and blood dripped from the side of his face onto the runt's face. "Idiot!" He smacked the runt and then they ran after Mary and Jan.

Marco caught up to Mary and grabbed her! "Got you!"

Mary got her small, but heavy bible from her bag and swung it at him! "Get your filthy sinner hands off of me!" The leather was supple and much like the leather on a well-used whip. The bible's spine landed dead on his cheek and the impact rippled across his tattooed face!

"Du idiot!" He shook his head to recover from the smack down.

"How dare you call me an idiot!" Mary kicked his shin, "get your filthy hands off of me, sinner!" The bible went up and then she looked for place to strike. "Praise be to the glory of God!"

He grasped his shin and then looked at the bible. "Please, no hit."

"The cable car!" Mary pointed and they ran off.

Elliot watched Jan and Mary head his way. "C'mon girls." He ducked back into the bathroom and got the cane. Then, he struck a Russian thug with his cane and the thug went down! "Go!" He yelled at Jan and Mary.

Moments later Jan and Mary were in line for the cable car.

Shots rang out! Screams erupted and the girls got on the cable car back to Murren.

"What about Aaron?" Mary asked frantically!

"He's been here before." Jan said and looked at the cable car operator who hid behind the metal frame of the car. "Are we going or not?"

The operator pressed the button; the doors to the car closed, the locks released, and the car slid out of the cradle headed to Murren.

"Thud!" Something hit the roof of the car.

The operator looked up. "What the hell was that?"

Other Russian agents slammed their hands on the glass at the station!

Jan filmed them. "Ha, we got away."

"No, we haven't." Mary tapped Jan's shoulder and turned her to look at the back of the car.

The cable car, with nearly seventy people in it, descended toward the town of Murren.

Jan squinted and then realized that the tattooed thug and his buddy were on board. "Oh shit."

Yuri stared at them.

Marco took his leather jacket off, took his shirt off, and flexed his muscles. He handed his jacket to

Yuri.

The operator looked at Marco. "Sir, you must be covered."

Marco used his shirt to wipe himself off. "Da." He slowly drew the shirt over his face to get the sweat and blood off. Then, he wiped the sweat from his chest. Finally, he got his jacket from Marco.

Jan grinned and videoed him. "Wish I had a dollar."

Mary smacked Jan's arm. "Really!"

A woman next to Mary tapped her shoulder. "Do you know those men?"

Mary caught her breath, "no." She snapped and then sighed. "They are nasty, evil men."

"Oh, then you've done well to get away from them." She said and looked at Jan. "And your friend?"

Mary looked at Jan. "Her? She's nasty and evil too."

Marco put his jacket on, zipped it up, and then sniffed his shirt. He whistled at Jan. "You don't forget me." He threw the shirt at her!

Jan smiled and grabbed the shirt. "Who's evil?" She tapped the camera icon and then snapped a

photo of Marco.

Elliot sat atop the cable car and the icy wind blew hard against him. "Jesus, it's cold." The escape hatch was a few feet away and he thought about what to do next. "Could drop in and fight with Marco and Yuri, no."

He pondered. "Wait until we get to Murren and then fight, probably."
Then, he pulled the wig off and threw his disguise from the top of the car.

Mary looked up and then at Jan. "I think there's someone on the roof."

"What?" Jan looked up and then everyone in the car looked up.

Marco and Yuri hesitated, then they looked up.

"Maybe it's Aaron." Jan said.

"Right, he leapt onto the top of a moving cable car nine thousand feet up." She shook her head and huffed.

"Being gay doesn't mean he isn't courageous." She smiled. "He's in good shape too."

"You're crazy." Mary said and looked at Marco. She leaned over to Jan and whispered. "We get off at Murren and then shove people back."

"That's rude." Jan videoed

"Yeah, but they'll bunch up into those guys." Mary winked at her.

"Oh, good." Jan looked back toward Schilthorn. "What about Aaron?"

"You didn't care about him ten minutes ago!" Mary bellowed.

"C'mon guys." Aaron and the thugs stood by the door to the cable car. "I don't know what you want."   "The tablet." He huffed. "We have you and you come with us." The waited for the next car.

Mary and Jan looked at Marco and Yuri who looked right back at them. Mary pondered, "what to do?"

"Huh?" Jan asked.

"Nothing."

Beth eyed her body guard. "Why haven't we heard anything?"

Savarine and Natalya got up just as Beth got up. Everyone caught the other one and they stopped.

"Savarine … Natalya." Beth said smugly.

"Beth and her little dog." Savarine's face was smooth, without an expression. "This is going to get ugly unless you people back off.'

"You back the hell off." She took a step toward the door.

The guard with Beth had his hand on his gun.

Natalya had her gun in hand and hidden behind her purse. "A shootout in a café, how much like an American western."

"Yes," Beth said. "The bad guys always lose."

Savarine dipped her head and they rushed out the door.

Beth and her guard followed.

The cable car slowed as it approached the Murren station.

Mary nudged Jan and whispered to her. "I have an idea."

Elliot smiled at the people who looked at him atop the car. He got up and got ahold of the metal arm to the roof and waved. "Oh boy."

Mary pulled at her coat. "Just trust me." She slid through the people. "Excuse me, my friend is sick."

Jan coughed. "I'm sick."

"I should have said, sinner." Mary stopped near the doors.

Marco and Yuri pushed their way toward them.

The car stopped and Mary turned to face the crowd that anxiously waited to exit. She yanked her coat open and yelled. "Ballah backbar!"

Everyone screamed and ducked for cover!

"Terrorist!" The operator yelled and huddled in the corner.

The doors opened! Mary grabbed Jan and they rushed out of the car!

The crowd shoved back into Marco and Yuri!

"Move!" Marco yelled and pushed scared riders out of his way.

Elliot swung from the top of the car down to the sidewalk. "That was good thinking." He looked around and saw Jan and Mary fast walking out of the station.

"That was horrible." Jan said and looked back. "Ballah backbar? That doesn't sound right."

"What are you talking about? God *is* great." She laughed.

Jan said. "We have to get to the police, Mary."

"Yeah, we do." They stopped a block away. "Here, go here." They ducked into a side street.

Elliot walked up. "Ladies."

Jan and Mary's jaws dropped. "You!"

Jan raised her tablet to hit him. "Get back!"

"You're the reason they're after us!" Mary shouted and had her hands up for a fight.

"Me?"

"Yeah you." Jan shouted. "Every time something weird or bad happens, you're near it."

Elliot put his hand to his mouth to stop himself from saying what had to be said.

Marco and Yuri shoved their way through the crowd and onto the platform. They looked for their people at Murren. Two Russian rushed up to them. "Where are they?"

"We didn't see them." The puzzled look on his compatriot's face infuriated Marco.

"What the hell!" Marco smacked the man. "Two old women run past and you don't see them!"

"There was trouble with a terrorist." He looked at his buddy and the other two men across the lobby.

"Idiot, they *were* the terrorist!" He shoved the man back and pointed at the doors. "Go!"

Elliot sighed. "Look, this … this *is* all my fault."

"I wondered." Jan looked him over from head to toe.

"Tell you what." There was a commotion just up the street. "I'm an Uber driver by day. You come with me and I'll explain it all."

The two other SEAOPS agents, Ryan and Sal, waited at the train station.

"No." Mary said and got her bible in hand for another strike.

"It's that or you fight off six angry Russians, including the tattooed one you smacked down with your bible. His name is Marco." Elliot looked around the corner. "The clock is ticking."

Jan looked at Mary. "It's him or them."

They followed Elliot down the street and he stopped suddenly to talk to two police officers. "Yes, they have guns and are coming this way."

The police officer radioed it in. "We heard of the trouble at the Schilthorn."

"Okay, we'll just wait down here." Elliot motioned for Jan and Mary to move on.

"Nein. You wait." The police officer demanded.

Then, Marco, Yuri, and four other Russian thugs came around the corner.

Elliot and Marco locked eyes. "Gun!" Elliot yelled. "He's got a gun!"

The police officers and the Russians ducked for cover. Everyone drew their guns. "Halt!" "Polizei!"

The Russians and the police were in a stalemate at opposite ends of the street.

"Place your guns on the ground!" The policeman yelled.

"Go!" Elliot rushed Mary and Jan down the hill toward the train back to Lauterbrunnen.

Marco looked at Elliot. "I will get you!" He looked his man, Yuri. "Go, that way!"

"Your hands!" The policeman yelled and then radioed. "Backup!"

Marco nodded and then motioned for his men to fight. "Now."

A shootout erupted!

Marco grabbed Yuri, dodged behind a house and then they ran down the alley. "Must get the tablet!"

Aaron and the thugs stood by the cable car, but weren't going anywhere. The place was on lockdown. A police helicopter rushed up the mountainside and several skimobiles with police approached from the other side of Schilthorn.

The thugs looked at each other and the leader listened to his earpiece. "They have the women." He shoved Aaron against the wall. "Today, you are lucky." He nodded at his men. "Poyekhali!"

At Murren, Russian agents on two skimobiles waited for their que, but wondered about the police traffic. Another police helicopter zoomed by! Gunshots rang out in the distance.

Twenty or more Swiss special police, armed with machine guns, stormed Schilthorn!

Aaron was in shock. "I will never, ever bring anyone on a trip with me again."

The police were all over the building and the Russians fled outside.

"Halt!" Other police came in and arrested the Russians. "Polizei!"

Beth stood by her car and shook her head. "Ryan, what the hell is going on!" She huffed. "A simple takedown is an international incident; there's Swiss security services and police all over."

"Ma'am?" Her guard kept a lookout.

"Not you." Beth shook her head and held her phone close to her ear. "You better get that tablet or go home, Ryan."

"So, who beat the hell out of you?" Jan asked. "Hey!" She realized who was who. "You were in a fight with that guy at the ferry!"

"Have to hurry." Elliot said and the train station was just ahead of them. "Yeah, well at the end though who was on top?"

"I thought the tattooed guy was." Mary said. "You know the life guard carry thing."

Elliot grinned. "Time to go ladies and the tattooed guy didn't do this." He pointed at his bruised face.

Marco and Yuri ran toward the station.

Elliot, Jan, and Mary turned the corner and headed to the gate. "I've got the tickets!" He swiped them and the girls went through.

"You should pay for all the trouble." Mary said.

"I will." Elliot stopped in his tracks. "Damn."

Ryan and Sal, SEAOPS, stood between him and the train with their guns drawn. Ryan stepped forward and looked at Jan. "Heard about the trouble and figured we'd meet you here at Murren instead." He looked at Mary and then Jan. "The tablet, Elliot."

Marco and Yuri got to a corner street. Marco looked around. "To the station."

Yuri pointed, "That way!" They ran off.

"So, you want the tablet?" Elliot got between them and the girls.

"Just kill them and take it." Sal said.

The train from Grütschalp slowed and then crossed the changed track to enter the station.

The watchman radioed for help.

Marco saw the two men, Elliot, and the women. He stopped and jerked Yuri back. "There!"

"What of our people?" Yuri held his gun and looked on.

"If there are no more gunshots, they are run or they are arrested." Marco eyed the man with the gun in the station. "We take them by surprise, get the tablet, and make for our people."

"Da." They jogged up to the station.

"Can't let you kill anyone. They're innocents." Elliot looked at Jan, Mary, and then turned to Ryan.

"We haven't done anything." Jan said and held her tablet close to her chest.

"Why do you guys want the tablet anyways?" Mary asked. "You can buy one anywhere."

Ryan stepped up. "He didn't tell you:" He raised his gun and pointed it at Elliot's head. "Hell, we have a minute." He chuckled. "Elliot put a chip, a stolen chip inside your tablet and used you as a mule to carry it back to the good old United States."

"What?" Jan felt sick and turned to Elliot. "Why would you do that to me?"

"You don't mean a thing to him." Ryan said. "It was all about the chip."

Elliot turned to her and didn't know what to say.

Sal looked at Jan. "But the Russians figured it out. Didn't they, Elliot?"

Mary got ahold of Jan and looked at the men. "So just take it then."

"Oh, we're going to take it." Ryan said. "And then we're going to clean up Elliot's mess."

Mary looked at him and her face was hot. "What's that supposed to mean?"

Ryan smiled and cocked the hammer to his gun.

The train stopped and the doors opened; tourist poured into the station.

"Hey!" Marco shouted and aimed at Ryan.

Chapter Seventeen: Detente Comrade

Yuri pointed his gun at Sal. "Don't do it."

Sal looked behind him at the crowd and then he ducked! "Down!"

"BANG!" Ryan shot Yuri!

People screamed and dove for whatever cover they could find!

Marco shot and wounded Sal! "Elliot!"

Yuri and Sal groaned in agony from their gunshot wounds!

"Run!" Elliot got ahold of Jan and pulled her toward the train. They stumbled over people who crawled to safety. "C'mon!"

Jan fought to keep going! "My knees!"

Mary helped her along! "I've got you!"

Ryan huddled for cover and looked for his partner. "Sal!"

"I'm hit." Sal said. "Get the tablet!"

Marco leapt over the guardrail and then fell onto some tourists. "Move!"

Elliot got Jan and Mary aboard the train. "Stay down!"

The train operator looked at Elliot. "I can't move this train." He huddled behind the dash.

Ryan got to his knees and aimed, but there were people in front of him who screamed!

Elliot pulled his gun out and aimed it at the driver. "I know." He walked up. "Get off."

The driver trembled.

"Now!" Elliot looked through the windshield for Marco or Ryan. "Go!"

The driver ran to the doorway and leapt out!

Marco got up and saw the train. He and Elliot locked eyes. "Elliot!"

Elliot looked at the control panel, tapped a few buttons, and the doors closed. Then, the train rolled out of the station and he tucked his gun into his backside.

Marco aimed and shot the train's windshield! "No!"

People screamed and ran from the station!

Marco shot again! "Pop!" "Pop!" "Pop!"

The train's windshield cracked and then shattered! Glass fragments burst into the car and flew around like tiny crystals that fell from the sky.

"Ah!" Jan screamed and covered her face.

"Dear Jesus!" Mary held her bible up to cover herself. "Save us!"

Elliot ducked and half-crawled, half walked to the other end of the train where there was an identical panel. "Stay down!"

Marco jumped over a rail and then jumped over another rail! He kicked the gate open to the train tracks and ran down the tracks after them! "Elliot!"

Elliot looked back and then looked at Jan and Mary. "Are you hurt?"

Jan trembled and covered her head. Mary looked up and her eyes were as wide as a deer facing a monster truck's headlights!

"Hey!" Elliot waved at them. "Are you hurt?"

Mary looked at Jan. "No, I … I think we're okay." She touched Jan's shoulder. "Jan, honey?"

"What they hell is this shit!" Jan blurted out. "I came here for a tour, not a God damn shoot out!"

"She might be in shock." Mary said and got her arms around Jan. "It's alright."

Elliot looked back and Marco was hotfoot after them, but the train moved along much faster than Marco. He let the controls go and went to Jan. "Hey."

Jan slowly looked up; her eyes were soaked with tears.

"I'm sorry about …" He sighed, "all of it."

She sniffled and then sat up with Mary and Elliot's help.

"It was never supposed to get this far." Elliot said. "Truly, I am sorry."

The train cruised down the mountain toward Grütschalp.

Savarine looked at Lev, the driver. "To the station and wait."

"Da!" He leapt in the driver's seat.

Savarine and Natalya got in and slammed their doors.

Beth got her guard and they went to their SUV. "This thing has gone sideways."

"Sorry, ma'am."

"Don't be sorry yet. Let's see what the next hour brings." She pressed her fingers against the bridge of her nose. "It's only after midday."

"Where to ma'am?" He started the SUV.

"Well, it looks like it's just you and me. So, go to the station and we'll see what comes out." She sat back and studied her phone.

The train hummed along as it descended toward Grütschalp.

Marco jogged along the tracks and tourists who used the hiking trail next to the tracks stopped and looked at him.

"You can't hike the tracks!" A man yelled.

"Da!" Marco yelled back.

"Russians, they can never follow the rules." The man sneered at Marco. "Let him get hit. Maybe knock good sense into his head."

"Papa!" His daughter said and studied Marco. "He's good looking."

"So is your mother's dog." The man said and ushered her off.

Jan wiped her tears away. She couldn't bring herself to look at Elliot, not yet. "So, you took my tablet that first time."

Elliot looked at Mary and he got a cloth from his jacket. He handed the cloth to Mary to give to Jan. "Please."

"And that other woman you were with in Petite Venise." Jan held her hand to her face and looked at the back of the train.

"I stole your tablet the first time, yes." He gritted his teeth. "The woman's name is …"

"Natalya or is that a lie?" Jan asked. "And your name?"

"No, that's her real name and my name *is* Elliot." He looked away. "She's part of a Russian spy group called SVR-RF; it's the spy agency of the Russian Federation." He brought his legs up to his chest. "It was a simple thing." He pondered about his mistake. "Put the chip in your tablet and I was the only one who knew." He looked away. "Then you go home and I'd get it back."

"Why not do it yourself?" Mary asked.

He thought about it. "They knew I had it, the Russians knew."

Jan turned and faced him. "So, you put it in my tablet, a grandma on vacation." Her soft, tear stained complexion turned red. "Help me up."

Mary got up.

Elliot offered his hand.

"No! Not you." Jan demanded, got Mary by the hand, and got up.
The train cruised down the mountain and picked up speed.

"Jan, I am sorry." He took a step closer and held out his hand. "I never meant for it to get this dangerous, this out of hand."

"Do you even know where our friend is?" Jan asked. "Or if he's okay?"

Elliot drew in a heavy breath. "He's probably still at Schilthorn, but I got through to the police on a landline; the Russians jammed everything else."

Jan reeled back and slapped the hell out of him. Then, she brought her hands together and clutched the tablet tightly. "You get my tablet when I get my friend back, alive."

Elliot rubbed his jaw. "Okay." He shook it off, went to the control panel, and slowed the train.

"Jan." Mary said and wrapped her arms around her.

"I'm a grandma." She looked at Elliot. "Shame on you!"
They went to a seat and sat down.

Elliot bit at his lip. Just then, his phone vibrated and a pop up showed. "Blue Moon." A thought about what was going on and how much time did they have before Grütschalp? "Hey."

"How are you?" His mother asked.

Jan looked at Elliot. "Probably talking to a spy to give us up."

Mary looked at Elliot. "I don't know."

"Yeah, I'm good. Just busy, you know." He looked down and the floor was covered with pieces of glass.

His mother sighed and then cleared her throat. "I just wondered if you might make Christmas."

Elliot looked up and at the large rearview mirror.

Jan chatted with Mary and she looked out the window at the beautiful mountains and valleys.

"It's alright or at least it will be." Mary said.

"Probably get killed." Jan said. "Already been shot at, chased, and all I got was a sweaty shirt from that one hot guy."

Mary laughed. "For a vacation though, it's been different, fun."

Elliot thought about it, thought about his mom. "Hey, I have to go." The station was a few miles ahead of them.

His mother sighed sadly. "I understand, government work."

"Yeah, mom." Two indicators were red, because the train was going too fast, so he pressed the brakes and slowed the train. "Yeah, government work."

"If I don't see you, we'll talk on Christmas day." She said and choked back the tears. "Be safe."

"Of course, I love you." He pressed his fingers into his eyes and then swiped "End Call".

Jan looked at Elliot. "Probably setting up the trade or something."

Mary turned and looked at him too. "He doesn't come across as the bad guy."

"How many bad guys do you know?" Jan's brow rose.

"For starters, he didn't wipe blood and sweat on his undershirt and throw it at you."

Jan smiled slyly and then her lips slowly drifted apart with a response.

"Don't even say it." Mary got her bible in hand and tapped Jan on the arm.

"Well." Jan said.

Elliot swiped the call and ended it. His mind wasn't here, wasn't in the now, and it wasn't ready to face what lay ahead of them at Grütschalp or Lauterbrunnen.

Mary cleared her throat. "So, do you have a plan to save us?"

He forced himself to smile. "I'm working on it."

Jan had a stern look, much like a mom who has said, 'I told you so.' "You better."

Savarine and Natalya had their guns in hand. Lev checked his sub machine gun.

"They don't leave with that tablet." Savarine said.

More police showed up at the Lauterbrunnen station.

Beth looked at her gun and then at the guard. "Just keep your cool, follow my lead, and don't kill anyone until I do."

"Yes, ma'am." He swallowed a gulp of fear the size of a baseball. "Who's left from the team?"

"We are the team sport." She laughed. "For the life of me, I can't remember your name."

He turned to face her. "Riley." He smiled and it was a nice smile, a boyish smile with charm. "Riley McDermott.'

"Riley McDermott, you may be killed in the next hour." She turned her attention to the Swiss state police who drove up. "Pull down the road a block and set up facing away from the station."

"Yes, ma'am."

The Swiss state police set up barriers at Lauterbrunnen. Then, two military armored SUV's pulled up and parked.

Natalya looked at the military. "This is out of hand."

"If you had competent people to do the job, we wouldn't be in this!" Savarine yelled.

Lev lowered himself in the seat.

Natalya and Savarine looked at each other, two cats that growled and hissed at each other over a bull.

Lev answered a call. Then, he looked in the rearview mirror. "Yuri is down."

"Diplomatic immunity." Savarine said. "Tell them to tell the Swiss."

"Da." Lev passed along the declaration and then listened. "So, two teams are in Swiss custody." He listened intently. "Marco is on the track running toward Grütschalp."

"Of course." Savarine shook her head. "This fool is done after this mission."

"Our Murren teams fled and the Swiss are in pursuit." Lev said.

"Tell them to stop and give themselves to the Swiss, diplomatic immunity for them too." Savarine's phone vibrated. "General Amosovo, just perfect." She swiped and dismissed the call. "I'm busy."

"I get the chip, hand it off to you, and you leave." Natalya said. "This will make it good."

Savarine thought for a moment. "Fine."

The Grütschalp station was ahead of Aaron, Jan, and Mary, about a kilometer ahead. He got the shift and slowed the train. "Okay, here's what we're doing."

Jan looked at him. "Getting the hell away from you."

He sighed softly and pursed his lips. "Soon." Then, he looked ahead. "We're coming into the station at Grütschalp. We'll take the mountain train down and then go to safehouse."

"And then what?" Mary asked.

"I'll get Aaron to you and you give the tablet to me." He studied Jan's face for a feel of what she thought. "Then, I'll leave you alone."

Jan looked at Mary for her thoughts; Mary smiled and nodded. "He better not be hurt."

Grütschalp station had many tourist and locales who were jammed together because the trains were on hold. Some people cheered when they saw the train on the track.

Elliot pulled back on the brake and the train slowed until it coasted along the tracks.

"You said that guy with the tattoo on his face was who?" Jan looked up the tracks. "Is he still chasing us?"

"His name is Marco and, yes, he's chasing us." Elliot looked at the crowd. "We're going to get off and go to the mountain train to Lauterbrunnen."

Marco jogged along the tracks. Sweat dripped from his forehead and carried blood with it down his cheeks in dark lines. "Kill Elliot." He mumbled.

"Marco!" A Russian drove along the foot trail on a four-wheeler. "Marco!"

Marco turned and then stopped. "Anatoly?" He smiled and ran to him. "Yes!"

"C'mon, Natalya said to get you out of here." He slid up so Marco could get on.

"No, you take me to Grütschalp, now." Marco hovered over Anatoly.

"Marco," he turned and faced him. "Natalya said …"

"You take me or I take bike and go my own." His face was riddled with streaks of wet and dried blood. The cut on the side of his head was brown and crusty.

"Da, Marco." Anatoly revved the bike. "No problem."

"I'm get my vengeance on Elliot." He clenched his fist tightly.

People pointed at the front of the train and asked about the windshield.

"Ladies, we get off quietly and make our way to the other train, nice and easy." He pulled the brake and the train stopped. Then, he pressed a button and the door opened. "Ready?"

Jan and Mary stood and walked to the door.

"After all the crap today, I'm ready for anything." Jan said and looked at Elliot. "Well, c'mon." She walked ahead of him.

One of the train managers stood by the exit gate and looked at the three people who got off the beaten train. His mouth was open and he stepped up to see all the damage. "What's happened?"

Elliot looked at the front of the train and then back at him. "The driver leapt through the window."

"Stephan leapt to where?" The manager asked and was at a loss.

"Crazy, isn't it." Jan said and walked past the manager with Mary in tow.

Elliot smiled at the manager. "He's fine though, good man Stephan."

They worked their way through the crowded station toward the mountain train. Most of the people were more interested in going up, not down. Swiss police patrolled the station.

So, there were just two people in line to go back to Lauterbrunnen. As it turned out, it was the couple that saw Elliot punch the Frenchman in Petite Venise and the same couple who took their picture at the pizzeria with Natalya.

Elliot saw the couple and laughed. "Things come in threes." He pulled at his torn jacket.

Jan looked at him. "What does?" Then, she saw the couple and smiled. "Hello."

The husband's eyes widened in terror and his wife clung to him.

Elliot's face was bruised and battered. "Hey." His clothes were disheveled and torn in places. "What's the holdup?"

The man and his wife were filled with horror and shock.

Elliot got the gate and pulled the lock. "Ladies?" He held the gate open and waited.

Jan stopped, "would you take our picture?" She held the tablet up.

Mary shook her head. "Be glad when you get a regular camera."

"I haven't taken a picture since we came down." She smiled at the terrified man.

Elliot looked at the poor man whose face paled in fear. "Take the picture."

"Yes, of … of course." His hand trembled and he got the tablet from Jan. "Fromage?"

"Ah, to hell with that." Mary said. "Cheese."
"Cheese." He barely got the word out.

"Cheese!" The threesome said.

"You riding with us?" Elliot asked and fanned his hand toward the mountain train.

The man handed the tablet back to Jan. "No, we …"

His wife stepped up, pulled him away, and then spoke. "We wait."

"Okay." Elliot smiled and then looked down the track. "May be a while for the next train."

"Yes, it's no problem for us." He said, got his wife and stepped further away from them.

Jan and Mary walked through and got on the mountain train.

"You know there is no driver yet." The wife said.

Elliot smiled. "Oh, I'm a certified, licensed drive … whatever it takes kind of guy." He boarded with Jan and Mary. "Sure you don't want to come?"

"Yes, we are sure." The husband clutched his wife tightly in his arms and stepped back again.

Elliot waved at the terrified couple, got to the console, and tapped a few buttons. The doors closed and the brake released. The train slowly picked up speed and went downhill to Lauterbrunnen.

Mary looked Elliot over. "Do you have a license?"
He laughed, "No, I'm lucky to have one to drive a car."

Marco and Anatoly zoomed down the path and were near the Grütschalp station.

"There!" Marco pointed at the station a kilometer ahead of them.

Anatoly looked on and saw the trains. "There is no place for them to hide here."

"Go around the station to the mountain train and see if they are there." Marco sat up and looked at the crowded station. Swiss police were in the shot-up train.

"Okay," Elliot turned to Mary and Jan. "We'll get my car and go to the safe house. I'm going to call a friend and get some help to find Aaron."

"Sounds good." Mary said.

Elliot got his phone in hand and tapped away. Then, he put the phone to his ear and waited.

"At least he hasn't given us up." Jan said.

"Yep." Mary wiped the sweat from her brow. "Next trip, let's go to the beach."

Jan laughed. "Alright."

"Or Disney World." She sat back and tried to relax.

"I'm not paying to park at a resort; it's such a rip off." Jan shook her head.

"That is." She smirked. "How'd you hear about it?"

"Aaron told me." She brought her hand up to her mouth. "God, I hope he's okay."

Aaron sat on the back of a snowmobile with the Swiss police. "This is fun, cold, but fun."

"Christina." Elliot said. "Yeah, we're on our way down."

The train clicked away down the track toward Lauterbrunnen and the views were beautiful.

"What time is it?" Jan asked and tapped her tablet. The screen flickered and was made up of hundreds of tiny boxes. "Great."

"It's nearly four." Mary said.

"So, he's with your people." Elliot smiled and looked at Jan. "Aaron's with the Swiss police."

"I get him, you get the tablet." Her tone was firm, decisive.

He chuckled. "You will. I just wanted you to know that he's okay."

"He's okay when I see him for myself." Jan said.

Mary sat up. "Me too."

Then, Elliot's smile faded. "What?" He looked ahead at the station.

Christina told him that there was an audience waiting for them. "Not just us, but the Russians, the Americans too."

"We're getting off." Elliot said and slowed the train. He looked ahead. "Lauterbrunnen, my …it has to be on my terms, not theirs."

"What?" Jan asked and looked around. The village of Lauterbrunnen surrounded them.

"We're in the middle of the track." Mary looked around. "Who are all those people?" She looked at the station and platform. "Tourists?"

"Hey, I've got to go." He listened. "No, I have my own safe place. Thanks." He swiped to end the call.   "Uh, there's military police, Russian hitmen, American spies and … I think there are a few teen skiers too." Elliot forced a smile. "Jan." He held his hand out. "Aaron is safe, but I have to ask you to trust me and let me have the chip now."

She gave him the evil eye and then held up the tablet. "What about my pictures?"

He held his phone up. "Quickly." Then, he looked ahead and there was his red Audi parked off to the side of the tracks. He pulled the brake and stopped the train. "Time to go." He forced the door open. "Stay close to me."

The police radioed for their people to go to the train!

"Hurry!" He got the tablet from her. They left the train, crossed the tracks, and stopped at the fence.

"Good God." Jan said and threw her hands up. "I can't cross that!"

Mary's skin paled. "Um, they are coming."

Elliot looked at the police, "they're a half kilometer away." He looked around. "Look scared and just move with me." He got his gun out and held it up. "Stay back!" He shouted at the military police who hopped down from the platform and onto the tracks. "I'll shoot!"

"Dear Lord." Mary said. "I am scared!"

The military police held their machine guns at the ready. "Halt and drop your weapon!"

"Okay, down the side here, just go down to that car." Elliot pressed on the fence and pushed it down.

Jan ripped her pants on the fence and then rolled over it. "I've had enough."

They went down the embankment.

"Halt!" The police ran toward them. "Halt!"

Sirens wailed in the distance!

"Okay, they're coming." Elliot said.

"I can't run." Jan said.

"I know, but for this thing to work." He looked up the strasse. "Car's right there." The red Audi was parked just a few feet away. "We've got seconds here."

The police ran up the tracks and shouted, "Polizei! Halt!"

Jan and Mary hurried to the car. "I liked that black BMW."

"Black, everyone's got black." Elliot said and pressed the key fob. "Get in, c'mon, both in the back!"

Mary looked at the front fender of the Audi. "It's wrecked. What happened?"

"Ask Marco." He shook his head. "Let's go ladies!"

They got in and slammed the doors shut. Elliot pressed the starter button and the engine roared to life.

"Guttural." Jan said. "Nice."

"Reminds me of my husband's Harley." They buckled up.

He jammed it in drive! "Black is boring too." The tires spun wildly and smoke billowed from them! "Okay, here we go!" They ripped out of the spot and down the strasse. "And red is hot, sexy hot, Jan. Any guy can have a boring black car, but a red one with an 'S' eight like this has, that's the guy to get wild with."

Jan and Mary shifted from one side to the other as Elliot jerked the wheel to make the roundabout!

"Sorry, got to make some quick turns here." He gripped the wheel tightly.

Marco, dirty and bloody, rode up the foot path with Anatoly until they saw the police on the track! "Stop!" Marco shouted.

A red Audi roared down a side strasse! "Elliot!" He shoved Anatoly, "go down to the station and then get on the road!"

"This is not for the street, Marco!" Anatoly revved the motor and raced down the foot path. Many tourists hiked up the path and leapt out of the way!

"Move!" Anatoly shouted.

Beth's phone beeped and she read the text. "Damn him." She grabbed a phablet and studied it. "He's in his car!" She pointed down the strasse. "Go! That way!" Riley raced down the strasse! "I know the safe house." She looked at her phablet and watched the blip on her screen. "Red damn Audi."

Savarine looked at the black SUV as it tore out of the parking space and onto the strasse. "The hell."

Natalya looked on. "They know."

"Lev!"

Lev jammed the BMW into drive and they took off!

"Yes, ma'am." Riley turned into a roundabout and nearly flipped the SUV. "Sorry!"

Beth grabbed the handle above her head. "That's alright, just catch up!"

Behind them and in hot pursuit, Lev chased the black SUV!

"Stay with them!" Savarine yelled. "Americans and their big trucks, easy target."

"The drone?" Natalya asked.

Savarine looked ahead. "Drive on!" Then, she looked at her phone. "It's up and near them."

Lev nodded and skidded around the roundabout!

"Yes, a black SUV." Officer Landau told Hans.

"I understand." Hans said. "This damn thing." He shook his head and ended the call. "Someone will get hurt or killed if we don't stop it."

An agent walked with him to a waiting undercover car. "Tell them we pursue the Americans and the Russians." Swiss police and the military raced after them at the very back of the chase with their blue lights and sirens wailing!

Anatoly and Marco drove off the trail and onto the strasse. "Go! Go! Go!"

Several police waved their hands at Anatoly and shouted, "Halt!"

"We're not going to make it anywhere." Mary said.

Elliot looked ahead, turned, and the Audi skidded around another roundabout and then onto a highway. Several other cars drove off the road to avoid a wreck with them.

"Hey, she's right." Jan thought for a moment. "An Uber driver eh?"

He smiled. "Glad to be of service."

A drone zoomed by!

"Ah!" Jan yelled.

"What the hell was that?" Mary asked.

"A drone." He looked hard at the road ahead. "They're following us."

"Gosh, Aaron won't take another trip with us again." Jan frowned.

Mary smirked. "With you."

Elliot chimed in. "He hasn't been hit by an ambulance, surely."

"You saw that?" Mary asked.

"Yeah, I was nearby." He smiled.

Aaron talked with the Swiss state police at Murren and drank a gin martini. "It's shaken, not stirred."

Elliot looked in the rearview mirror. "Beth."

Jan turned in her seat. "The Americans, the Russians, and the police."

Mary tried to laugh about it. "Oh my."

Then, a helicopter came over a mountain toward them.

Mary sighed. "Elliot, all this for that chip?"

Elliot looked at his phone that rested on Jan's tablet. There was a status bar with green indicators that filled the bar. "Your pictures are on my phone now." He handed his phone to her between the seats. "They know that the chip is in the tablet."

"So …" Jan got his phone.

Elliot skidded around a corner, slammed on the brakes, and then fishtailed onto a snow-covered road.

"Ah!" Jan screamed. "You're going to get us killed!"

"No way, Jan. Audi's have an airbag for everything." He smiled the best he could and watched the SUV swerve onto the road behind them.

"So, this car has all the options." Mary said.

"This car will do everything but wipe your ass." He said firmly.

Jan smiled heartily. "I'm going to get one when we get back."

"You would." Mary shook her head. "Maybe, I'll get one too."

"He said red is hot." Her brow bounced up and down. "Sexy hot."

The Audi lots is traction and fishtailed! The traction control light flashed repeatedly!

"Hang on!" The car zigged that way and then zagged the other way!

"Ah!" The girls screamed.

"Okay!" Elliot shouted and tried to get control of the car.

The tires brushed the edge of the pavement and were half on, half off the snow-covered road!

"God, we're going to go over!" Mary yelled and looked down at the valley.

"Not yet!" The Audi hit a snow bank and they were in a cloud of white flakes.

"Stay with them!" Beth yelled and held her phone. "Can the drone hit the tires?"

Two Swiss military attack helicopters flew by. The pilot in one of the helicopters targeted the drone. "Ja." The guidance system targeted the first drone and the pilot fired!

"BOOM!" The Russian drone burst into hundreds of pieces!

"Lima one, target is down." Both helicopters zoomed past and then circled around.

Savarine slammed her phone down. "Damn!"

"What's happened?" Natalya asked.

"Lev, do not lose them!" Savarine looked out her window. "They shot down our drone."

"Da!" Lev punched the pedal and zoomed up to the SUV.

"Natalya, the tires!" Savarine pointed.

Natalya nodded, put the window down, and leaned out of the BMW. The snow cloud hung in the air.

"Got it!" Elliot, with both hands on the wheel at ten and two, fought to stay on the icy road. "Whoa!"

"Where are you going?" Mary asked.

"You'll see." In the rearview mirror, the SUV was nearly on them.

"Is it me or is it arrogance that keeps you going despite the odds and danger?" Jan said and held her hands up to her face.

Elliot looked at the rearview mirror and studied Jan and Mary. Then, he looked at the army of cars behind them. Slowly, he let his foot off of the gas pedal and let out a sigh of relief. "You're right, Jan."

Riley nearly rammed them and let off the gas. "They're slowing down."

"Good, ram them!" Beth shouted.

Lev tapped the brakes. "What the hell!"

Savarine leaned up and looked at the taillights of the SUV. "Look out!"

The Swiss police jammed their brakes too.

"Ma'am, I know you're my boss, but if we ram them … both of us are going to go over the cliff; that Audi weighs over two tons." Riley eyed her in the rearview mirror. "I'm new, not stupid."

Elliot crawled along at fifty kilometers per hour. "Okay," he looked at the terrified women in the backseat. "I'm … it's enough. It's over." The car slowed to forty kilometers per hour.

A Swiss military helicopter zoomed by!

Beth looked ahead and then took a call. "Get it out of their airspace, now."

Too late, the drone turned and headed south. The Swiss helicopter pilot fired. "Missile away!" The SEAOPS drone dodged right and then left, "BOOM!" Then, it was blasted into a hundred pieces.

"Damn it." Beth said and tossed her phablet aside. "Don't ram them."

"Lost the drone?" Riley asked and tapped the brakes.

"You think." She rolled her eyes.

Elliot turned onto the summit, drove past a small cabin, and drove to the edge, five thousand feet up. The Audi idled and he put it in park. Then, he turned to Jan and Mary.

Jan rubbed her cheeks. "So, what was I right about?"

"Me, my arrogance to go until the job is done." He looked around them. "No matter what the odds are or who may get hurt." He pursed his lips and then huffed. "Wow."

Behind them, Riley skidded to a stop on one side! Lev slammed the brakes in the BMW on the other side! The Swiss military and police skidded to a stop all over!

Elliot smiled and then sighed. "So, this is it."

Jan and Mary turned and looked behind them.

"Oh my God." Jan said.

Mary looked around at the flashing blue lights, the men and women who got out and pointed their guns at them. "Sinners."

Savarine got out with Lev and Natalya.

Beth and Riley got out too.

Everyone had their guns drawn!
The Swiss police announced, "Halt! Put down your weapons!"

"So, stay here and it'll be fine." Elliot got out of the car with the tablet and took a casual walk to the edge of the summit. Around them, beautiful snow-capped mountains that glowed in the sunset.

Beth walked up and looked him over. "Elliot, it's over."

Swiss military helicopters flew past.

Savarine looked at Beth. "You don't leave here with it; I promise that." She pointed her gun at Beth.

Beth pointed her gun at Savarine and Riley wondered who to point his gun at.

The Swiss police moved up and pointed their guns at everyone else.

Elliot took in a refreshing deep breath. "It's a terrible way to spend Christmas." Then, he mumbled, "I should be with my family."

Beth turned her gun on Jan and stood by the Audi. "It's her or the tablet, Elliot."

"Lower your weapons now. You are not permitted to be armed in Switzerland!" The police said. "We are authorized to use lethal force!"

Elliot tucked the tablet against his chest.

Natalya walked up and pointed her gun at Mary. "They both die. It's ours."

Mary put the window down. "Hey, we had pizza together and were nice to you!"

Natalya smiled at her. "Yes, but it was just to get the tablet. I don't care about you." She cocked the hammer.

"Slut sinner!" Mary put her window up.

Elliot looked at the crowd of armed people around him. Then, he looked at the helicopters. "Wow, all this." His fingers tapped the tablet and then he gripped it firmly. He looked at Jan and Mary and then mumbled to himself. "To save them, no one should have it." In a split second, he spun around and threw the tablet off of the summit!

Savarine, Natalya, Beth, and Riley ran to the edge of the summit!

"No!" Beth and Savarine yelled in unison!

They stood at the precipice as the Swiss police rushed in!

The tablet danced on the wind on its way down and then it smashed into some jagged rocks! It was shattered into tiny pieces and destroyed!

The pieces disappeared into the mountain's vast snow-covered side far below them.

Elliot turned and held his hands outstretched.

Savarine got her phone out and studied an app on the screen with a blip.

Natalya, Beth, Riley and Lev pointed their guns at Elliot.

"Net!" Savarine raised her hand. "No."

Elliot smiled. "That's détente comrade." He motioned at the army of Swiss police behind them. "You don't have it and we don't have it."

Savarine studied her phone and the blip faded away. "So true, so clever Elliot."

Beth shook her head.

Riley, Beth, Natalya, and Lev lowered their guns and were arrested.

Savarine tried to reach into her jacket. "I am a Russian diplomat."

Hans knocked her hand away. "Not yet."

Beth looked at Elliot. "You're sure know how to make a fantastic finish."

"Elliot, I don't forget you." Natalya said.

"Good." He waved and blew her a kiss.

The Swiss police did not arrest Jan, Mary, or Elliot.

Beth looked at Hans. "How are you going to arrest me? You know who I am."

Hans smiled politely. "Perhaps, over an espresso, you can tell me all about yourself."

Savarine and Beth were taken away anyway.

Marco and Anatoly pulled up in the four-wheeler and walked up to Natalya. "Natalya?" The police grabbed him too!

Elliot walked back to the Audi and opened the door. "Ladies."

Jan and Mary were as white as the snow around them. "Are you okay?"

"I have to pee." Jan said.

Mary leaned up and looked around. "I'm scared to move."

Officer Landau walked up and nodded at Elliot. "So, it's ended well."

"Has it?" He knelt and leaned against the car door. A huge sigh of exhaustion bellowed from his mouth. "Wow."

"He's into younger women." Jan said and pursed her lips. "Damn the luck."

Mary looked around again. "Why are we sitting in here? Let's get out."

"Alright." Jan forced the door open and shoved Elliot onto the ground.

Elliot lay face first in the snow.

Jan looked at him and got to her feet. "What are you doing there?"
An unmarked police car skidded to a stop nearby.

"I know now what Aaron felt like in front of the ambulance." He spat snow from his mouth.

"Jan!" Aaron got out of the unmarked car. "Mary!"

He ran to them and they hugged each other.

"What happened to you?" He held his hand out to Elliot.

"I fell." Elliot got Aaron's hand.

Jan held her hand out and they lifted Elliot up.

The police cleared the area.

"It's Christmas eve, right?" Jan said.

Elliot was taken by what she said and looked at his watch. "It is."

Jan walked up, got Elliot by the arm, and walked away with him. They stopped near the edge of the summit. "It would never work." She said.

His smile faded. "I wondered."

"She's cute though." Jan dipped her head at Officer Landau.

"She's more than that." He admired Landau and they locked eyes. "She's my sister."

"No shit." Jan said and had to catch her breath. She licked her dry, cold lips. "I think there's another woman who you need to see." They hugged.

"Oh?" He held her.

"You love your mom and she hugs like I do." Jan let go and eased back. "Surprise her, but not with a phone call."

Elliot's eyes welled up and he cleared his throat. "How'd you know?"

"You've got time to get there by Christmas." Jan raised her hand and touched his chin. "Merry Christmas, Elliot." She smiled wide, turned, and walked back to Mary and Aaron. "What about the rest of our tour!"

"No shit." Mary said. "Sinners just about ruined it for us."

Hans, Swiss Intelligence, walked up, and shook their hands. "I'm Hans and I'm going to take you back to your apartment tonight."

"But we didn't get to see the rest of Schilthorn." Jan frowned.

"Not today, no." He shrugged his shoulders. "But the day after Christmas we will bring you by helicopter to Schilthorn and give you a fantastic lunch followed by an exclusive tour."

Aaron eyed the man. "Why?"

Elliot spoke up. "Take the freebee and don't ask."

Jan, Mary, and Aaron looked at Elliot, smiled and winked at him. Then, he walked up and they did a group hug. "Alright."

That night, Hans drove up the hill to the Dolder Grand. Zurich's most exclusive residence. The doorman and a bellman rushed to the car. "Hans

Dietrichite."

"Ja!" The bellman got their small things from the trunk.

"We're here." Hans opened the door.

The Americans were passed out in their seats and turned slightly.

"Lime green apartment, blah." Mary rubbed the sleep from her eyes and sat up. "Oh." She rubbed her eyes again. "Get up!"

Jan sat up and caught her breath. "What?"

Aaron wiped the drool from his mouth and looked at the entrance. "Where the hell are we?"

The doorman tipped his hat. "The Dolder Grand, sir."

"What?" He sat up and turned. "Really?"

Hans helped Jan out. "Compliments of your new friend."

"What friend?" Mary asked and yawned.

Hans grinned. "You know."

"You are in the Maestro Suite." The doorman said. "Frederick, your butler, will show you in."

Aaron shook hands with Hans, "thanks and Merry Christmas."

"Merry Christmas," Hans said. "To all of you."

Frederick, a handsome young man, nodded at them. "This way please."

They went into the lobby and many eyes looked at the disheveled, dirty Americans.

Frederick slid a card into the elevator and they got in.

The elevator doors opened and they went to their suite. Frederick got the door and their breath was taken away at the sight of such a beautiful home.

"Ah." Jan said and brought her hands up to her mouth. "My gosh."

Mary looked the place over. "For once, I'm going to sin."
"Me too." Aaron said and smiled at Frederick. "Me too."

The wood in the fireplace cracked and spit as it burned.

"It's after ten, perhaps you would like to rest and then have a late dinner?" Frederick asked.

"I think I need to lay down, for a month or more." Aaron looked at the ladies.

"Yeah, I have to pee." Jan said. "Bad."

Frederick blushed. "All your things were brought here from your other apartment."

"She does." Mary said. "I'm too nice a person to say I have to pee."

They were far too exhausted to hear anything Frederick said. "Of course, I'm at your call, whatever you need." He looked at Aaron and nodded. Then, he left.

"Okay, I don't care who gets what bed, but I've got to lay down." Aaron walked off and bumped into a wall.

"Me either." Mary made her way to the other room.

Jan looked around. "Where's the toilet?"

The next morning, Christmas morning, Jan was up and in her nightgown. "Gosh, it's nearly ten." She walked into the living room and her breath was taken away. "Oh!"

In the center of the living room stood a warm and well decorated Christmas tree with gifts under it.

Jan walked up to it and smiled. Her eyes welled up and then she heard paper rustling. "Hello?"

"Oh." Mary sat in a corner and tore open a gift. "Had my name on it."

"Really?"

"Yeah." She ripped the paper off and looked at a new camera and a new zoom lens. "Oh wow."

"Didn't you smash yours against that guy's head?" Jan looked through the gifts for her name. "Hey!"

"Merry Christmas." Aaron said.

"Merry Christmas!" The ladies said.

Jan got her gift in hand and sat down.

"Frederick's bringing two Americanos and one espresso." Aaron said and had a small box in hand. "And since we slept through our late-night dinner, he's bringing a lot of breakfast food."

"Good, I love those Americanos." Jan said and pulled the paper from the box.

"Let's open gifts!" He tore the paper off and looked at the white box. "Okay."

Frederick walked in. "Merry Christmas!" Two staff members followed him in with silver serving trays filled with eggs, bacon, sausage, toast, jams, croissants, fruits, butter, and juices.

"Merry Christmas, Frederick." Aaron looked at the staff. "And friends."

Frederick set the coffees down and then went to the kitchen with the staff.

"So, what did you get?" Mary asked Aaron.

"Don't know." He cut the tape and then pulled the box apart. "IWC Schaffhausen."

Mary looked over. "Hey, isn't that the watch we looked at in Zurich?"

"Jesus, it is."

"Ah!" Jan took out a new tablet. "Got a tablet."

"Elliot." Mary said.

"No sh … kidding." He looked at the watch and held it up. "Wow, unbelievably beautiful."

Jan looked at Aaron and then Mary. "Let's hope that Elliot got what he wanted for Christmas."

Mary set her camera down. Aaron put his watch on his lap.

"What did he want, Jan?" Aaron asked.

Mary got her coffee and took a sip.

"To see someone special." She smiled and nodded at them. "Now, I'm going to put my pictures on here."

"Your tablet was smashed." Aaron looked around her.

"No," Mary said. "He put the pictures on his phone and gave it to Jan."

"I wonder how many watch lists were on." He put the watch on.

"Watch lists?" Mary asked and sniffed a bottle of perfume.

"Like spies or something." Jan said.

Mary laughed. "Three fools for spies." She shook her head and spritzed perfume on herself.

"I'll be right back." Jan took her new tablet, went to her room, and got the phone. There was a text message pop up and she looked at the word, "SLIDE TO OPEN". She gently placed her finger on the screen and slid it across. The phone unlocked and there was a picture of Elliot with his mother, his sister, Christina, and a Christmas tree to the side of them.

"Greetings and Merry Christmas from Blue Moon, Kentucky! Miss you, Elliot."

Jan smiled. "Miss you too, Merry Christmas."

The end.

About the Author:

Michael S. Lachance writes fiction and loves his unique and wonderous characters that bring life to each scene. He lives in Iowa near Council Bluffs. He enjoys writing about drama, historical fiction, love, and action/adventure.

The Treaty of Versailles, The Power of Love is a story that evolved out of a trip to Poland and a prison camp. This story is about Erich and his love, Nikki. Prior to World War II, Nikki is arrested and imprisoned at a concentration camp. Erich will not let the man he loves die in the camp. In order to save Nikki, Erich must become what he hates most, a Nazi.

21 Windows is about a family who buys an old farm house in the country. They discover a painted over window and a room hidden in the house. After they knock a wall out to get into that room, bad things happen.

The Camera is about a priest, Father Leauvin, who is sent to the front during World War I & takes pictures of the dead & dying. He is torn between his love for Christ & his love for a woman that he met in Paris.

The Long Short is about two people who don't know each other until their flight to the US crashes. They end up on an atoll and have very different goals they want to achieve. Bill wants to find treasure and Claire wants to be rescued. One of them will get what they want at the expense of the other

Currently, Michael's working on *The Adventures of Skipper Pete* (YA-four books in the series), *Butch Roberts and The African*

Adventure which is about a gay man who travels to south Africa in search of fun and adventure, but winds up on the run from a rebel army.

Published works are available in eBook or paperback!

To connect with Michael, please visit

Facebook – www.facebook.com/skipper.pete

Twitter - https://twitter.com/skipperpete1

Website: www.skipperpete.com

Please join him on his website blog for updates about novels in the works, pre-orders, and Q & A. Upcoming works include: Skipper Pete Adventure Series, So Happy, and Butch Roberts and The African Adventure.

Michael's books are available as eBooks and in paperback at all major book sellers: Amazon, Barnes & Noble, iTunes Book Store, Smashwords and other sellers.

Thank you for your interest and enjoy.

9 781799 071587